Tanaka,

Thank you for your support, your friendship, and your kind words over the last few years. I hope this character will be worthy of your namesake in this book and those to come.

Ghost

A. ZAVARELLI

Ghost © 2016 A. Zavarelli
Cover Design by Lara at Coverluv
Photo by Wander Aguiar
Formatting by Champagne Book Designs

All rights reserved. This book or any portion thereof may not be reproduced or used in any manner whatsoever without the express written permission of the author except for the use of brief quotations in a book review.

This is a work of fiction. Names, characters, businesses, places, events and incidents are either the product of the author's imagination or used in a fictitious manner. Any resemblance to actual persons, living or dead, or actual events is purely coincidental.

Playlist

Dark Paradise—Lana Del Rey

Angel of the Morning—Skeeter Davis

Enjoy the Silence—Denmark + Winter

Breathe Me—Sia

Sober—Pink

Dance with the Devil—Breaking Benjamin

Save Me—Shinedown

Hurt—Johnny Cash

Comfortably Numb—Pink Floyd

45—Shinedown

Paint it Black—The Rolling Stones

The Monster—Eminem

Born to Die—Lana Del Rey

The Sound of Silence—Disturbed

Dear Agony—Breaking Benjamin

Even Though Our Love is Doomed—Garbage

My Least Favorite Life—Lera Lynn

Beautiful Pain—Eminem

Lucky Ones—Lana Del Rey

What Lies Beneath—Breaking Benjamin

Unwell—Matchbox Twenty

GLOSSARY OF TERMS

Avtoritet—authority, captain

Boevik—warrior, soldier, strike force

Pakhan—leader, boss

Lyoshenka, Lyoshka, Alyoshka—diminutive forms of the name Alexei

Solnyshko—little sun

Sovietnik—councilor, advisor to the pakhan

Vory v Zakone—thieves in law

Prologue

Talia

Hope is for suckers.

That's what Mack and I always like to say.

So I guess I'm a sucker too.

Because when Dmitri asked me to go to Mexico with him, I couldn't say no.

There was a part of me that wanted to. The part that keeps my shields up and my armor in place. We've only been dating for a month. Not enough time to vacation together.

Not that I would know. I've never even been on a vacation.

Mack and I have always done it tough. Growing up in foster care and then on the streets. Scraping by every day. When the majority of your life is consumed by the thought of your next meal or a safe place to sleep, places like Mexico might as well be on another planet.

But things are different now.

I'm twenty-two. And perfectly capable of taking care of myself.

Mack doesn't agree.

And even though I'm here in paradise with this man who promises the world, I can't stop thinking about her.

She's like a sister to me. She's the only family I've got. I hate that we argued before I left. We're always arguing these days, it seems.

She hates my job. She hates all of my life decisions.

And it hurts. Because I miss her. She should be here with me, in this beautiful place, experiencing it with me. But instead, she's back in Boston… completely oblivious to where I'm at. I couldn't bring myself to tell her about this vacation. I knew she would argue. I knew she would tell me that I was making another mistake.

She doesn't like Dmitri, even though she's never met him. Mack always sees the worst in everybody. It's her way of protecting herself and me.

But sometimes, like right now, I just want to see the good.

Dmitri has done nothing but treat me well since I met him. And I have this crazy idea in my head that maybe someday Mack will meet him and understand that. That she'll be able to see what I see when I look at him.

I want to call her right now. I want to tell her all about this place. How beautiful the weather and the drinks and the beach are. These last few days have been the best of my life, and I want to share that with her.

But my phone is up in the hotel room and Dmitri and I are down by the pool. So it will have to wait until tonight.

I'll get the courage to call her tonight.

"Hey." Dmitri reaches over and touches my face, turning my attention to him. "Why so sad, kitten?"

"I'm not," I lie.

He smiles, and I do too.

"Good," he answers in his Russian accent. "Because tonight, I am taking you somewhere you will never forget."

My heart rate slows and some of the anxiety in my chest ebbs away. I feel like I could trust Dmitri. And I haven't felt like that in a long time.

"Tell me, Talia," he brushes his fingers down my arm and breaks away, watching me carefully. "Have you enjoyed our time together so far?"

"Yes," I answer.

And that isn't a lie. I feel like he's different. Like he can read me better than most. I've told him things about my life that I've never told anyone. I've opened up to him. I've given him a piece of myself that nobody else has ever earned.

It isn't just my body, but a part of my heart too.

"I've enjoyed our time together as well," he says wistfully. "Very much."

The expression on his face confuses me, but it vanishes quickly. A moment later, he's checking his watch and taking me by the hand.

"Come," he says. "The car is waiting out front."

I follow him through the resort and into the back of the car. He gives instructions to the driver in his native language, which surprises me a little. I didn't realize that he'd brought anyone else down here with him. But it is apparent that this man works for Dmitri.

Something nags at the back of my mind. A sinking feeling takes hold of me as we drive, and I can't be sure what it is.

When I glance at Dmitri across the seat, he is lost in his own thoughts. And distant. He is never distant. It worries me. As does the landscape up ahead. Which is looking less like a tourist area by the moment.

Dmitri seems to sense my panic though as he always does.

"It's okay," he assures me.

He reaches out and takes my hand in his, and I try to focus on organizing my thoughts. I'm at war again. In my mind. Looking for demons in everyone the way that I always do. I told myself that I wasn't going to do this anymore. I told myself that I was going to forget the past.

"You trust me, don't you?" Dmitri asks.

I look up at him and give him a nervous smile. Half of me is screaming no while the other half nods on autopilot.

"Good," he says. "Because you know I'd never do anything to hurt you, Talia. I'd never put you in danger. You have nothing to worry about when you are with me."

I allow his reassurances to calm me as the car pulls to a stop. But one look outside the window, and all of his words mean nothing.

There isn't time to protest or question him. When I turn back, there's a flash of movement in which the only thing I see is his fist. Flying at my face. And then blackness.

Only blackness.

When I wake again, I am naked. And my senses are distorted. I'm dizzy and confused by the overwhelming sense of dread coursing through my body. There is vomit lying next to my face, which causes me to wretch. But nothing comes up. And I realize, it is mine.

And then I realize something else. When I feel movement on top of me. Inside of me.

There is a man's face above me. One I do not recognize.

I try to move. But my body isn't cooperating. It's sluggish and heavy. Something is wrong with me, but I don't know what it is.

There is a low murmur. And some movement. Hands on me, shifting me around. There is shock and pain at another intrusion. From behind.

There are two of them now. Two strangers inside of me.

And then I hear Dmitri's voice. My confusion and panic halts for a split second in which I believe that he's going to fix this. That he's going to make it right.

But when he enters my blurred vision, distorted from my swollen face, I remember the car. His fist. The place he took me to.

He's in front of me now. Expressionless as he unzips his pants. It isn't the same man that I knew. The same man that I've spent the last month with. He rubs himself on my face, and I try to pull away when he seizes my hair and slaps me in the same spot he hit me before.

The shock of pain causes my mouth to fall open, and he shoves inside, gagging me.

"You better get used to it, kitten," he tells me. "The pain is your new best friend. This feeling is what you will know now. The only thing you will know. It is better to accept it than fight it."

I can't move. I can't fight back. They've drugged me with something, I realize, as Dmitri watches the tears spill down my cheeks. He knows my resistance is futile as well. And he doesn't care.

"Now give me one more gift," he says as he uses my mouth. "For old times' sake."

He is rough with me. Rougher than he's ever been. And when he finishes, he does it on my face, smearing the liquid around with his palm before he spits on me and rubs that in too.

And then he's kneeling in front of me. Patting me on the cheek.

"It's just business," he tells me. "That's all, kitten. Don't make it any harder on yourself."

He disappears from the room, and from my life, as another man takes his place. It hurts for a long time. But the lines are blurred and I can't be sure if it's the physical or emotional. It never seems to end.

I don't know how many there are. I don't know anything but the pain.

And when I close my eyes, I try to find a way to transcend it. Thinking that it will help. But the only thing I can see is Mack's face. My best friend and my sister and the only person on this earth who loves me.

She doesn't know where I am. Because I was too angry to tell her the truth.

There's a well-known saying about everything becoming perfectly clear in hindsight.

In hindsight, I never realized exactly how pivotal that moment was. My best friend and I, sitting in a café together, eating lunch. About to have one of our many arguments. It was the last time I saw her.

People always say they wish they'd known what was about to happen before disaster strikes. I would have said that too, at the time. I would have told Mack where I was going. And then I would have let her talk me out of it.

But looking back on it now, I don't think I'd say the same.

I had to go to hell to find the person I am today. And in the end, the road through hell led me straight to him.

One

Alexei

Human emotion is not a linear experience. That which provokes emotion in one may provoke little, if anything, in another. I came to understand this at a young age.

I understand it even better now. As I trace my finger over the rough, cracked wood of the rook that sits atop my desk in these late evening hours. The profound pleasure I feel is at war with equal amounts of rage. And yet, to anyone else, it is merely a worn chess piece.

A chess piece I find myself revisiting far too often.

A shadow falls over the desk, alerting me to a presence in the doorway. When I glance up, Franco is there. He speaks in slow and succinct intervals, giving me adequate time and attention to read his lips.

"Katya is at the door again," he announces.

"Send her away."

He leaves without a response and I retrieve the bottle of cognac from my bottom drawer. By the time I have poured and finished the glass, Franco returns. He takes a seat across from me, his eyes on the chess board.

"Your move," I tell him.

He takes his time, examining every piece. I have already taken control of the center and captured his rook. In several more moves, he will be sunk completely. The thing that Franco always seems to forget is that in his desperation to protect the King, he often leaves the Queen vulnerable.

I would never make that mistake.

"Is everything in place for tomorrow?" I ask.

He looks up at me and gives a simple nod. "It is all in place. The shipment will disappear and Arman will be in your debt."

"And what of Viktor?"

"I've arranged for dinner tomorrow evening. You can speak to him then."

He makes his move on the board, a careless one at that. I follow suit with an equally careless move because I'm bored of this game and I'd like him to challenge me, at least once.

"He will be reluctant to have you leave the country," Franco notes. "He won't want to risk you."

"Then I will give him no other choice." I shrug.

"What do you have in mind?" Franco asks.

"A problem with the Russian bank. Frozen accounts, perhaps."

"Ah." Franco rubs his chin in thought. "A problem only you can fix. Then you will suggest… two birds, one stone?"

I nod, but it's only a matter of moments before Franco speaks the rest of what's on his mind.

"Do you believe this is wise, Mr. Nikolaev?"

"Are you suggesting I am unwise?" is my reply.

He shakes his head. "You are many things. Unwise is not one of them. But I feel as though you might be acting impulsively. It is out of character for you."

Out of character for me is leaving the sanctuary of my home. This is what Franco refers to. There have not been many occasions where I felt the need to leave. Every time I do so, I risk exposing my secret to those around me. To my fellow Vory.

Leaving the country is an even bigger risk. However, it is one I must take.

I meet Franco's gaze. "Sometimes we must do things that we'd rather not. Is part of life, yes?"

"You have lied to Viktor," he answers. "If he ever uncovers what you have done to retrieve this girl, there could be a war…"

"Considering that you and I are the only two souls who know, I find it highly unlikely. And besides, who would replace me?"

Franco makes a gesture with his hand, conceding.

"Nobody can replace you. This is why you take such risks. But this girl, I worry about her."

He does not need to tell me the many ways this could go wrong. I have gone over them myself ceaselessly. It will undoubtedly strain my relations with Lachlan Crow and our Irish alliance. I gave them my word I would find her, and I did. But neither the Irish nor Viktor are aware of my true intentions with the girl. He will be angry, as Franco so obviously reminds me. But my position within the Vory is secured for life. Perhaps this is why I take risks. But I have weighed all sides of this matter carefully.

The end result, and the only result that matters, is that I will not be chained to Katya for the rest of my life. Franco knows this. And yet, I indulge his worries out of respect. He always has my best intentions at heart, so he deserves to be heard, even though it will not change my mind.

"Tell me what has you so concerned," I suggest.

"She is likely to be highly unpredictable. It is impossible to say what state she will be in when you first meet her. The things she has been through. She will be damaged."

I glance at the photograph of the girl on my desk. The one her friend Mack gave me in the hopes that I could find her. That I could save her. It is the photo I have studied night and day for the last three weeks. I know everything about her. I have read all her files. Uncovered all of her history up until the point she was sold. And the things Franco says are true. She is broken. She is damaged. I know this better than anyone.

I pour myself another cognac and raise my glass in agreement.

"And that is why she will be perfect."

Two

Talia

Death.

The word has such a sense of finality to it. But it's more than just an ending. People die long before they ever make it to the grave.

They die in little ways, every single day.

A loss of feeling. A lack of caring. Sometimes it is slow. Sometimes it has the subtlety of a hurricane.

Death can inhabit the body long before the soul ever leaves.

In my case, this is true. It is the only truth I know.

And I am ready to embrace the death of this life with open arms. I am ready to fly. To find peace.

One more week. Seven days. One hundred and sixty-eight more hours.

Then I will have enough. Enough remnants of the white pills to set me free. If tonight goes as planned, I might even shave a day off that number. Arman is always generous with the pills when he is entertaining guests. To keep me placid. To keep me in line.

After he fucks me.

Because he never fucks me when I'm high. He doesn't grant me such courtesies. For him, I'm always stone cold sober.

He's inside of me right now. Fucking me like the filthy pig he is. The same as he always does before a party. This is so I don't forget who owns me when all of his friends are inside of me tonight. He finishes with a grunt and then tosses me aside onto the stained mattress that I spend my days on.

I don't look at him when he speaks. I already know what he'll say. The same warning I always receive. His accent is heavy and his breath is too. Only the words are different this time. I almost miss it through the haze of my despondency, but there's something in his voice that captures my attention.

It's difficult to identify exactly what it is. Something sounds off. I've never heard Arman nervous before, but right now, that's exactly how he sounds.

"Tonight is important," he says. "These men must be satisfied. You must put in effort."

I don't respond to him because I never do. He doesn't deserve my words. My words abandoned me long ago, around the same time my sanity slipped out the door. But the question is there in my eyes when I look up at him, and he answers.

"If you embarrass me tonight, I will flay you alive for all to see."

Nothing. I feel nothing when he says that. Because his promises of death, no matter how brutal, are always false. He treasures his ownership over me too much to let me go.

His trophy. His prized slave. The American with the pretty blonde hair and vacant eyes. Nothing else matters in this wasteland.

"Karolina!" he snaps his fingers and she appears a moment later, her hands folded in front and her head bowed in submission.

Karolina loves Arman. And she hates me. He always makes her wait outside the door while he fucks me. So she knows her place. She may have her freedom to roam the mansion and his trust, but she will never have Arman's heart. Because the man doesn't have one.

He jerks his head at her, and she steps forward without any further instruction. Her hand moves to the locket around her neck, and Arman holds up a finger, speaking to her in a language I still haven't figured out. Arman is not Russian. This much I know. And he told me once that we were in Bulgaria, but this is not his native land. The rest are just details that elude me.

I may not understand the words that Arman speaks, but I've come to understand his mannerisms well. And when Karolina takes one pill from the locket, panic takes hold of me. I need two. Two pills to equal seven days. I hold up two fingers in a plea, and Arman slams his foot into my stomach. My body curls into itself as I launch into a coughing fit and fight for air.

I have to resist the urge to squeeze my eyes shut and block everything out as he finishes his instructions to Karolina. There is still a part of me that hopes he will be merciful, but that part is foolish. He leaves the room without any further regard to me. It's for the best, I realize. Because I might be able to fool Karolina, but I can't fool him.

And there is still one pill.

One pill is better than nothing. She hands it to me and I slip it into my mouth and under my tongue. And then she shackles my legs to the hooks along the wall, leaving just enough leeway for varied positions. I want her to leave now, but she doesn't. Instead, she glances back over her shoulder, and a cruel smile takes over her features when she turns back. She kicks me in the stomach twice more and then leans down to spit on my face.

"Dog," she mutters in a heavy accent. "Enjoy your evening."

She sashays from the room and I'm left gasping for air, horrified as I realize that I swallowed the pill whole in my coughing fit. Seven. It was only supposed to be seven days. Now it's eight.

Tears blur my vision, and I collapse onto the fluid stained

mattress in a heap. My eyes land on the familiar lines etched into the wall by my nail, and I retrace the line from this morning with my finger. Repeating the same word over and over in my head.

Seven. Seven. Seven.

At some point, the music upstairs begins to vibrate through the ceiling. I know it won't be long now. Drinks first. They'll all be drunk when they come down here. Sometimes that's better. Other times, it's worse.

The door opens. I don't look. But I hear Arman's voice. And feel the eyes of his guests as they inspect me. This is Arman's version of a dinner party, his slaves offered up as dessert. They talk amongst themselves, deciding who gets to go first. Sometimes they share. Sometimes there are so many on me at once I can't breathe. And I like that sensation. The air slipping from my lungs. I want them to empty completely and steal everything away. But it never happens.

Because Arman would kill them if they killed me.

The door closes behind me, and I'm left with only one man. I can tell by his breathing. One breath, one man. It doesn't matter what he looks like. I rarely see their faces anymore. I rarely see anything, other than the lines on the wall and the numbers in my head. Seven. Seven. Seven.

A zipper comes down. And then the sound of foil tearing. Arman makes them wear a condom when they take me. And they don't get to hit me either. I wish they would. I wish they'd hit me so hard I could fade into the blackness. But that special privilege is reserved for Arman only. And he'll never let me go.

He's inside of me now. This faceless man. And everything is one dimensional. The pill has entered my bloodstream and I feel nothing. I only hear him. Grunting and cursing.

I count the lines on the wall. And the lyrics to Angel of the Morning by Skeeter Davis play through my mind like an old record. My mother's voice. I sing along with her. And see their faces. Three empty, vacant faces of my brother and sisters. Lying on the bathroom floor.

Water in my lungs. Air slipping away. Clawing, thrashing. And the soothing song my mother sings while she holds me under.

My eyes flicker open and shut, everything distorted and sharp all at once. Seven lines. Seven days. Angels in the morning. Mother's hand on my cheek. Gasping for breath as I cough up water and see the halo of her hair surrounding her in the bathtub.

They are all gone. All but me.

Four angels. Seven days.

A grunt. The man behind me finishes. I collapse. Another takes his place soon after.

Flickers of my foster dad swarm my vision. This man smells like him. Like tobacco and stale sweat. The song plays through my mind again and I sing along, trying to block it out. I need another pill. I need the whole bottle.

"So very sweet."

It isn't this man's voice. It's my foster dad. Number one. He was the first. He won't be the last.

I count the lines and time holds me captive. I don't know time anymore. It's distorted. Days, months, years, minutes. They are equal to me. I don't know how long I've been here. I never know how long it goes on for.

The only thing I know for certain, is that at some point, the sweaty pile of human garbage behind me changes. This one tries to get rough with me because he can't get his whiskey dick to cooperate. I don't make it any easier on him, and after throwing me against the wall, he leaves the room, unsatisfied.

The next one murmurs in my ear as he fucks me. He is gentle, fucking me like a lover would. Halfway through he reaches down and touches me, trying to get me off. It makes me want to puke and it's completely pointless. I feel nothing. Nothing but the void.

He leaves the room and I lie in a puddle of sweat and semen, wondering where the next man is. There's always a next one and this one is taking forever. I want it to be over so Karolina will give me another pill. The door opens again, and I wait.

But he doesn't approach me. He watches me. I feel his eyes on me and I don't know why. Why is he dragging this out? A prickling sensation crawls along my spine and time suspends in the long stretch of silence. There is an unfamiliar urge inside of me to cover myself. To hide my body in his presence. I don't like his eyes on me. I don't like anyone's eyes on me.

Not like this.

Finally, there is movement. And my heart-rate calms as his shoes clip across the cement floor in my direction. I think he's going to fuck me now. And then he will go, like the rest of them.

Only he doesn't. He stops just above me. And it's the scent that always hits me first. That's the one thing I notice about these men I don't look at. This one smells good. Earthy like warm oak and spicy like cloves. He is too clean to be in this filthy room. I know it right away.

From the corner of my eye, I glimpse his shoes beside me. Black leather oxfords. Polished and well cared for. Knots tied with precision, peeking out from beneath gray twill trousers. Expensive.

I'm curious. And yet my eyes resist the urge to travel further. Until he commands it. It's not the command itself, but the deep accented voice that I recognize. The voice with the hard consonants and soft melody. A contradiction.

That voice, I'm certain, is the same one I heard two nights ago. When Arman was eating dinner and the doorbell rang out. Arman never greets company in the middle of dinner. But that night, when one of his men came barging in, he did. Whoever had arrived that evening was important. This man had power over Arman, which made me curious. In this castle, Arman is King. And I'd never seen him bow to any other.

But on that evening, he did. He graciously allowed for the interruption and even offered for the stranger to dine with him while I sat on the floor. The man declined and chose to stand for the few brief moments he was there. I wanted to glance up at him even then. But that was breaking my own rules. I never look at them. So instead, I focused on his shoes. Black oxfords. And listened to the voice. Deep and melodic. Unmistakably Russian and laced with warning. A warning that Arman didn't seem to like.

He left, and I pushed the whole incident from my mind.

But now my resolve has abandoned me. So my eyes travel up. And up, and up, and up. He's tall, this man. Taller than most. Much larger than Arman. And that pleases me.

I wonder if he'll kill him. I wonder if he'll let me watch.

He looms over me, his shadow eclipsing my much smaller body on the mattress. He's broad shouldered and powerful. The type of man with a presence that can't be ignored. Athletic and toned. A fighter, I think… maybe. Most of Arman's friends are fat and old, and stink of cigars and vodka. But this one is sharp, both in dress and manner.

He wears a black suede jacket and a gray flat cap atop his head, which casts his face in shadow. I can't see him, but he can see me. The weight of his examination is heavy, and my pulse responds. I don't know why. Only that I'm anxious, and I want him to leave.

He doesn't.

Because he's here to fuck me. Only, he's drawing it out. Taking too long. My dissociative fortress is caving in on me. Emotion seeping in. One I haven't felt since Dmitri's betrayal.

Anger.

It's roiling around inside of me, catching my breath and stealing my peace.

I lift my chin and try to meet his gaze. I don't know this man. But I want him gone. I have rules. I don't talk. Because I'm afraid what might spill out if I do. The truth I won't be able to contain. The space inside of my head is the only sanctuary I have. And he's ruining that. I turn my focus back to the lines on the wall, but I don't want him to see. I don't want him to see me counting. Because that's private. That's mine.

"Get on with it, will you?" the words snap from my tongue in a harsh cadence, a shock to my ears.

My voice is rusty and foreign. Demented. I sound like an animal. Because I am.

The intruder remains silent. Nothing but silence, for a full minute. I know, because I count every second. And then his deep voice reverberates off the walls, surrounding me.

"Look at me when you speak," he demands.

I turn my head back towards him slowly, only to find him kneeling in front of me now. Breathing my air, taking up my space. The shadow is gone, and his face is unmasked. Harsh and serious, with the type of blue eyes that can only come from Slavic genes. Ice cold and shocking in their intensity.

It has been many months since fear has held a place in my head or my heart. But the presence of this man stirs it to life again. Pulling me even further from my dissociative state than I'm willing to venture. Not a single one of these men have ever had the audacity to get intimate with me. To get right up in my face and look me in the eyes. I am merely a body with three holes to them, and they make their choice and cause me several minutes of discomfort before it's all over. But not this one. I don't know what it is he wants from me. I don't want to find out either.

The way he is staring at me disturbs me on a different level. He isn't just looking. He's seeing. All of my darkest secrets. The part of me that nobody ever gets to see. But he does. My armor means nothing to him.

He is different than Arman. This man scares me more than Arman. He's too well put together. Too calm. His emotions do not show on his face for all to see. And his hands… they are huge. Heavily tattooed.

I imagine one of those hands around my throat, crushing my windpipe. It would only take one.

"Do not worry." He brushes the matted hair away from my face in a surprisingly gentle manner. "I'm not going to fuck you."

There's a haunted sadness in his eyes. And something else too. A flicker of guilt. It's a rare emotion in the men who come to visit me. It sets off all of the alarm bells in my head. If he's not going to fuck me, then I don't know what he has to be guilty for.

The confusion must be written all over my face, but he doesn't explain further. Instead, he holds up a packet in his hand and shows it to me. Pain killers. He releases them from the foil and signals for me to open my mouth.

For just a split second, my eyes dart to the left. In the direction of my stash. Where I have every intention of putting these two pills when he leaves the room. So that I can make my seven days a reality, and not eight.

But this stranger is watching me carefully. Too carefully.

My lungs cease to function when he stands up and walks to the other side of the mattress.

I flop over onto my side, pressing it down with my weight. As if that would stop him. The man is a tank. He could toss my entire body into the wall with one hand, should he so choose. But I can't let him win. Not this battle. The only battle I have left. My hands claw at his arms when he reaches down, but he's too strong. And I am too weak. And now I'm merely a spectator as my peace is snatched away from me in horrifying slow motion.

He finds the pills easily. Some half and some whole, and some only a fine powder. For sixty days I have saved those pills. I have planned so meticulously. And in five seconds, he has uncovered my secret. He has destroyed everything.

"Please," I find my rusty voice again. "Leave them."

His eyes meet mine, and now… now they are even colder than before. Frozen over with a disturbing level of hatred.

His fingers pinch my face and his lips part. But the words he means to speak don't come. Instead, he takes a breath. And then another. Calming himself. His brows draw together and his eyes search mine. I am a whore. A slave. A subhuman piece of merchandise that Arman will use until he finally tires of me. It should not matter to this man if I die.

He flicks the painkillers in his hand onto my tongue and then retrieves a flask from his jacket. He holds it to my lips and the liquid sloshes into my mouth, strong and rich. Cognac. It is not the thing Arman drinks, and I am grateful. This man doesn't let up. He forces me to drink what's left in the container. I know why. I know what comes next. But I don't want to accept it.

When the flask is empty, he pulls it away and pinches my jaw between his fingers, prying my mouth open. He looks inside, and without an ounce of finesse, he seizes my tongue and searches beneath it.

But the pills are not there. He ensured that with the amount of liquid he made me consume. When he eases me back down onto the mattress, I can only hope the combination will usher me off into oblivion. His fingers sweep over my cheek. Gentle again.

An abominable noise escapes me when he bends down and scoops up every last remnant of my stash. The thing that is mine—the only thing I had—is now in his pocket. The dying ember of hope, snuffed out by one careless mistake on my part and one man too cruel for words.

The door opens and he does not seem to notice. Only when my gaze moves behind him, his posture straightens and he rises. There is another man in the door. A man like this one, only older. With the same type of clothing and many tattoos peeking out from every seam. He's the type of man that upon first glance, people would cross the street to avoid. His eyes are without emotion when they land on me. He says something in Russian to the man in front of me while they both seem to appraise me.

My destroyer of hope replies and it makes the other man laugh. The older man slaps him on the back and nods before his face slips into a more serious expression. It appears as though they are trying to come to an agreement on something.

The older man takes a step forward, gripping my chin in his hand and forcing my gaze to him. He is inspecting me. Much the way that Arman inspected me when he first purchased me.

"I think you are correct, Lyoshenka. She will be the perfect gambit. Hit Arman where it hurts, yes my little dove?"

My chin jerks impulsively in agreement. The temptation of hurting Arman in any way makes me nod. I'm nothing more than a dog with a bone. A product of my environment. I want to hurt Arman, even at my own expense, which is probably what this man is referring to.

He releases me with a satisfactory smile and says one last thing to his younger companion before leaving the room. And then blue eyes is back in front of me, for a brief moment. He brushes the hair away from my face again.

"Go to sleep now, Solnyshko." His breath is hot in my ear, scented with the oak and vanilla of his drink.

Before I can even comprehend what any of this means, he is gone.

Throughout the evening, time creeps forward in the way that it always does during these events. Sluggishly. I'm waiting for my pill. The only thing that separates day from night anymore. Eventually, the door opens and the other slaves are brought in. The men have been sated and now it is time for them to conduct business and leave us here in the basement.

There are three other girls here this evening. They walk into the room like zombies in their drugged states and slide down the wall onto the cement floor. I could tell them what to do right now, and they would not argue. The addiction is the only thing that matters to them. The next fix. They do what they are told and then they get what they want.

We have common ground, but I don't trust them. I can't. Because the last time I tried to bond with another slave, she told Arman. My parting gift from that short friendship was a broken arm and a dislocated jaw. A reminder of what happens when you betray Arman.

I stare across the void that is my cell and examine the girls faces. They are all young like me. Thin and probably pretty once. Now their eyes are sunken and their skin dull. Cracked lips and dry, brittle hair. It makes me wonder what I must look like to them. What I look like at all. I can't remember anymore.

I want them gone, I decide. Because we are not alike. That's what I tell myself when they stare back at me too. I just want to be left alone where I don't have to worry who to trust or what to say. I want to go back to counting the lines on the wall, but then I remember the truth. My mind is too fragile to accept it right now. That my hope has been snatched away from me so easily. That I'm not getting out of here in seven days.

That I'm not getting out of here at all.

Unless I find another way. The chains around my ankles aren't long enough to wrap around my neck. I know because I've tried. Everything in this room has been considered. Examined. And when that failed me, I tried to leverage the only power I had. Provoking Arman and even Karolina into a state of violence that would finally set me free. But that never worked either. I've considered every option at my disposal, and the pills were the only thing that made sense. The only option I had left.

And now they are gone.

The numbness is dissipating again. The carefully constructed sanctuary I created to protect myself has been fatally wounded by the stranger with the blue eyes. I hate him. I hate him so much a tear actually squeezes from my eye.

I need the numbness to survive. And he took that from me.

Now all I have is this room. My silent thoughts. And these girls who stare at me like I belong here. Like we're the same.

"What did he do with you?"

The skinny brunette with an accent breaks the silence. It takes me a moment to understand her question is directed at me. I've seen her before, but she's never spoken to me. So why now? I don't want to talk to her. I don't want to talk to anyone.

She mistakes my silence for apparent confusion.

"The fourth man," she presses. "Mr. Nikolaev. Did he fuck you?"

They all lean closer, waiting for my response. I still don't answer.

The brunette turns to her friend. "See, I told you, a sadist."

"No." The blonde shakes her head. "I don't believe it. She doesn't have a mark on her."

"What does it matter?" the third girl asks. "Why do you want to know what he did to her?"

"Because," the brunette explains, "Alexei Nikolaev is a recluse. He never leaves his house. Never comes to functions. He doesn't own slaves, and he has never even been to an auction. Yet, he came here tonight. It is a huge thing. There are always rumors, but to see him in person… even Arman was surprised. He didn't want him in here with her due to his reputation, but nobody says no to him."

"What sort of reputation?" one of the other robots asks the same question that's in my own head.

"He is a Vor," the brunette whispers. "Red Mafia."

"He's not just a Vor," the blonde sneers. "He is the councilor to Viktor Sokolov. The boss. Alexei Nikolaev has a reputation of being ruthless to anyone who crosses him."

The Russian Mafia?

"I think he has business dealings with Arman," the brunette rambles on. "Something fell through and Mr. Nikolaev is not happy about it. Arman is trying to mend fences. But one of the other girls said she overheard Alexei asking about his slave at dinner."

They all look to me again, even though I'm nothing more than a silent participant in this conversation. I don't have an answer for them. I don't know what he wants. But I hope I never see him again.

The door opens, and this time, it's Arman. He's drunk and his eyes are lasered in on me. Which is never a good combination as far as I'm concerned. He stumbles over to me and grabs me by the hair.

"What did he do with you?" he demands. "Are you ruined?"

I don't answer. I never answer him.

He shakes my head back and forth, yanking some of my hair out in the process. "Don't play stupid with me, girl!"

And then to my relief, he lets go of my hair and moves around behind me. Then he promptly shoves his fat disgusting fingers right up inside of me.

"I knew it," he laughs mockingly. "The man is all show. You are still perfectly intact. You aren't ruined, little dog. So perhaps I will keep you around a while longer, yes?"

I turn away from his taunting words. The reminder that I will never be free of my cage. I wish for blackness. And it comes in the form of his fist in my face.

Three

Alexei

"How are things with Katya?" Viktor asks.

I observe him from my space across the table. The restaurant has been cleared out to accommodate him. To most, I'm sure he is as fearsome as the rumors would have you believe. The Pakhan of the Vory v Zakone. But to me, he is simply my friend. Someone I respect and admire and who has given me a place in this life when others would not.

He values me. And he is risking his life by traveling this far with me. But even though my position within the organization is officially as his councilor, I am also his most valuable asset. My job cannot be done by any other within the Vory. My ability to manage the gambling operations and fatten Viktor's wallet substantially is a skill set belonging only to me. There are hackers who pride themselves on their work. Who boast publicly under pseudonyms and taunt the authorities. I am not one of them. I simply fly under the radar as I have always done. As I learned to do at a young age.

My skills are unique. Forged over a lifetime of dedication and hard work. It is not talent. It is not luck. It is nothing less than perseverance that makes me the best at what I do.

For this reason, Viktor holds me in high regard. But I'd also like to believe he considers me a friend. And perhaps, as his role has evolved over the years, even a son.

I do not like lying to him. But when it comes to Katya, I must. Viktor would not stand for such a betrayal. If the truth were ever uncovered, he would surely have her slaughtered. She has made a mockery of me. And in the Vory world, there is only one punishment for such a crime.

As little as I care for her, I still cannot in good conscience sentence her to death. Viktor is old school in some ways, and modern in others. He does not follow the original Vory tradition of forsaking all family. To him, a family outside of the Vory is as important as the brothers themselves. A happy home makes for a loyal Vor, he likes to say. The organization is very old, but it has evolved to the times. Now it is common practice to marry suitable prospects within our own culture, or for the sake of alliances. For a man with my rank, Katya is the most obvious choice. The one who Viktor and her father Anatoly insisted upon. So this ruse continues. He wants my reassurances. And I will give them, for now.

"She is busy planning a Christmas party."

Viktor waves his hand and dismisses the idea as preposterous. "That is nonsense. She should be planning a wedding, Lyoshenka. Anatoly has asked me for a date several times already."

I take a spoonful of Borscht and bide my time. I am running out of reasons to give him.

"What is holding you back?" he asks. "You are thirty-five this year. Do you not believe it is far past time to start a family?"

"It is," I agree. "I want that very much."

"And yet, you hesitate," Viktor argues. "I'm starting to believe you have doubts."

The waiter comes and clears our bowls, and Viktor leans forward to study me.

"Does this have anything to do with your father?"

"It has nothing to do with him," I counter. My voice betrays the indignation I always feel at the mention of Sergei, but a man like Viktor doesn't heed warnings from anyone.

"You have never believed you were adequate, Lyoshenka. You must let these fears go. Katya will make a good wife for you. She is already aware of your condition. And she accepts it. She will be loyal. In that, she has no choice."

Only, she isn't loyal. She is a liar and a whore. One who seeks a high ranking husband but prefers to sample all of his Vory brethren behind his back. But I do not tell Viktor that. Instead, I only nod.

He sighs and leans back in his chair, requesting another drink. The waiter promptly fills it up and leaves us to our conversation.

"What of this slave?" he asks. "You plan to keep her in America until Arman comes through?"

His words stir to life the mental image of the girl. Talia. It is the same image I have thought of many times since I met her only last night. She is more damaged than even I had foresaw. Franco was right. I have been over every detail of her life. Of her photos. But meeting her in person… seeing her in those conditions… I was not prepared.

She is skin and bones. A tangled mess of blonde hair and a gaunt, lifeless face. Those empty gray eyes were a painful reminder of someone else. Another ghost. One that haunts me often. And already, Talia is provoking memories I have no desire to revisit. I have questioned my strategy a thousand times over since the night before. And yet, even now, I am anxious to retrieve her and bring her to my home. To carry through on my plans before I can doubt it further.

"Yes," I tell Viktor. "She will stay at my home."

"At your home?" he questions.

"Magda will care for her," I explain.

He does not challenge my judgment any further, and I am glad. But he does observe my obvious discomfort.

"You seem… impatient," he remarks.

"Only to get home," I answer.

He nods. "Ah, yes. Well that makes two of us. We will give Arman one week to come through. And if he does not, then we will move forward. And we can both get back to our sanctuaries."

"Agreed," I tell him.

I already know that Arman will not come through. Because I have designed it that way. And yet when Viktor holds up his glass to toast, the traitor inside of me toasts him back.

Four

Talia

Arman announces that he will be away on business. It's a rare break for me, and I should feel relief. But I never feel anything. My world has returned to normal. White noise. A dissociative static. Numbness blankets me, and I try to forget that I've only just started counting my pills again. There are too many days yet to replenish my stash.

I have this plan. It is the only thing I have. The only motivation that breathes life into me from one day to the next. I will be the one to set myself free. It will be my choice. Time does not matter. Time does not even exist in this place. Or in my heart. Only the light in the distance. The angels waiting for me on the other side.

I've built a wall of invisible armor around myself. And it works almost all of the time. There is no warmth, no fear, no pleasure. Not even in the smallest thing. But I do still experience sorrow on occasion, so deep and violent that it feels as if I am an endless chasm of despair. And anxiety. I experience that too from time to time. There is only one cure for someone like me. I accepted this truth long ago. But it's a hard concept to explain to anyone else. Feeling numb, yet sad and anxious at the same time. They are three conflicting emotions, and by definition, I shouldn't be able to feel them together. But I do.

I want there to be nothing at all. Ever again. No pain. No sadness. Just nothing.

It is the only way. And I won't let go of this notion. I won't give up. It's the only hope that lives in the barren landscape of my soul. The only true freedom I will ever have. The course has been set, and deviation is not an option for me.

This is the thought that carries me through. The only thing that carries me through.

There are seven days in Arman's absence. I don't leave my room, and the only time I see another soul is when Karolina comes to my door. She uses Arman's leave as an opportunity to take out her hate on me. I rarely get to eat when he's away, and she takes advantage of my already battered face by hitting me every time she pays a visit. Even if I wasn't shackled to the wall, I doubt I could find the strength to fight back anymore. My body is thin and weak. I don't need a mirror to know that.

It only grows weaker with every passing day. I welcome that weakness. And her fists too. There is always a chance she will go too far.

But it never happens.

On day four, I hear her arguing with someone outside my door. It's in Russian, so I can't understand the words, but it's the voice that's familiar. The voice that belongs to the man I now know to be Alexei Nikolaev. The door cracks open, and I can only recognize the distorted shape of his figure from beneath my swollen eyes. His footsteps are soft as they approach, but the words out of his mouth are harsh.

I don't know what he says to Karolina. But she doesn't reply.

He kneels before me, his fingers gentle on my cheek again.

"Did she do this to you?" he asks.

I don't know why, but I want to answer him. I hate him. But the kindness of his touch dissolves my armor, if only for a second. My lips open, but they are too cracked to speak. I haven't had water all day. It takes me several tries to get the word out.

"Both."

He nods. And then rises to his feet. There is a blurred flash as he moves towards Karolina and slams her into the wall with his hand around her throat. I can only listen to the harsh cadence of his words, not understanding them.

Karolina nods, the sound of her blubbering satisfying me in a way I have not felt before.

And then, he is gone.

For the next three days, Karolina delivers three meals a day and does not touch me again.

When Arman arrives home, his mood is fouler than usual, and I don't even see it coming. He blasts into my room, spewing something about what I told Nikolaev, and how I will regret it. He beats me all over again and then chokes me until I pass out.

When I wake up, I'm a bloody fucking mess, and Karolina is hunched over me, cleaning me with a sponge, a smirk on her face.

"It is for your own good," she says in her thick accent. "Soon you will get out of this place, make us both happy."

I try to process her words, but my head is still spinning and nothing makes sense. My eyes are too heavy. And I can't keep them open any longer.

When I do wake again, it's with a stinging slap to my already sore face. I draw in a sharp breath, only to realize I'm now propped in an upright position against the wall. Arman is standing in front of me, with another man behind him. It takes me a second to recognize Alexei. His lips are pressed together, those steely blue eyes boring into me.

"Did you hear me, *pizda*?" Arman growls, raising his arm again.

Alexei clips out a quick string of words which causes Arman to halt, and I can tell it burns him. Arman does not take orders from anyone. And yet he is taking orders from this man. So perhaps it's true what those slaves said. Perhaps he is ruthless. A man not to be crossed.

But what interest does he have in me? His eyes move over me in a calculating pattern, observing every bruise and scrape. Arman takes this as his cue to start poking at my body. He seems to be pointing out all the things that he considers my flaws, and he is none too gentle about it. But Alexei is not looking where Arman points. His eyes are on Arman, watching his face intently. The noxious thumping of my heart tells me this can't be good.

Alexei steps forward, absently running a strand of my hair through his fingers. I flinch at the pain in my scalp, and he frowns.

"She is American, is she not?" he asks.

I glance up at him curiously. He already knows I'm American, since he spoke English to me last week. So why is he pretending he doesn't?

Arman replies, but Alexei doesn't seem to hear him. His gaze is still focused on me, and mine on him. It's only after I break contact first that he turns back to Arman.

The room is silent for a few awkward moments before Alexei repeats his question.

"American?"

Arman appraises him and then nods. "Yes. An American gem. So you must be able to understand my hesitation in parting with her, even temporarily. She is worth a lot of money this one, and she is very valuable to me."

"Valuable indeed," Alexei replies. "Like the shipment I was expecting."

Arman's face sours at this, and for the first time since I've known him he actually looks speechless. And it's then that I realize that if Arman is afraid of this guy, I probably should be too. Here they are, talking about pawning me off on this man who already fucked up all of my plans. And for what?

"You've put us out," Alexei states. "You can either part with her as collateral, or I can inform Viktor that you have cut the deal altogether…"

Arman growls out his frustration and throws his hands into the air. "Trust me when I say I'm doing you a favor. This girl cannot be trained. She is worthless in that aspect. I have tried everything. I think the *shalava* actually likes the beatings I give her. But I have another slave, who…"

"No," Alexei objects. "I am not interested in other slaves, Arman. The idea of collateral is to part with something of value. Any of your other slaves will not do. It has to be her or nothing."

"Yes, yes." Arman nods obediently. "I understand. We are all friends here… no need for threats. You can take the girl."

The room is quiet while Alexei looks me over once more. Arman is still nervous, evident by the sweat on his forehead, and it makes me nervous too. But then I think of the possibilities outside of this room. This man does not know me. He may have found my pills, but he can't predict all of the thoughts running through my mind. Leaving here means more options. More opportunities to find another means.

"I will take her," Alexei breaks the silence. "Until you have fulfilled the order for the lost shipment, plus three additional…"

"Three additional shipments?" Arman's eyes bulge. "But that could take…"

"The price of doing business," Alexei responds. "You have inconvenienced me, and I am growing tired of you already. Do we have a deal or not?"

"Very well," Arman says. "I can have her sent over this afternoon."

"No." Alexei shakes his head. "I will take her now."

Arman sullenly undoes my shackles and attaches a leash to my collar. He jerks me to my feet and makes me walk outside without a shred of clothing on. He hands Alexei the leash, stroking my face one last time. I shudder, refusing to look at him.

The low sun stings my eyes, and they begin to water. It's the first time I've been outside in over a year. It's so overwhelming I have to fight the urge to cover my eyes. To hide in the darkness like the animal I am. Alexei ushers me to a car where another man is standing guard. He opens the door and I slide into the back seat, Alexei following suit. Once Arman is back in the house, he removes the leash from my collar. Then he frowns and shrugs out of his jacket, handing it to me.

I don't understand the kind gesture at all, even if it is cold. I hesitate, but ultimately decide to take it, since I desperately need a safe cocoon. It's warm and smells like him, but it does not bother me.

Alexei says something to the driver who eyes me in the rearview mirror before cranking up the heater and driving off. As we drive, I feel Alexei's eyes on me but I am too transfixed by the scenery outside to pay attention to anything else. I don't even know where I'm at. When Dmitri left me to my fate, I was drugged for many days, maybe even weeks. That time—everything except for the horrifying realization of his betrayal—is a blur.

It does not matter, I realize. Wherever I am makes no difference. My heart and body are sluggish, but I need to keep my mind sharp. To focus on any opportunity that presents itself before I descend into the next level of hell.

I scan my surroundings carefully. Outside the window, there is nothing but landscape. We are on a long, lonely stretch of highway. And Alexei is now focused on the scenery outside. So I peek over the collar of his jacket, appraising him. I hate him for taking away my pills. My freedom. But he has also been kind to me. I know better than anyone that kindness always comes at a cost. Kindness is merely an illusion. Like Dmitri.

This man is no different. He is graceful in his movements as he shifts in his seat and stares out the window. He is cool and collected, like he has a force field around him that nobody can penetrate. He is still as well dressed as I remember, and he is clean, which is more than I can say for Arman, who bathed only when it suited him. But I would rather deal with Arman over this man. At least Arman doesn't hide his true nature beneath nice clothes and a fake exterior.

"My name is Alexei," his voice fills the tiny space when he turns and catches me staring.

I don't reply. But still, he persists.

"Now it is customary for you to tell me your name," he states.

I don't have a name. I am nothing. No one. If I ever was, I do not know her anymore. So I remain quiet. Safe in my fugue. He cannot take that from me. He will not.

He frowns, and silence returns to the car. With it, my anxiety. I cannot read him. He's trying to get inside of my head. Trying to hurl every weapon at his disposal into my already tattered armor. When he is near, the feelings come back. The things I told myself I would never feel again.

I need to get away. I need to fly away. By any means possible.

The driver turns the car off the highway and onto a gravel road, slowing his speed. My sluggish heart is pumping too hard. Too loud. I glance back at Alexei, and all of the uncertainty I feel about him fuels my fear. I make a split second decision before I can give it any more thought.

I fling open my door and thrust my torso out of the car with every ounce of strength I can muster. But it isn't enough. Something strong catches my leg and the vehicle screeches to a halt. The momentum sends the door crunching into my ribs, choking all the air from my lungs. I try to kick and scream, but my body is frozen in white hot pain.

I'm being pulled back into the car, my gaze colliding with the most volatile of blue. He is cursing in Russian, shaking me as he stares at me with wild eyes. When I don't respond, he changes to English.

"What are you thinking?" He clutches me tighter beneath his grip. "You would rather kill yourself than come home with me? Do you really think I'm worse than Arman?"

The way he says it makes it sound personal, but I don't know why. I don't know what to say, so I just continue to stare at him in silence. There isn't an explanation I could give that he would ever understand. There are no words to convey that the very life essence has been siphoned out of me and the wreckage in his arms is all that's left.

I was supposed to die in that bathtub twelve years ago. And I did. Only my body came back to life. What remains now is merely an apparition.

"Answer me!" Alexei shakes me again, and I flop around in his arms like a limp noodle.

His eyes betray his disgust with me. His resentment. I have seen those same things many times in Arman and it did not bother me. But on this face and this man, they bother me.

"Why couldn't you just let me go?" I yell back. "You took my pills from me! You took everything from me."

He stares at me in disbelief. And in a single moment, all of the humanity dissolves from his face. He yanks my body across the seat, pinning me belly down in his lap. His hand collides against the cheek of my ass, hard.

I don't make a sound. Or even flinch. Because his spankings are nothing compared to Arman's fists. This only angers him further. He rains down a series of hard slaps, grunting each time he does. It's the man in the driver's seat who captures his attention when he turns around and taps him on the shoulder.

"Lyoshka."

Alexei freezes, his hand still on my ass. I'm staring at the door handle, still mourning the loss of my attempt. And then he yanks me upright, into his lap. His eyes meet mine, and his hand comes up to my face. Gentle. So very gentle. There's remorse in his gaze. But I don't know why. He didn't hurt me. He could never hurt me. Nothing can anymore.

When he recognizes that in my expression, the anger returns. His fingers grip my face and his breath is hot against my lips when he speaks.

"Do not ever try that again, Solnyshko. I am not a man you want to test, and you will not like what happens next."

He pushes me back to my seat and buckles me in before locking the doors with the controls. And, just like that, we're off again. For the briefest of moments, something passes between him and the driver in the rearview mirror. Some unspoken thought.

There is guilt in his expression. The driver speaks to him in Russian, but Alexei focuses on the landscape as though he didn't even hear.

The remainder of the drive is quiet and tense. My ribs ache, and I can barely breathe. A deep, throbbing sorrow blooms inside of me, overwhelming the numbness.

I have tried and I have failed again.

And I know this man will never let me go. I have only traded one hell for another.

The car pulls to a stop, and outside I see that we are at a private airplane hangar. In the time that it takes me to turn back towards Alexei with questioning eyes, he's already got a needle in my arm.

"Shh…" His fingers move over my panicked face. "Go to sleep."

And I do.

Five

Talia

My eyes flicker open and shut, a groan vibrating through my lips as I peel my face off the slab of leather it's resting on. My head throbs and my mouth is too dry. I'm laying still, but something is moving beneath me. Tires, I realize after a moment. I'm in a car, sprawled across the back seat.

I attempt to flop over and my head bumps against something when I do. A trouser clad thigh. My eyes move up to find Alexei peering down at me.

"Where are we?" I croak.

"Just outside of Boston," he answers. "Almost to my home."

His answer sends a small wave of panic through me. And the words leave my mouth without a chance for my brain to filter them.

"I don't want to go to Boston."

He raises a brow at me and shrugs. "You are not."

And that's it. That's all I need to hear to slip back into my comfortable state of numbness. The walls resurrect themselves, my emotional fortress restored.

I manage to sit upright, noting that I'm now fully clothed. In leggings and a sweater. There's a brief question of who dressed me, but it disappears quickly. My attention is focused on the scenery outside.

I'm back in Massachusetts. My mind is too fragile right now to accept that. So I tell myself it isn't real. That none of this is real. But even so, my lips repeat the words again.

"I'm not going back to Boston."

Alexei gives me a curious look, but does not answer. And so I am satisfied with his silence. My thoughts slip away into the cavernous spaces of my brain and I just watch. The rolling expanse of trees outside of the window are an explosion of colors to my dull eyes. It is Autumn. And this is how I know Alexei's words are true. There is nothing like Massachusetts in Autumn.

But it's not real. And I'm not here.

The drive is long and quiet. Almost to Alexei means over more than an hour. I just watch the scenery fly by outside the window until my eyes hurt too much and I have to rest them again.

When we finally arrive at our destination, comfort surrounds me. The house is a fortress in the middle of nowhere, surrounded by nothing but wilderness. I am away from the people. Away from everything. Everything but him.

The car pulls to a stop and I try to get out on my own. I realize soon after that my legs don't work. Alexei heaves me up into his arms like a child and carries me inside. He's wearing a soft blue sweater that rubs against my face with every step. It smells like him. Like oak and cloves. And cognac too.

He leads me through a series of halls and rooms before we reach his destination. I don't have time to absorb the details of the house in the time it takes for him to open the door and set me onto a bed. A real bed, with two mattresses and a frame.

The softness is alien to my body, and everything about this room overwhelms me. I have lived in darkness so long, and this room is bright. The curtains are drawn back, sunlight spilling across the floor. I want to shut them. To stay in the darkness. But I don't move.

My eyes roam over the room, taking it all in. There's a bookcase, stuffed with books. And a table with art supplies. An oversized chair next to the window. Rich colors and cold stone walls. It is too big, and still too small. And it all caves in on me.

I claw at my throat, feeling claustrophobic, but stop when Alexei calls out to someone in Russian. When I flinch, he steps in front of me and frowns. And then an older woman enters the room with a flourish. She gives a little smile and bow, her eyes darting straight to me.

She is older than Karolina. And she does not look at me the way that Karolina did. She has soft brown eyes and dark hair speckled with grays. She wears it in a bun, and an apron covers her floral dress. If I had a grandmother, I imagine this is what she might look like.

"Talia, this is Magda," Alexei tells me. "She keeps the house in order."

I frown and move my attention back to him. Because he said my name. And I never told him my name. I'm confused and my head hurts, so I rub my temples. I haven't had a pill in a long time, I realize. Not even half of a pill. And everything hurts.

I need at least half a pill, to keep the numbness. And the rest I can save. I wonder how many Alexei will give me, now that he knows my secret. It worries me, but I don't have time to consider it.

Magda steps in front of me, giving me a small sympathetic smile. "Hello, Talia," she greets me in English, though her accent is very much Russian.

I stare blankly at her.

Alexei clips out a few short sentences in Russian and then moves towards the door. But before he goes, he stops, his gaze drifting back to me.

"Remove anything sharp from the wash room," he tells Magda. "And no baths either."

Magda frowns at me, but nods. And then Alexei leaves. I'm still staring at the door when Magda takes me by my hand and leads me to the walk in closet.

"There are clothes in here," she says. "So you can choose what you like, until…"

I don't hear the rest of her words. I stare at the clothes but don't touch them. There's too many. Too many colors. That claustrophobic feeling is back, so I move away from them, bumping into the wall.

"Miss Talia?" Magda asks, concern evident in her voice. "Are you okay? Do you need to sit down?"

I shake my head.

"Very well." She nods. "Mr. Nikolaev wants you to get cleaned up. There is a shower you can use, and I'll be right outside if you need some assistance."

She leads me towards the door of the adjoining bathroom, but I halt before I step inside.

"Miss Talia?"

I can't look at her when I speak. I can't allow her to see that the numbness is slipping away again.

"Is there a mirror?" I ask.

"Yes, of course," she answers. "I will show you."

"I don't want to see."

The room is quiet. She's considering my words. And then she slips away, returning a few moments later.

"There," she says. "I have covered it over. No more mirror."

This time, I let her lead me inside. The bathroom is large, and like everything else, overwhelming. But when my eyes move to the bathtub, there's a sense of familiarity and longing. The same lyrics begin to play through my mind. My mother's voice. Angels in the morning. Four angels. And me, too.

Soon…

"No baths," Magda destroys my reality with two simple words.

She urges me towards the shower and turns it on for me. And then I watch her remove the razors and anything else I might hurt myself with.

"Once you have washed, I will tend to your wounds," Magda states.

And with that, she takes a seat in the chair across the bathroom where she can reach me quickly if she needs to. It only confirms that thought echoing through my head.

This man is never going to let me go.

Six

Talia

I take my time in the shower, letting my sore muscles soak up the warmth. I cannot remember the last time I felt hot water on my skin. When Karolina bathed me, she spared me no luxuries.

There are a lot of toiletries in this shower. The choices overwhelm me, and pressure builds behind my eyes. The numbness is slipping away from me, and pain is taking a greedy hold of my body and mind. I don't want this. I don't want any of this.

I just want to be free. Like them. Like my family.

But he won't let me.

I reach for a bottle without checking the label and use it on every part of my body. I keep squirting the flowery scented gel into my hands and washing, over and over, but I never get clean. When I blink my eyes open, my skin is raw and I'm shivering.

"That'll do," Magda tells me, appearing outside the door with a towel. "You've scrubbed too hard."

When I step outside, my knees nearly buckle. Magda grabs me

by the arm and helps me to the chair across the room. She wraps the fluffy towel around me, but it doesn't help. I'm still shivering. It's getting worse.

"Miss Talia, are you alright?"

"I n-n-need a pill." My teeth clack together.

She shakes her head and frowns. "No pills. It will pass."

"It won't," I argue.

She ignores me and gathers a few items from the cabinet before she makes her way back to me. She starts to dab at my wounds. Her touch is gentle, but it feels like fire on my skin. I cry out everywhere she touches, and the pain is unlike anything I've ever felt before.

"It hurts," I tell her. "It hurts so much."

I know something's wrong when I blurt those words. My pain tolerance is high. Usually, I can dissociate. Float away to somewhere else. But not now. My heart is racing. I'm sweating. And the room is spinning.

"Give me something," I beg. "Anything."

Magda presses her hand to my forehead and grimaces. "You're burning up."

She opens a bottle of Tylenol and hands me two. Instinctively, I know they aren't what I need. But I take them anyway and wash them down with the glass of water that she hands me. And then I promptly heave myself over the toilet and vomit them back up a moment later.

This is when Alexei reappears, frowning at the scene before him. I'm sprawled out on the tile floor, naked and shivering as my brain spews words out of my mouth.

"Just let me die!" I scream. "Give me something. Anything. End it. Please."

I'm crying. For the first time in too long to remember. There's no numbness, no comfort for me. I feel everything now. Even the weight of his concerned gaze as I writhe on the floor. I don't want his concern. I want his mercy.

He takes four quick steps and kneels down to scoop me up into his arms. He clips out something in Russian to Magda before she scurries out of the room to do his bidding.

"You are going through withdrawal," he tells me. "It will pass."

I shake my head and sob into his chest. "I can't. I can't do it. Please…"

"You can and you will."

His voice leaves little question. He's sending me straight to hell.

And then we're moving. He carries me into the other room and places me into the bed which Magda has prepared just now. The covers are folded down to the end, and he gingerly places only the sheet over my skin. It still feels like knives, so I kick it off, and he doesn't argue.

"The doctor will be here soon," he tells me. "It won't last forever, Solnyshko."

"I hate you!" I scream in a demonic voice.

He flinches, and it surprises me. There is something on his face that looks familiar. Pain. It hurts him to look at me this way. It hurts him to hear those words. The fucked up part of my brain latches onto that information and takes note of it before he gives me one last glance and then leaves the room.

Magda sets a glass of water on the nightstand and smooths back the tangled hair in my face the way that I've seen mothers do to their children. Not mine. Mine kept us locked away where we couldn't disturb her.

I squeeze my eyes shut and tell Magda to stop. She does.

"It's okay, child," she murmurs. "Everything will be okay now. Mr. Nikolaev will take very good care of you. You are safe here."

Her kind words anger me and I want to tell her so. I want to tell her that she's a liar. That you are never safe. That you can never count on anyone to protect you. Only yourself. And even then, you will fail. But I don't say anything. Because another sharp jolt of pain seizes my body and I flop onto my side and curl up in a ball.

"Try to get some rest," she tells me in a soothing voice. "I will be right here."

I hear her soft footfalls move to the chair by the window, and a weak thought enters my mind. Even though I lashed out at her, I am grateful that she is there. Because if I'm going to hell, at least I won't be going alone.

Pain.

I understand now that the word truly meant nothing to me before. The thing I thought I knew well was merely a shadow of the demon that courts me now. Howling inside of me, clawing at my insides, desperate for more poison. My body is at the mercy of this demon. The sanctuary inside my head no longer exists. Nothing exists. Only the pain. The want. And the demon I cannot control.

I continue to beg Magda to end it for me. To kill me. I say horrific things that I didn't even know I was capable of. At one point, I hear her sniffling from her chair across the room.

I think I black out for a while. Everything is fuzzy when I wake, and Magda is shaking me.

"Miss Talia," she says, "This is Dr. Shtein. She is here to give you an exam."

A groan is my only answer. I can't move. I can't even see anything but the fuzzy figure of a woman hovering over me.

"She isn't going to hurt you," Magda says gently. "Just making sure you are alright. It won't take long."

The poking and prodding that takes place over the next twenty minutes barely registers. The pain is gone, and now there is only exhaustion. I think I'm hallucinating too. My limbs don't feel like my own as she lifts them and examines every inch of me. I'm still naked. But there is no shame anymore. There is nothing.

The numbness is starting to return, and I am grateful. Magda and the doctor speak in murmured Russian and then Magda translates to me.

"She will give you something for the pain. Something to help with the withdrawal."

The pain is gone, but I don't argue. I'll take anything I can get.

"It will be back," Magda adds. "She says this is normal. This liquid will help you."

They help me sit up long enough to ingest whatever it is they are giving me. And then I flop back onto my pillow, my eyes rolling up towards the ceiling.

"She needs to do a vaginal exam as well," Magda says.

There is a note of concern in her voice. As though I might react unfavorably. There is nothing they can do that is worse than what's already been done. My body has not been my own in so long, I don't remember anything else. So I keep my eyes fixed on the ceiling and come up with a new number in my head. Thirty. I will give myself thirty days to find another way. By then, Alexei will let his guard down. I will convince him I am better.

There's a snap of latex gloves, and then an instrument inside of me. It doesn't hurt. But then the doctor is moving the IUD around inside of me, and I cringe at the sensation. Arman had it placed when he purchased me.

Dr. Shtein murmurs something in Russian, and her and Magda talk quietly for a few moments, coming to some sort of conclusion. And then Magda squeezes my hand tighter and says something in English that I don't hear.

Something shifts inside of me, and then the Doctor pulls away and pats me on the leg. Magda covers the lower half of me over while the doctor prepares for something else. My eyes fall shut, and a needle enters my arm.

"A blood test," Magda explains.

When that part is over, Magda covers me completely.

"You did very well." She pats my hand encouragingly.

I don't want her to be kind to me. I don't want any of this. Those are the last things I tell myself before I fall asleep.

Seven

Alexei

I'm pouring over the reports on the computer screen when Franco taps on my desk to get my attention. I glance up at him through bleary eyes.

"You needed me?" he asks.

I nod and use the remote to pull up the information I've retrieved on the monitors across the wall. Franco turns to examine the faces on the screen as well as the names and addresses beneath them.

"What is this about?" he inquires.

Another click brings up the screenshots of the bets I flagged a month ago. While Viktor does not trouble himself with what kind of bets make him money, I do. There are certain things in this life even I will not abide by.

"They are running a sports bet under a false category."

I bring up the images of the illegal dog fighting ring I uncovered, and Franco doesn't ask further questions, except for the most important one.

"What would you like?"

"Make theirs a double." I point at the men to the left. One in the head, one in the heart. "And then bring Abbott to me."

Franco nods, but before he goes, he gestures to the monitors again.

"Nikolai is waiting for you downstairs."

My fingers contract around the glass of cognac in my hand as I flip over to the house cameras and observe him on the screen.

"What does he want?"

"To speak with you," Franco replies vaguely. And then he leaves the room, allowing my rage to consume me in peace.

I temper it with the rest of my drink before I am calm enough to face him. My half-brother, Nikolai. Though we do not carry the same surname. My father's shame of me was too great to allow such a thing. So I carry the name Nikolaev of my dead mother's heritage, while he carries our father's name Kozlov. It is fortunate for my father that we look nothing alike, to avoid speculation. His greatest fear is that the truth will be revealed to his brothers in the Vory. That they would know he has a son who is defective. Nikolai is his pride and joy, and I am nothing.

When I reach the sitting room, Nikolai is waiting for me, hands folded in his lap. He has fairer hair and complexion than I do, and when I meet his gaze, his eyes are an exact replica of my fathers.

"Is this a business visit?" I ask.

"Yes." He stands up and extends his hand, which I ignore.

I gesture to the bar across the room. "Help yourself to my drinks if you like. As you do everything else."

The insult does not go unnoticed, but he ignores it. Viktor is unaware of the tension between us, and this is the only reason I allow his presence in my home. He has only been here one other time since the incident six months ago, and then he left with a broken arm and a blackened face. If Viktor had been aware of the incident,

Nikolai would be lucky to escape with the loss of a few appendages at best.

But despite the bitter rivalry between us, he is my brother. And he has never dared to share my secret to the Vory or anyone else who could easily use it to their advantage. For that reason alone, I feel I owe him the same courtesy.

"Anatoly sent me to inquire of a good date for an engagement party," Nikolai states.

"Then this was a wasted trip," I inform him. "You should know that."

"I have no excuses to give for my actions," Nikolai tells me. "It was a mistake, Lyoshenka. I know I deserve to die for what I have done to you. And sometimes, I wish you would tell them. Tell them the truth. I don't want to carry on this way. I want to repair the damage I have done. So please tell me how."

"This discussion is over," I inform him. "So unless you have other business with me, you can leave."

Nikolai frowns and stuffs his hands in his pockets. "What should I tell him then?"

"That is up to you," I reply. "I'm sure you will think of something."

An odd expression takes over his face, and his eyes move to the ceiling. Though I cannot hear it myself, I know exactly what it is. The girl. She is having another episode. Which I've watched from the monitor on my wall for far too long today.

The tension in my body is at the point of exploding if I don't release it soon.

"What is that?" Nikolai asks.

"That is none of your concern."

He frowns, but does not argue when I gesture to the door. He pauses one more time to listen to the sound above and then leaves as I requested.

By the time Franco returns with my captive, I am even more on edge and entirely too drunk. But his repentance cannot wait. Because at this moment, it is exactly the thing I need.

I nod at the gagged man tossed over Franco's bulky frame in approval.

"Take him to the basement." I grab the bottle of cognac from the bar. "I'll be down in just a moment."

Eight

Talia

The days blend together in a repetitive pattern of pain and sleep. Magda feeds me broth and the prescribed medication every morning. Everything is too vivid and sharp to my fragile eyes, and I beg her to shroud the room in darkness.

She agrees to my request and allows me to sleep. There is no other choice. I cannot move from the bed. Or at least I believe. Until one night, I find myself on the floor, curled up the way I used to at Arman's when he took my mattress away. It's hard and uncomfortable, but familiar. I want to stay there.

When Alexei picks me up and returns me to the bed, my murmured protests are met with his harsh words.

"You sleep on the bed in my home," he tells me. "Always."

And then he leaves me to my own special form of hell.

Three weeks pass before the symptoms dissolve and my mind is clear. The first time I sit upright in bed and glance around the room, I have to remind myself where I am. With sober eyes, everything looks different. More expensive.

The walls are made of stone. And the colors around the room are rich and dark. Golds and burgundies throughout the drapes and area rugs to match the mahogany furniture.

It is large. Too large for me. And the curtains are drawn back again, allowing natural light to invade the space. It still feels too bright. When I swing my legs over the side of the bed and put weight on them, they are stiff and I have to hold onto the mattress for the first few steps.

Soft material brushes against my skin, and I glance down. I am wearing pajamas, I realize. Soft pink cotton. It is a strange sensation against skin that has been naked for so long.

I move around the room, touching everything that is foreign to me. Things I have not seen or felt for longer than I can remember. Books, canvases, paintbrushes. The textures feel bizarre against the pads of my fingers. On the back of the canvas, I find a staple which I pry off with my fingers.

Instinctively I press it into the flesh of my palm, easing the tension in my chest with the familiar comfort of pain. Then the door opens and I toss it to the floor.

Magda meets my gaze, her eyes following the movement, and she frowns. There is a tray of food in her hands. Real food.

"You should be in bed." She gives me a sad smile as she places the food on the nightstand. I observe the brightly colored fruit on the tray and my mouth waters at the sight of it. There is also soup and some crackers.

Magda gestures for me to come back to the bed, and I do.

"Eat slowly," she instructs me, "and stop when you are full. You don't need to worry about food here, Miss Talia. Any time you are hungry, you can eat."

I nod, unable to focus on her.

As soon as she leaves the room, I disobey by gorging myself. It isn't long before I'm in the bathroom purging it all back up. It's only after the fact that Magda's instructions begin to make sense. I brush my teeth and make it as far as the soft rug in the bathroom before I lay down to rest. I fall into a deep sleep, only waking when Alexei retrieves me once more.

I can tell by the oak and cloves in his scent that's it's him. He picks me up and carries me back to the bed again. I open my eyes and stare up at the ceiling, tracing over the patterns there with a finger while he watches me.

"What will you do with me?" I ask.

"I am keeping you," is his reply.

His words don't affect me one way or the other. Which seems to disturb him more than anything when I meet his concerned gaze. I'm back to myself now. To the familiar state of despondency. Even without the pills. And it pleases me. That I can stay numb forever, maybe. It will make it easier this way.

"Would you like to call Mack?" he asks.

"I don't know who that is," I answer.

He tilts his head to the side, examining me. After a moment, he seems to have decided something.

"You feel she has betrayed you?"

"I don't feel anything."

His lips press together and he nods.

"I will come for you tomorrow," he tells me.

And then he leaves the room.

Nine

Alexei

Franco and Magda are both watching me with matching expressions of concern on their faces. I ignore them and toss back the cognac in my glass.

"Everything ready?" I ask.

"Yes, sir," Franco replies. "He's waiting in your office."

"Talia is bathed and dressed," Magda adds.

I nod and check my reflection in the mirror. I'm nervous, but it isn't obvious to anyone but me. If there was another alternative, I'd like to believe I would take it. I tell myself that what I'm doing is best for the girl. For Talia. She will be safe here with me. Out in the world full of monsters and wolves, she would not survive.

This is what I tell myself as I make a gesture with my hand for the others to move to my office. Magda hesitates.

"Mr. Nikolaev, may I be excused from the occasion?"

Her face leaves little doubt to what she thinks of this. She does not agree with it. Magda has strong maternal instincts, and she feels protective of Talia. Just as she was protective of me when I was a boy with nobody else to rely on.

"No," I tell her. "Talia will want you there."

She wipes her hands down her dress, smoothing it out before giving me a soft nod. "Very well."

Her and Franco head to my office and leave me to gather Talia. When I step into the threshold of her doorway, I find her curled up in the chair by the window. Her ankles are crossed, and her pale white fingers clutching a book between them. She's staring at the pages, but I don't think the words are even registering. Her mind is far away. Somewhere that nobody else can ever hurt her again. The chair swallows up her tiny frame, and the deadness in her eyes scares even me. There is still much work to be done with her.

Her gaze moves from the pages to me. The expression on her face never changes. She is always flat, despondent. Just as I knew she would be. It is the very reason I told myself she would be perfect. But looking at her now, I need more from her. I need to see a spark in her eyes. Something that tells me there is still a sign of life inside of her.

"I need you to come with me," I tell her.

She doesn't argue. Her thoughts and actions have not been her own for so long, it is an automatic response on her part when she rises and moves towards me. I could be leading her to her death, and still she would not argue. In fact, she would probably celebrate. It is the thing she believes she wants.

Magda has dressed her in a white lace gown. She looks pure, even though we both know she is not. She also looks like a haunted angel. Still too thin and sporting dark rings beneath her eyes. But she is beautiful, nonetheless. Her blonde hair is long and falls into her eyes, like a shield against the world. She doesn't want others to see her. She can't even stand to look at herself. A fact evident by the still covered mirror in her bathroom.

These are all things I knew and expected in my mind, but I'm not certain I can accept them as I once thought I could. I want to shake her out of it. Demand that she feel something. But I know it is not yet time for that.

So instead, I reach forward and smooth the errant strands of hair back behind her ears, leaving her face fully exposed. A flicker of unease moves through her eyes, and I can tell she wants to pull it back into place. I do not allow it, my fingers gripping her chin and moving her gaze up to me.

"Do you question if I will send you back to Arman when this is over?" I ask her.

She blinks, but doesn't reply. I can see the answers in her eyes. She would die before she allowed that to happen. It is what she believes I will do, and anything I say or do to prove otherwise is a wasted effort. Talia has been betrayed by everyone who was ever supposed to love her. Words mean nothing to her. I suspect even actions themselves, she will always second guess. Always seeking out the true motives beneath them.

The truth is, she will never trust me. Nor I, her. It is the way we are programmed. Duped by too many in the harsh school of life. She is my equal in this regard. The perfect partner. Emotionless. Someone who can stand beside me for the benefit of tradition without the complications. I need to remember that when I look at her.

"You are at a precipice," I explain to her. "Wolves nipping at your heels. I think you already know this, yes?"

She bites her lip and gives me a tiny nod.

"And then there is this wolf in front of you. One whom you already know wants something else from you. It is this simple."

She doesn't argue. Instead, she waits for me to explain. To carry on as she considers every word carefully.

"You could go back to Boston…"

She flinches involuntarily at the very mention of it. As I knew she would.

"Which I cannot in good conscience allow you to do," I finish. "Knowing what you would do there."

Her gray eyes search mine, wordlessly. So many questions, but she does not voice them. That would show me that I have power over her. She already knows I do, but admitting it is something else. This is the spark that makes me believe all is not lost in her. There is still fight, even if she cannot accept it herself.

"I will not be sending you back to Arman," I tell her. "Because you will be staying right here with me. As my wife."

The only response from her is a vacant expression. I want more. I need more. My chest is tight, but I forge on.

"With me, you will be safe. I will provide you anything you could ever want. Clothing, shoes, jewelry… you will have the best of everything. And you will be protected. As my wife, nobody will ever touch you again."

She accepts her fate without a fight. It should not disappoint me, but it does. Her only question is an honest one.

"What do you get in return?"

"In return, I will have fulfilled my duty and maintained tradition for appearances. You will stand by my side when I have guests, and at all other times, you will be free to do as you wish. Within the boundaries of the house."

There is no reply from her. The words mean nothing to her. It would be easier if she told me she didn't want this. But she doesn't. So I take her by the arm and lead her down the hall.

The door to my office is open, and everyone is waiting. Magda's eyes move over Talia, searching for some sign of protest. For a sign of distress. Anything. But there is nothing to be found there.

I meet the officiant's gaze and nod. "We are ready to begin."

Since he is on the Vory payroll, there is no need for vows or any other long drawn out procedures. He simply nods to the desk where the certificate waits. I help Talia into her seat and then take mine beside her. Then I hand her a pen and show her where to sign.

She glances at the tip, probably considering if she can do any real damage to herself with it. And then she presses it to the paper. Her fingers tremble after the first swoop, and I close my hand over hers to guide her. We sign her name together, and then she looks up at me. There are more questions in her eyes, but she doesn't voice them. How do I know her name? What else do I know about her?

I feel as though she needs something from me in this moment. So I praise her in the only way I can think of.

"Good girl."

I clear my throat and take the pen into my own hand, signing my space on the paper. When it's all said and done, the officiant pronounces us husband and wife.

Alexei and Talia Nikolaev.

Franco and Magda watch as I slip the black gold wedding band onto my finger and then repeat the action on hers. Her band is also black gold, featuring a large ruby and a selection of black diamonds on the side. I could not imagine my wife wearing a simple ring like so many others. I could not imagine Talia blending in when she was born to be noticed.

She is beautiful, this wife of mine. With her dove gray eyes and pale skin. She will be the one every other Vor notices at parties. The woman that every other Vor covets. But she is mine now.

Still, it will not be official for me until she bears a permanent claim on her hand. One that she can never remove and nobody can ever question. I am anxious to mark her, but first, we must have at least several photos. Viktor will undoubtedly want them. As will anybody else who questions the legitimacy of my marriage.

My Vory brothers will want her. Even at the risk of death, they will want her. It is up to me to let them know that she is mine. That no secrets will live between us, and that she will never betray me. Even if I cannot believe it myself, they must believe it. Talia must believe it too. That death is the only result of such an action.

I have been weak once. But I cannot ever show that same weakness again.

So I request Franco to take exactly ten photos of us. Which he does. The ten photos which I have already strategically allocated places for around my home. Places that all of the other Vory will see them when they visit. The reminder that if they touch her, they will die.

Talia poses with me without any fight. There is no smile on her face, and no emotion either. But when I tilt her chin up to look at me, she does not turn away. I hold her in my arms and then kiss her cheek. Even after the last flash has gone off, we cannot bring ourselves to look away.

I ask the others to leave, and they do. And then it's just Talia and I, facing each other. My gaze moves to her lips, and my own mouth is telling lies before I can even question it.

"It is bad luck not to kiss your bride."

"I don't like to kiss," she replies.

But she doesn't move away, even when I lean into her space, feathering my fingers over her jaw. My breath fans across her lips, and she shivers.

"You will kiss your husband," I tell her.

And then my lips are on hers. At first, it is cold. There is nothing from her. But when I tangle my hand in her hair and demand more, she gives it. Her hand clutches at my shirt and she parts her lips for me. Allowing me in. I take from her, for far too long. Until she can barely hold herself upright. And when I pull away, I regret doing it at all. Because I want more.

Her eyes move over my face, seeking out answers that I don't have. I need to tell her my secret. She needs to be aware. It's on my tongue, but I can't force the words out. I don't want her to know that part of me just yet. I don't want her to think me weak when she needs my strength. When I promised to protect her, there needs to be no doubt in her mind that I am able.

So instead, I remove the tattoo kit from my drawer and set it on my desk while she watches.

"You would like some pain?" I ask her.

She nods.

Again my fingers move over her face, hard against her silky skin. "Then I will give it to you."

She sits through the process of the tattoo on her hand without so much as a twitch. This girl is accustomed to pain. She likes the pain. It is probably the only thing that feels good to her anymore.

I enjoy giving it to her this way. Marking her as my own. Seeing my star and my name carved into her flesh stirs a sense of pride in me when I wipe away the last of the blood and bandage it.

"Now, everyone will know that you are the wife of a Vor," I tell her. "And if they touch you, they will die."

She does not question it. She just watches me, quietly. Thoughtfully. Waiting to see what I will do next. So pliable.

"This star you wear has meaning in our world, Solnyshko. You do not yet trust me. You may never trust me. But that star gives you power. Protection. And so I want you to do something for me."

I take her other hand in mine, so small and delicate and cold, and brush her fingers over the bandage.

"When you feel anxious or uncertain, I want you to touch that star. Always. Remind yourself, Solnyshko, of the one thing you can be sure of more than anything else. That you are safe if only for having that on your skin. You do not require any other armor when you wear my star."

Her eyes meet mine, and there is doubt in them. Uncertainty. Even still, her fingers are moving over the bandage as she battles her thoughts. And I know in this moment, this is a step towards progress. That she can be reprogrammed. That I have given her something to believe in, no matter how small.

I am hard, from touching her. From being so close to her. And what I really want to do next is pull her legs apart and bury myself inside of her. To fuck her and fill her and claim her in that way. I do not think she would protest.

"You would let me fuck you," I say aloud. "Right now, if I wanted to."

"Whatever you want," is her reply.

I gather the material of her dress and slide it up the skin of her thighs. So creamy and soft beneath my palms. But there is no response from her, even though I am on fire for her. She knows I am using her. She does not see me when I look at her, but another faceless man.

And that is not how I will fuck my wife for the first time. I let the material fall back to her ankles and retreat, holding out only my hand for her.

"Come," I tell her. "Time for you to sleep."

Ten

Talia

I'm staring at the pages of a book when Magda comes in with lunch. When I take one look at what's on the menu, I frown. Fish, again. With another heaping of sour cream. Always with the sour cream and fish.

"I'm not hungry," I tell her.

She shakes her head. "You must eat every meal. At least a little bit."

"I don't like fish."

"Mr. Nikolaev insists you eat it until you are feeling better."

I don't reply, so she sets down the tray and moves towards the door. There's a part of me that wants to keep my distance. But Magda has been kind to me. She has seen me at my worst, and when she looks at me, there is no judgment in her eyes.

"Magda?"

My soft voice stops her, and she turns in surprise. "Yes?"

I want to tell her something. But I don't know what.

"Why are the windows bulletproof?" is the thing that comes out of my mouth.

Magda glances at the window. "How could you tell?"

I tap on the glass. "Because Arman had the same."

What I don't tell her is that I discovered this when I tried to throw myself out of one of them unsuccessfully.

"Mr. Nikolaev will not take any chances with your safety," she says. "It is for all of our protection. This house is more secure than any other place you could ever imagine."

To demonstrate, she pulls back the heavy door to my room that is never fully shut. "Do you see these strips?" she points out. "They are magnetic. Reinforced steel. This room is for your protection, Talia, although you do not need it. Mr. Nikolaev would never allow anyone to get this close to you."

I nod and she smiles. There's hope in her eyes, which is a dangerous thing. I can't allow her to think she will fix me. I have disappointed anyone who ever looked at me that way before.

I reach for my tray and focus on the food. Magda leaves, and only once she is out of earshot do I tell her thank you.

Eleven

Talia

Another two weeks pass with the monotony of the same pattern. Wake, eat, sleep, repeat. My body has returned to a healthier state, but my mind is the same as it always has been. Diseased. Toxic.

I'm growing restless. Alexei has not come to see me since he made me his wife. Sometimes, I venture outside of my room. Not very far. Only the level I'm on so far. The house is large, and inside it looks like a castle. Stone floors and walls and rich colors and furnishings. There are three bedrooms on the second floor as well as Alexei's office. And when I pass him, or even linger just outside the doorway, he doesn't seem to notice me. I'm like an apparition in this house. Moving around unseen.

But I notice him. I'm starting to notice more about him the longer I am here. The blue of his gaze when he settles his eyes on me. The line of his jaw. The scent that seems to linger around the house even when he isn't in the room. The ever present reminder of him.

I am curious.

He is mafia. But he never leaves his house. There are computer screens that take up an entire wall in his office. I don't know what he does. Something with computers. He is smart. I can tell by the way he examines the numbers and makes notes. Often, he and Franco can be found playing chess in his office too.

Magda takes care of all of us. She cooks and cleans and keeps the household running. Franco does as Alexei bids I gather as he leaves the house more frequently. They all have their jobs. Their reasons for being. All except me.

I pretend to read. And contemplate my own plans. Sometimes, the urge isn't there anymore. To hurt myself. To free myself. And that worries me.

I need to bring it back. I can't get too comfortable. This is not reality.

So when I step out of the shower, I do something I haven't done before. I move to the mirror above the sink. The one still covered with a towel.

With a trembling hand, I reach up and pull it down. And staring back at me, is the stark cold reminder of my true reality. I don't recognize that woman. She is gaunt, with protruding bones and pale skin. Covered in scars and fading bruises.

I touch my cheeks, and so does she. And I hate her. I hate her so much I wish she would just disappear. I ball my hand into a fist and slam it into her reflection. The glass shatters, and blood drips from my knuckles when I stumble back a step. But it isn't enough. It's not enough for the rage that's bubbling up inside.

So I lean down and scoop up one of the fragments and drag it over my arm seven times. Before I can count eight, Alexei is in the doorway, his expression horrified and angry.

His eyes flicker down to the shard of glass now aimed at my wrist.

"Don't," I warn him as he takes a step.

He ignores me. I dig the tip into my skin, but I am weak. Because he pries it from me easily and tosses it to the floor. When I look up at him, my lip trembles. The veil of numbness is gone now, and my knees are about to buckle. He senses it and grabs me just before I fall.

I'm pulled against his chest, smearing my blood all over his shirt. He holds me tighter, and his hand comes up to smooth over my hair. His touch is gentle and kind even though his eyes were angrier than I'd ever seen them. And it's all that it takes to send me over the edge.

I cry. I cry hard, clinging to his chest for support. In the tiny part of my rational mind, a voice is whispering to me. *Don't get too close. Don't let him see you like this.*

But the emotions are too strong. He holds me and whispers in my ear. It's in Russian, so I have no idea what he's saying. His voice is soothing. And it scares me. Magda comes into the room and gasps at the sight before her, and I am grateful for the interruption.

"Talia," she says. "Come, come. I will tend to your wounds."

"I will take care of it, Magda," Alexei informs her.

She glances at him, and something passes between them.

"Are you sure?" she asks carefully.

He nods, and she seems hesitant, but she goes. And I wish it was her staying instead of him. It's dangerous to be alone with this man who right now feels like a source of comfort. Like he could be the remedy for the chaos inside of my head. My calm in the storm.

He told me himself that this marriage is for the sake of tradition without any of the complications. This is a complication. The wife he married is damaged and broken. Unrepairable.

How could he not know that?

He leads me over to the same chair that Magda sat me in when I arrived. I focus on the tiny rivers of red on my arm. Alexei returns and cleans the wounds thoroughly and harshly. He wants to punish me, I think. When I peek up at him from beneath my hair, I notice the anger has returned to his eyes.

His thoughts are faraway. And I wonder what it is about this that reminds him of something else. He stitches the wounds next, with a steady and practiced hand. It sparks my curiosity further, but I don't ask him about it.

When he is finished, he leads me to the closet and chooses a set of pajamas for me.

"Put those on," he instructs me.

I do as I'm told and he doesn't watch. I wonder if there is any part of him that finds any part of me attractive. He is handsome. With strong cheekbones and a prominent jaw. Pale blue eyes that fascinate me at times and annoy me at others. But at times he seems as dead as I am. Like right now. In a closet with the half-naked woman before him. He does not flaunt his good looks, but he does seem to hide something else behind them.

When I am dressed, he puts me back to bed like a child. The disappointed expression on his face irks me. He has no right to be disappointed in me.

He calls out for Magda, and she appears in the doorway as though she were waiting just outside. He speaks to her in more Russian. Words I don't understand, but get the gist of anyway.

She's not to let me out of her sight.

Twelve

Alexei

I tip the bottle of cognac towards my glass, but nothing comes out. Through unfocused eyes, there's a vague understanding in my mind that I drank it all.

Both of their files are laid out on my desk. Like a puzzle I cannot figure out. I've studied each of them closely, and the only conclusion I have reached is that I need more cognac. Part of my brain tells me this is the process. That it will be worse before it gets better. The other part, the logical one, tells me that I have failed already.

A shadow falls over my door, blocking out the light from the hall. When I look up, Magda is standing in front of my desk.

"Alyoshka."

There is pain in her eyes. For me. From anyone else, I would not tolerate it. But Magda knows me better than anyone else. She reaches for the empty bottle on my desk and shakes her head in disappointment. And then her eyes move to the files, side by side.

She takes a seat across the desk and appraises me. "They are not computer data," she says. "You cannot analyze these files and find an answer."

"I already have the answer," is my drunken reply.

She looks at me with disgust and maternal outrage. "The answer is not you."

The photos from my past tell me otherwise. My gaze moves to the drawing inside the first folder. In my childlike brain, I believed that some pencils and paper could make up for the damage I had caused. The scratchy lines compose a house, in a field of purple flowers. Her favorite color. I told her I would buy her that house someday. And she rejected my gift. My last gift to her.

Magda reaches over and closes the file, obscuring my past behind thick brown paper.

"They are not the same," she tells me.

When I look at the woman across from me, with the kind eyes, I wonder how I have not failed her too. She took me in. She cared for me in my darkest hour. And still, here she is. The only person in my life I have not tainted.

"You need to keep her alive," I order.

This only angers her further.

"You know better than anyone that you simply cannot force someone to have the will to live. Especially not after what she has been through."

Her words frustrate me too. If anyone can save her, I know Magda can.

"I worry about you," Magda tells me. "This girl is bringing your past back. You believe you can save her with material things. But this is not the way."

"Then what is the way?" I ask.

Magda sighs and stands up. "She needs the one thing that nobody else in her life has ever given to her. The one thing that even you are not willing to give."

There's a pause where a deep sadness flickers through her eyes. "She needs love, Alyoshka."

Thirteen

Talia

Alexei is avoiding me.

My cuts are healing, and every time I touch the stitches, I think of him. About the look that passed between him and Magda that day. About the secrets he is keeping.

These thoughts help me not to focus on myself.

True to Magda's word, she brings me food any time I'm hungry. But it's always the same things. Fish or chicken. Berries and nuts and greens.

I waste some time painting since Alexei obviously intended for this to be some type of therapy. I paint every canvas blood red. When Magda sees them, she frowns. There is disappointment in her eyes, and it irritates me.

"I need more red paint," I tell her.

"Why don't you go explore the house," she suggests. "I could give you a tour if you like."

I fidget with the paintbrush in my hands to avoid her hopeful expression.

"I might go later."

She nods and then does something unexpected. She pats me on the shoulder and gives me a little squeeze.

"You remind me so much of him at times," she says. "When he first came to live with me."

"Who?" I ask.

"Alyoshka," she answers. "Alexei. You two are more alike than either of you realize."

There is warmth in her eyes when she says it. And pain too.

I look away, and she leaves the room.

After lunch, I do as Magda suggested and explore the rest of the house.

There are three levels, and I suspect a basement as well. After exploring the first, I discover something new. A gym. The only piece of equipment inside is a solitary punching bag hanging from the ceiling. It isn't the bag, but the man punching it that captures my attention.

Alexei.

He is wearing a pair of black pants and nothing else. And for the first time, I see his extensive tattoos. Some intricate, some simple. There are a mixture of black and other colors climbing up his back, chest, and biceps. There is an urge inside of me to study them. To explore him. Like a puzzle, I want to decipher each and every one of his mysteries.

I want to know the feeling of his body beneath my hands. The chest and back that are broad and strong and glistening with sweat. It is an urge I have not had since Dmitri. This kind of want is unfamiliar. This kind of want is dangerous to me and alluring in the worst kind of way.

He doesn't seem to hear me, even when I step inside and the mat creaks beneath my foot. It is only a moment later that his gaze catches mine in the mirror. He freezes, and then slowly turns toward me.

"Talia?"

There is concern in his voice. He wants to know what I'm doing in here. I wish I had an answer.

"I'm sick of fish," I tell him.

"Is good for brain chemistry," he replies.

I tilt my head to the side and examine him. "Is that the polite way of telling me that I'm crazy?"

A ghost of a smile appears on his lips, and he shrugs. "Maybe a little bit."

I smile too. And it scares the ever living shit out of both of us. My hair falls in a cascade around my face when I tilt it down and tap my toes against the mat.

"Don't hide from me," Alexei says.

And when I look up, he is in front of me. His fingers find my chin, and he pushes my hair away from my face.

"Never hide from me."

His face is close to mine, and we are both studying each other. I want to know things about him. Things that I'm not privy to.

"I need you to take my stitches out," I say.

He picks up my arm and smooths his fingers over the healed cuts. "Magda…"

"I want you to do it."

His pale blue eyes search mine for answers, but I don't have any to give. So he simply nods and takes me by the hand, leading me upstairs to my bedroom.

"Sit on the bed," he instructs.

And I do. My legs dangle over the edge since the bed is tall and I am short. I watch Alexei disappear into the bathroom and return a moment later. He kneels before me with the scissors, and I hand over my arm freely. While he works, I study his tattoos.

"What do they mean?" I ask him.

He looks up at me, and it seems like he didn't hear me. There is concern in his eyes, but I'm not sure why.

"Your tattoos," I clarify.

Again, he remains silent. The way he did at Arman's. He seems tense. And I can't help but feel like I'm missing something here. Either he doesn't want to talk about them, or he didn't understand me.

"You want to know about my tattoos?" he asks.

I nod when he looks up at me.

"The stars on my shoulders I received when I became a Vor," he tells me. "I have them on my knees, as well. And it is the same reason you also wear my star. To let others know you belong to a Vor. But, more importantly, to me."

My pulse beats a little faster when he says those words. So full of ownership. But not like Arman. With Alexei, it is different, and I don't know why. I feel like those words mean he will protect me. Like he promised he would. But that's a dangerous thought to allow.

"What about the ones on your hands?" I ask.

"These signify my crimes. The time I spent in prison. The rose on my shoulder means that I turned eighteen in prison."

"What for?" I ask.

"You are a curious kitten," he remarks, but there is the hint of a smile on his face. "Now that you are speaking."

I shrug and wait for him to answer. He watches me carefully as he speaks, gauging my reaction.

"You must serve time in prison to become a Vor. It is the old way of doing things. The tradition was still valued at the time I wished to be inducted. So I hacked into a bank at sixteen and diverted the funds of a corrupt politician."

"So you got caught on purpose?" I ask.

"Yes. But it was nothing. Just a few years. Every Vor must do his time."

I don't understand it, but it makes sense to him. He finishes quickly. Too quickly. And I don't want him to leave yet. So I lean forward into his space and kiss him. The tools in his hands are discarded on the floor, and then he's on top of me, pressing me back into the bed.

It happens fast. And he kisses me hard. I kiss him back. My hands are in his hair, and his tongue is in my mouth. He is hard against my stomach. And my body aches for him in a way that terrifies me.

But he pulls away abruptly, his eyes wild and confused.

I press my fingers to my lips, never allowing my gaze to leave his as he hovers over me.

"Not yet," he tells me.

And then he gets up and leaves the room.

Fourteen

Alexei

Viktor has paid me a visit as I knew he would when he received the news. The pakhan rarely makes personal house calls without a good reason. But I gather as he sits in my office that this is the exception.

"I'm beginning to think that I'm losing my own hearing," he tells me when I finish pouring his drink. "Surely, I've been given some misinformation Alexei."

I fold my hands across the wooden desk and study him. Talia is asleep down the hall. I don't want her to hear this. Outwardly Viktor appears calm, but inwardly, I can see his anger. I was supposed to marry Katya. It is what everyone believed would happen, even though I never agreed to it.

"I have fulfilled my duties as your councilor and I continue to secure the future of the Vory through my work. But when it comes to who I marry, the choice was mine to make. Katya did not suit me."

"Why?" he demands. "Because she is well bred? Beautiful? Or

is it the fact that she was brought up to do exactly as she was told? Which is remain loyal to this family."

Loyal, Katya is not. But Viktor is right. She was raised with one purpose. To marry a Vor. Perhaps this is what makes her greedy to sample as many of them as she can, but it is not my place to determine. I will not be responsible for her death, so I keep my lips sealed on the matter.

Which only serves to irritate Viktor further.

"You cannot possibly care for this girl," he tells me. "She is a whore, Alexei."

"Enough." I warn him. "That is my wife you are speaking about. It is done."

Viktor smirks. He has always found it amusing that I speak freely with him. Most men would not attempt it. But most men don't know all of Viktor's secrets. And they are expendable. I am not.

"I am just stating facts," he says. "No self-respecting man would want other men's…"

He makes a gesture with his hand, searching for the right word. "Leftovers."

Beneath the desk, my hand is shaking with the force of my anger. Outwardly, I remain calm. This is the way Viktor speaks of all women. Normally, it does not bother me in the slightest. But I don't want him speaking that way about Talia.

"She had no choice in the matter," I tell him.

"And she does now?" he raises a brow at me. "I would like to speak to the girl myself. Understand what it is that made her agree to such an arrangement."

"You will not be speaking to her."

He finishes his drink and rises to his feet. "I will," he says. "But it can wait. Perhaps another time. Meanwhile, you will need to break the news to Anatoly."

"There are plenty of suitable matches within the Vory," I inform him. "Perhaps even Nikolai."

Ghost

Viktor gives me a curious look, but I maintain a neutral expression.

"Yes, perhaps even Nikolai," Viktor says. "After all, he has Sergei's approval. And his ears are intact too, no?"

"It has nothing to do with that."

"I certainly hope not," he tells me. "Forever is a long time to lie in the bed you've made."

When Viktor has gone, I chase his departure with two glasses of cognac. And then I go to check on Talia.

Only, I find her in the hall. Her hand hovered over a burning candle, searing her skin. Emotionless eyes meet mine, and she does not attempt to hide her self-mutilation. Her face is once more cast in a shadow of despondency.

She heard.

I move towards her and remove her hand from the flame before leaning down to blow the candle out. I take her by the arm and walk her back to her room.

Not a word is spoken between us as I apply salve to the burn and she watches me. The questions are in her eyes, but I don't know how to answer them.

Why did I marry her?

She wants to know. I owe her answers. I want her to know that I do not believe what Viktor said of her. I should tell her. What I give her instead is a soft kiss on the forehead before tucking her into bed.

Yesterday, she smiled. And today, she wants to die all over again. Because of me.

Fifteen

Talia

I've taken to roaming the house at night. When everyone is asleep, and it's only me and the moon to keep me company. Sometimes, Alexei is still in his office. Passed out on his desk.

He drinks often at night, reliving his own memories, I think. I want to know the ghosts of his past. The things that haunt him. If only to take the focus off of my own demons for once.

Tonight, when I peek through his doorway, hidden in shadows, I find something else entirely.

He is sitting at his desk, but he is not asleep. His pants are unzipped, and he is gripping his cock in his fist. Pleasuring himself. His eyes are closed, his head leaned back against the chair. The muscles of his forearm tense with each harsh pull, and a jolt shoots through my body at the sight.

Sex has always been a coping mechanism for me. The only way I could connect to a man. I want to connect with Alexei. I want him to want to fuck me.

But then his friend Viktor's words filter through my mind.

Dirty. Filthy. Whore.

That's what I am. Why would Alexei want me?

I wonder who it is he thinks of when he pleasures himself. My husband.

Katya?

I don't know who she is. But the very name produces a fire inside of me that I can't put out.

Alexei grunts, and his hips flex upwards. I slide my fingers into my shorts and breach the barrier of my panties. Already, I am wet for him. I touch myself while I watch him.

His breathing is changing. Growing harsher. Faster. He's almost there. And I'm nowhere near it.

I can't get myself off anymore. It's been too long since I've even tried. But I want to touch. To feel. To watch this secret part of him that he keeps hidden away. Someone in their most vulnerable and intimate moments.

He is jerking himself roughly. Angrily. At war with his lust. Something is holding him back from his pleasure. With a frustrated groan, he fumbles for the remote on his desk and opens his eyes, focusing his attention on the screen for a brief moment.

And that's all it takes. He comes with a harsh growl, spurting into his fist. I'm transfixed by the sight of him like this.

Exhausted, he leans his head back against the chair and closes his eyes again. And I finally move my attention to the screen, to see what it is that pushed him over the edge.

What I find scares and thrills me.

The girl on the screen is me. Standing in his gym two days ago, smiling. For only the briefest of seconds. A freeze frame from a security camera I never knew existed.

My mind cannot handle the overwhelming emotions that spring up inside of me. So I retreat. The same way that I always do.

Sixteen

Talia

Alexei has given me a computer.

Not directly, but through Magda. It is small and thin, with a silver casing. I have not opened it. But I like to feel the smooth surface beneath my palm.

Magda explained that if there were clothes or anything I'd like to purchase, that I could do so through this device. Before any hope sprang up inside of me, she informed me that all the packages would be received by her and Franco and not to try anything questionable.

There isn't a single purchase that I'd like to make. But there is something else inside of that computer. An answer to a question whispering at the back of my mind.

I'm tracing over the tiny apple emblem when Alexei's voice cuts through my thoughts.

"You have not used it."

I don't answer him, but I do look up. Today, he is dressed for going out. The same black jacket and gray flat cap on his head as when we first met.

Alexei never leaves.

In my eyes, nothing else exists outside of this world he's built for us. These walls and this space which harbors me and keeps me safe. But he is the gatekeeper. And when he is gone that safe feeling flees with him. And the thought of him doing so now sends a small sliver of fear through me. I don't understand why. He doesn't miss it. And like always, I wonder how he reads me so well.

"I will only be away for a short while," he says. "Franco will remain here to look out for you, as well as Magda."

I nod, though his words do nothing to dissipate my fear. Every breath I take feels forced, stilted… as if my lungs have given up. I've lost the will to breathe. He promised he would keep me safe. But then I think of Arman. How unlikely it is he will ever let me go. What if he came here? I haven't been counting. Or planning.

I need to do that.

Because Arman will come. Alexei's words mean nothing to me. Just as Dmitri's and all of the others before him. Words are nothing. Even the vows of marriage cannot protect me. Shield me. Or even repair me. And I must die.

"Talia?" Alexei's voice is closer now, and when I blink his fingers are on my face. Warm and strong. I don't say anything, but I don't need to. He seems to understand what I'm thinking, and I don't like that. He is hesitant to leave now.

"I'm tired," I tell him. "I want to lay down."

He nods and pulls back the covers for me, helping me into bed. And then he pauses. His eyes on mine. My eyes are on his lips. Wondering if he thinks they are dirty now because I kissed him. Wondering what he sees when he looks at me the way he is looking at me right now. My fingers are moving over the star on my hand. Exactly the way he taught me to. He doesn't miss it.

"I'll be back soon," he repeats softly.

And then he retreats.

I lay in the stillness of the house, waiting for the sound of the front door to close. In the time it takes the organ in my chest to beat sixty times, he is gone. And I'm staring up at the ceiling. Thinking of Arman. And the questions in my mind. The desire to know more of Alexei, and the emotions I feel rising to the surface the longer I avoid the thing that needs to be done.

Before I can really question what I'm doing, I move down the hall to his office. I know he has alcohol in there. I tell myself that's what I'm seeking out.

I can hear Magda downstairs in the kitchen, and there is no sign of Franco. The door is open. All of the screens are off. And I step inside.

His scent still lingers in the space. The large oak desk is well worn, with lines that tell a story of who this man is. A constant companion over the years, it seems.

I sit down in the chair and glance at the drawers. They are all locked. One of the few things that poses no obstacle to me. I had a good teacher. A friend. A distant face that I think of sometimes, but pretend doesn't exist.

Because it's easier that way. It's easier to die knowing that nobody cares.

I retrieve a bobby pin from my hair and go to work on the first drawer. It doesn't take long for the skill to come back to me as if it were yesterday. When I was just a kid on the street. Always looking for my next meal. My next aversion to the constant well of pain inside of me.

The drawer yields nothing but a black notebook and some pens. Addresses, names, and a makeshift ledger with neat scrawls of penmanship across the blank pages. I put it back and move to the big drawer. The one on the bottom. A file drawer.

Ghost

It opens. That organ in my chest beats again. Harder.

There are only two files inside. Two brown paper files.

My fingers hesitate to touch, but my brain demands answers. So I pick them up. Neither has a name. Or anything noted on the blank space where it should be. My mouth is dry when I glance at the door and open the first.

What I find is worse than I expected. More than I can handle.

The pages of my life. Summarizing my existence into a series of mercilessly blunt chapters. Birth certificate, health records. But worst of all are the photos of my family. Of my mother and my siblings. The newspaper records printed in black and white. And then the careless notes of the case worker who handed me off to anyone who would take me.

I keep flipping through the pages. Catching only words and fragments of sentences as they collide with images in the story of my life.

Murdered. Tragedy. Children. Monster.

Disappeared.

Then there are photos. My airway is choking the life out of me. I can't breathe.

That little girl. It isn't me. I don't know her. That isn't me.

Those faces. Four angels. My mother's halo of hair in the bathtub, her eyes open and the only smile I ever saw on her face. My lips are singing the words as I examine the photos I never knew existed. Angels in the morning.

Crime scene.

My eyes are flickering open and shut, and my body is rocking back and forth in the chair. Footsteps move in time to the beat inside my head.

Muffled words. A curse.

And then a hand, reaching out to take what isn't his to take.

I claw at the files, and he pulls. The paper rips, and pieces of my life rain to the floor. I'm on my knees, crawling around in a frantic effort to conceal them. He doesn't deserve to see. He doesn't deserve to know these things. And I don't want to remember.

I reach for a photo just as a strong arm wraps around my waist. But it's wrong. It's all wrong.

This is not my mother in the bathtub. This is someone else. Another woman in a different bathtub.

And there's blood. So much blood. Murky red water and a face I don't recognize. The photo is snatched from my hand before I have a chance to make sense of it.

"Breathe." I hear through the haze of my confusion.

My chest is heaving hard. Deep in the grips of a panic attack. Something I have not experienced since I was a child.

There is no breath in my lungs. I'm clawing at my throat, and he grabs my hands.

"Shh, shh, shh…." The words are whispered into my ear as his hand rubs my back.

The attack ebbs away with the soothing tide of his voice. I open my eyes and meet pale blue. And something else returns as I jerk away from him.

Anger.

My lip trembles when I speak. "This is why you took me."

It's the only sentence I can manage to get out. But it means so much more. And the guilt and shame in his eyes leave no doubts to the answer.

He could never love me. Because I'm damaged beyond repair. And he wanted a wife in name only. I don't want him, I tell myself. I don't want any of this.

"You had no right to know me!" I scream. "You don't know anything about me!"

"I know everything about you," he answers.

"I hate you!" I charge at him and the surprise makes us both tumble to the floor in a heap. "I want to cut your name out of my skin!"

I want to hurt him, the way he has hurt me. But instead, a split second of luck gives me the opportunity I need. He's wearing his shoulder holster. And a gun. I take it before he regains his composure and scramble backwards on my legs, into the corner of the room.

He's watching me.

And smiling. It's not a normal smile. And it doesn't fade even when I shove the gun up beneath my chin, meeting his gaze.

He moves closer. Slowly. Daring me with his eyes. Challenging me. Like he doesn't believe I'll do it.

I want to do it. It's what I've been wanting for so long. So I don't know why I'm frozen. Why I can't let go of his gaze and just pull the trigger.

"Your move, Solnyshko," he taunts me.

I don't reply. And I can't stop shaking. He moves closer still. And now my hand is trembling. Watching him watch me with disbelieving eyes.

"You want me to do it?" he asks.

Alexei sees the indecision on my face. And he revels in it. He moves too close. Capturing my wrists before I can do anything, trapping me in place with his too large body. Then he's lying on top of me, pinning me against the floor. Rejoicing in my failure. Mocking me with his eyes.

"Do you want to drown, baby?" he asks.

"No," I answer. "I want to fly."

"You know I'll never let you go," he tells me. "Maybe I need this angel here with me, yes?"

"I hate you!" I scream in his face again.

I don't expect anything from him. But he flinches. A visible reaction to my words that proves he isn't the only one with power. I take this knowledge and run with it. I keep screaming the words over and over. His hand comes down on my face and he squeezes hard, forcing my lips together so I can't speak. The gun in his hand caresses my cheek and down the sensitive flesh of my throat, soft and deadly.

"Do it," I murmur beneath his hand.

He digs the gun into my flesh, holding my jaw in place with the force of it. For a minute, it looks like he is actually debating it. But instead, he grabs me by the hair with his free hand and holds me in place while he kisses me.

It isn't nice. It isn't sweet.

It's pure rage and chemistry. He wants to hate fuck me right now. I would let him.

In fact, I want him to.

But in the end, he decides against it.

And then the only sound in the room is his heavy breathing and my angry sobs. He saw my weakness. He saw my past. And now he thinks he knows me. Thinks he can use me. Just like Dmitri did. Like everyone has always done.

"Go to your room."

He moves away from me. There is still anger on his face as he gathers up the photos, but he has no right to be.

"I hate you!" I tell him again.

His shoulders tense, and my body trembles under the anger in his gaze. Directed at me.

"As you should," he answers. "Because I will destroy what is left of you."

I blink. And there are tears on my cheeks. Wetness. I hate that he's made me cry in front of him. That he's made me feel things he has no right to. Dug around in my past and my life. I need validation. That my thoughts are right. That my deepest fears are right.

That people will always disappoint you. And that hope is the most dangerous thing of all.

"You picked me," I tell him. "You picked me because of those things. You took a whore for a wife because you knew you could never love me."

His face is blank. Devoid of the hurt I thought I saw only a few moments ago.

"Yes," he answers.

The tiny bit of peace I thought I'd found in this sanctuary withers under his words and turns to dust. My feet are moving and my mind is repeating the only words that can bring me comfort now.

One day. One line.

One angel.

Seventeen

Alexei

I am in the gym. Piss drunk and with bloody knuckles when Magda finds me. I meet her panicked gaze in the mirror, and my heart beats too hard in my chest.

"What is it?" I demand.

My body is moving from the room before she can even explain. I find the cause for her concern when I walk into the sitting room and see the sofa cushions piled onto the floor.

My gaze moves up to where Magda points. Where on the ledge of a beam across the roof, Talia sits. Her back is facing us, her long blonde hair a halo around her white pajamas. Her legs dangle freely as her white knuckles grip the beam and keep her steady.

"She is singing a song," Magda informs me. "I cannot get her to answer me."

My body is stiff as I move forward. Towards the front of her body where I know I will find lifeless eyes if they meet my gaze. Because I put them there.

"Talia."

The word is a command. One hidden behind the veil of fear I feel inside.

Her eyes flutter open, dead and empty, to collide with mine.

"You can't catch me," she says.

"I can," I tell her.

"But you wouldn't."

"I always will," I insist, my throat working to get the words out. "Come down from there."

She takes one hand from the beam and uses her fingers to trace my face in the air. My heart is beating too hard. Too fast. I know she's going to do it this time. Before she was unsure. Now, there is no doubt in her mind.

I've seen that expression before. That peace on her face is hauntingly familiar.

And for a moment, I am no longer thirty-five, but ten. And powerless.

My mind knows every dimension of this house. The height from the floor to that beam. But right now, the calculations are failing me. The pillows Magda has carefully placed below will not be of any help. Not from that distance.

"I was the wrong choice," Talia says. "You picked wrong."

There's a moment where she meets my gaze again, and I try to find the words I desperately need. The words I have sought all my life. The ones that could save us both. They do not come. They have never come.

"You can't destroy what's already broken," she says.

And then she lets go.

I step forward.

In front of me, Magda screams.

She is falling too fast. But she is light.

When I catch her in my arms, we both hit the floor, and her head bounces against my chest. There's a momentary pause of silence before she blinks open her eyes and stares at me in confusion.

My relief is swiftly chased away by rage.

Magda is already hovering over us, attempting to coddle her. But I am done coddling the girl. I speak to her in Russian, telling her to retrieve my bag from the closet.

She does so reluctantly, and I heave the girl into my arms. She yelps when I grab her by the hair and yank her head back, forcing her gaze to mine.

"We are done with these games."

Her throat bobs and tears threaten at the edges of her eyes. But she holds them in, like the brave girl she is hiding beneath the illusion. The one who has no choice but to go on because I will not allow any other option.

I carry her up the stairs and throw her onto the bed, her slight body bouncing against the mattress when I do. When Magda comes in, her expression worried, I instruct her to leave the bag and go. She hesitates, and it only fuels my anger.

"Go!" I roar again.

They both flinch, and Magda gives Talia one last glance before leaving. I dig around in my bag and find the rope. I use it to tie Talia's wrists to the bed posts and her ankles to the base. When I finish, I step back to examine her. Spread open for me, her eyes wide and her chest panting.

My cock is painfully hard.

I want to bury myself in her now. To fuck her and fill her with my come. To impregnate her with my child. To prove to her that she is never leaving me. That the contract she signed with me is signed in blood. To remind her whose name and star she has carved into her flesh.

Instead, I settle for hovering over her body, my hand gripping her face when I speak. She smells of my drink, and it makes me want to fuck her until she can't walk.

"You are my wife." My fingers dig into her jaw. "I own you. And you will never disobey me again."

Her eyes move over my face, and no argument spills from her lips. So I take it a step further by kissing her. Hard and punishing, my body pressing hers into the bed. My cock insistent that I sink inside of her.

"You've been into my cognac," I tell her. "Do you like the taste of me on your lips as you fall to your death, my sweet?"

I grind against her, and she does not retreat. She is breathing heavy. Her chest rising and falling. Her nipples are stiff beneath the fabric of her soft white chemise. No bra. The swells of her breasts heave with the force of her breaths.

"My little Juliet." I nuzzle into her skin and suck on her flesh. "You will taste of me for all of eternity. Because you don't get to leave me."

"You will grow tired of me," she replies.

"I will not ever love you," I tell her as my lips move down the snowy skin of her throat. "But I will have you, Talia. In every way. Make no mistake that you are mine. And I will do as I please with you."

A puff of air leaves her lips and ruffles my hair as I nudge her top down to reveal her breast. She is watching me, her eyes no longer dead. But curious. Curious about what I will do. And impatient.

I swirl my tongue around her nipple and then suck her into my mouth. She shivers against me, biting down on her lip hard.

My hand cups the heat between her legs, rubbing the material of her shorts with my thumb, soaking it in wetness.

When my gaze meets hers, there is shame there. But want too.

And this is how I know she is not lost. That perhaps the thing she needs is not love but want.

My thumb rubs circles around her shorts, using the material for friction as I free her other breast and suck the soft skin into my mouth. She bucks her hips. And cries out.

"It won't work," she tells me.

My fingers yank the material of her shorts aside and shove inside of her bare pussy. Soaked and ready for me.

"It works just fine."

I finger fuck her and eat at her breasts.

"I can't." She keeps telling me. Even as her body contracts and expands around me.

"You will."

But she isn't letting go. And I know what she needs from me. I also know that I want to give it to her.

I reach down and fumble around in my bag until I find what I need. The flick of the switchblade causes her eyes to shoot open. It has the immediate effect of calming her. As I knew it would.

My angel thinks she wants death. But what she wants more than anything is to trust. In me.

I reach up and drag the blade down the sensitive flesh of her throat, scratching at the skin but never puncturing. Beneath the milky soft flesh, her pulse beats wildly for this. For me.

"Harder," she pleads.

The blade travels lower, down over her breast and ribcage as my fingers continue to move inside of her.

"Do you want some pain so that you can have your pleasure?" I ask.

"Yes, please."

Her hips are straining up against my palm, her body coming alive for me as I stroke the blade over the tender place on her stomach. And then lower. Down over her hip and against her thigh.

The anticipation is freeing her from the prison in her mind. But I know she will not give in until she has what she thinks she wants. What she thinks she needs.

"You don't need to be ashamed, my angel," I tell her. "I want you to let go for me. It is okay to enjoy this."

She meets my eyes and shakes her head, biting into her lip.

"I need more."

"I know what you need," I tell her.

There's an argument already prepared to spill from her lips. She thinks I will deny her. But I won't. Not now. Maybe not ever.

I like my fucked up wife. I like everything about her. And I'm going to keep her.

I take the blade and retrace the path back up her body. To the pale flesh of her fingers and over her knuckles until I reach her thumb. I press the tip into the flesh, and her breathing halts. I'm fingering her harder, and she is so wet for me I know she can hold out no longer.

"Now," she pleads.

With a flick of my wrist, I slice into her thumb. She hisses, and then her head falls back against the pillow as crimson spills from her flesh and she lets go. The orgasm is neither small nor weak when she finally comes around my fingers with her lips parted and cheeks flushed.

Immediately, she closes her eyes and tries to hide from me.

I toss aside the knife and lean over her, my lips a breath away from her face.

"Look at me."

She does.

"You will like it," I tell her. "You will like my eyes on you by the time I'm through with you, Solnyshko. Get used to it now."

She does not reply. But when I take her thumb to my mouth and wipe her blood across my lips, there is relief in her eyes. She craves this from me. My acceptance. And I crave the need she has for me. The need that only I can give her.

I push the material of her shirt all the way up beneath her throat and move up to straddle her hips. My body is much larger than hers, and she looks so small beneath me. So soft and sweet and fuckable.

But breakable too.

When the sound of my zipper reaches her, she opens her eyes and meets mine. Her tongue wets her lips, and I watch them as I reach inside my briefs and fetch my aching cock. It's in my fist, and her eyes expand as she watches me stroke it.

Once. Twice. And then three quick, hard pulls.

Neither of us says a word. She watches, her eyes flicking from my cock back up to my face again and again. My eyes are on her lips. And then my thumb is too. Pushing inside.

I close my eyes and groan at the feeling of her wet, hot mouth wrapped around me. I want all of her wrapped around me. And I tell her as much as I jerk myself off on top of her.

When I come, it's on her stomach. Hot and thick, marking her the way I have wanted to since I brought her home with me. I take what's left on my fingers and push them to her lips. She licks them without being asked, and it makes me want to fuck her all over again. The urge even stronger than before.

I use her shirt to wipe up the mess and then cover her over with the blanket. Ropes still tied, keeping her in place.

When I lean down to whisper in her ear, her eyes are sleepy and the fight is long gone.

"I may not ever be able to love you," I tell her. "But I can want you. And let there be no doubt, Solnyshko, I am keeping you."

Eighteen

Talia

Alexei keeps me tied to the bed for three days.

Magda comes to help me to the bathroom and allows me to bathe. And then I am returned to my binds. She will not meet my eyes. And I can't tell if it's because of her shame or disappointment.

I disappointed her. The way I always do.

But it's better this way. I tell her as much when she is adjusting my binds this morning.

"You should never expect anything from anyone," I say. "And then you can't be let down."

Her soft brown eyes meet mine, and she shakes her head.

"Talia." Her hand strokes my cheek, and I try to pull away. "I could never be disappointed in you."

She sits back on the bed, watching me with quiet worry. I watch her back, wondering why she is nice to me. Wondering why she cares at all. And then disbelieving that it's true. Because nobody ever cares. Those emotions are only the cover for something else. Something sinister.

I want to lash out at her. To push her away. Because that would be the easiest thing to do.

These aren't the words that leave my lips though.

"Who is she?"

She blinks, and then asks, "who?"

"The woman in the bathtub. In the photo."

She glances over her shoulder quickly and then shakes her head. All of the kindness has disappeared from her face in an instant, and instead, something else has taken hold. Fierce protectiveness. Devotion and loyalty.

"You must never speak of that photo," she says. "Or that woman. Forget you ever saw it."

I don't answer her. Because I won't make promises I have no intention of keeping.

"He's avoiding me," I say instead.

Magda nods, but gives me no explanation.

"He's been drinking."

Again, she nods.

And that's the end of the conversation. She moves to go back to her chair, but I stop her.

"I want to look at something on the computer."

She hesitates, checking the door again. Not that it matters. Alexei has cameras in every room of the house, I believe. I'm sure he can see what I'm doing any time he wishes to. But the whole point of avoidance is not to, so I doubt he's doing so now.

"Only for a few minutes," she says. "And then I must return you to your binds."

Magda frees my hands and sets up the computer for me. She has to help me get to the web browser since I've never used this type before. Once she's given me a brief explanation, she gives me the privacy I desire by going back to her chair.

My fingers are shaking as I peck at the keys. My stomach is churning, and my throat tight.

M-A-C-K-E-N-Z-I-E W-I-L-D-E-R

I don't expect much. I don't expect anything at all. She doesn't have facebook. But she does have an email. One I don't have any intention of using. I just want to see her. I just want something.

We have so much history together. For as long as I can remember, Mack has been at my side. She was the first person to see past the walls I'd erected around myself. She befriended me in foster care and then took it upon herself to look out for me.

And when we got separated and she discovered what my new foster dad was doing, she came to my rescue. She left her warm bed and a comfortable home to live on the streets with me. So that we could be together. And she taught me everything I know about being tough.

We don't have to be blood because we are sisters. No matter what anyone says. The only warmth I've ever felt in my heart has been for her. She's the toughest, craziest bitch I know and I love her.

I miss her.

I miss her so much the thought of never seeing her again makes me sick. But how can I?

How can I face her like this?

When she was right about everything. She was right to believe that there are monsters in everyone. I can't even imagine what my disappearance must have done to her. How much it would have hurt her. And it isn't fair to go back now when I'm still in pieces. When I can't even promise her that I want to live to see another day.

None of that would be fair to her.

So I tell myself as I scroll through the results that I am only seeking validation for those thoughts. That she is happy now. That's all I need to know, and then it will be okay. No matter how much misery lives inside of me, as long as she is happy, it will be okay.

But what I find hurts more than I expect it to. And it's also the thing I wanted most. For her to move on with her life. Forget I ever existed or dragged her down with the problems she couldn't fix for me but desperately wanted to.

It's her name, on a wedding registry. Mackenzie Wilder and Lachlan Crow.

The name is not unfamiliar. He is my old boss. The man who ran the club I worked at when Dmitri locked me in his sights. I was an easy target.

I always have been.

That's the dangerous thing about hope and want. Believing that this one might be different. That this one might not hurt you too. Other people have happy endings. But I never will. I was never born to.

Mack is different. She deserves her happy ending. But I can't understand it. Why him? Why Lachlan? And how?

I know the answers. Deep down, I know she went looking for me.

And she found him instead.

There are no photos of them. I want to see her face. But I know it's asking too much. My fragile mind can't handle that. I would want to see her and believe that somehow it would be okay.

That can't happen.

She can't ever see me like this. What I've become. She will still try to fix me. And I can't be fixed.

It's better this way.

Magda looks up at me, and I realize I've said the words aloud.

"It's better," I repeat. "I'm happy for her."

I tell myself those same things over and over as I shut the computer. And it's true.

So I don't know why it feels like I'm dying inside.

Nineteen

Talia

When Alexei comes to see me again, any reminder of what happened between us is gone. His face is calm, vacant of emotion as he studies me.

"Have you learned your lesson?" he asks.

"Have you learned yours?" I reply.

He moves to stand up and leave me again, and I stop him.

"I can't make any promises," I tell him. "But I won't do that particular thing again."

He returns to sit beside me. The soft gray of his sweater stretches across his muscular frame, and my fingers itch to touch it. To touch all of him. To have him make me forget.

His fingers find my face, hard and unyielding as his eyes bore into mine.

"You won't try anything again," he tells me.

It isn't a question, or a threat. Simply a command. As though he believes I will obey. I have no question about his authority. His power over me is absolute. But it still feels like maybe I have some power too. Like I remind him of his darkest wound. As if I am the very salt that burns it and brings all of that concealed pain to the surface.

He takes my silence for approval, and undoes my binds, rubbing my wrists and ankles when he finishes. His eyes are on my body. Moving over the pale expanse of my legs and the skin hidden beneath the shorts and cami.

These pajama sets are the only thing I've worn since my arrival. He's seen me in them every day. He's seen everything beneath them too. But right now, he looks like he wants to see it again. I want him to. I want to forget. I want to be reckless and feel the small thrill and warring hatred for myself that I feel when he touches me. When anyone touches me.

But he does not allow himself to give in this time.

"We are having dinner guests this evening," he tells me as he rises. "They will not like you, but they will respect you."

No sugar coating. Maybe that's what I like about Alexei.

"You will need to play the part," he adds.

I splay my legs apart a little wider, drawing his attention there as I speak. "The doting wife? Or the reformed whore?"

His eyes flash to mine, his lust barely concealed by his equal annoyance.

"Clean yourself up," he orders.

"Do you have a fire?" I reply. "Because I'll need one for that."

I don't know why I'm baiting him. But his indifference towards me today is annoying me. And all of the emotions I don't want to feel are bubbling to the surface.

"A shower will do," is his terse reply before he leaves the room.

I don't know where Magda is at. She must be busy preparing dinner. Because usually, she is always near when I have a shower.

Today, she is nowhere to be found. And since Alexei stomped back to his lair, I am left to my own devices.

My eyes move over the bathtub with a dark sense of longing and despair. My fingers trail over the white porcelain, and like clockwork, I hear my mother's voice in my head.

I kneel and put the stopper in. The same way she must have done that day. I wouldn't know. Because I was last. But I should have known. Because she was happy that morning. And she was never happy.

I hum the song to myself as the water fills the basin, ripples distorting my reflection on the surface. The water is lukewarm when my fingers weave through it, just like it was that day.

My clothes come off in a heap beside me, and I grip the edges of the tub as I lower myself inside. Flashes of my mother's face emerge from the darkest places of my mind. She was smiling and singing. And I was still dressed.

There was nothing on her face when I saw them lying on the bathroom floor. The horror washed over me when I realized what she'd done, and I wanted to die too. I didn't even put up a fight.

I was in a daze when she pushed me under the water. I grasped at the distorted sound of her voice beneath the water. But then it was in my nose. My lungs. Choking me. I thrashed, and she held me under.

Like I'm doing now. My eyes are closed, and I'm floating. Perfectly still.

Silence.

I can't hear her voice anymore. I can't see the angel's faces. The memories have stolen them from me. Distorted them.

I only remember their innocence.

And that it was my job to protect them.

I failed.

And that's why I'm still here. Being punished. My little brother and my sisters got to fly away, but I never will. Because I didn't protect them.

In this moment of clarity that's what it all comes back to. I always thought that it was punishment. That's why I survived. Why I was left behind.

My hair is a halo around me, like silk beneath the water, tangling over my face and arms. Just like mom's was that day. A bubble of air escapes my lips. A test.

An urge to be close to them.

But something keeps pulling me back. Into the light and away from the darkness. A nagging hope. That maybe I'm wrong. Maybe I've always been wrong. And maybe it wasn't my fault.

But hope isn't what saves me today.

This time, it's a strong pair of hands, heaving me out of the bathtub and shaking me from my stupor.

When I open my eyes, it isn't Alexei I find. It's someone else. A small boy. Horror and unforgiving pain etched onto his face.

"Why are you doing this to me?" he roars.

The force of his grip is painful. His muscles are shaking, and it isn't me he sees when he grips my face and screams at me.

"Why?"

When I don't answer, he discards me on the floor and bends over to drain the tub. And then he pauses, breath heaving, and punches his fist into the porcelain with a level of violence even my eyes have not seen before.

When he turns around again, I'm in the corner, watching him cautiously. His fist is bloodied and swollen. Fingers probably broken. Because of me.

But it's the expression on his face.

Hurt and rage.

I did that.

It bothers me. And it is my fault.

As soon as I come to grips with that, he is gone.

Twenty

Talia

Magda's radio silence is bothering me.

She's dressed me carefully. With a flashy black dress and tiny sheer strips of fabric that show my skin beneath. Black heels, and jewelry too. My hair is washed and curled and falling in a veil around my shoulders. Makeup carefully applied.

And yet I'm not looking at myself when she pulls me to the mirror. I'm looking at her, in the reflection.

"I told you," I say to her reflection. "I told you I would disappoint you."

She meets my eyes in the mirror, and her shoulders sag.

"You have not disappointed me," she states. "You have reminded him."

Of what, she doesn't say. But I know now that it's true. I'm the salt in his wound. And I should have seen it before. That Alexei is a masochist, like me. Trying to drown his sorrows in the cognac he drinks. Trying to lock himself away from the world and whatever it is he doesn't want to face.

People cope in different ways.

And when those ways are not what society deems respectable, then you are pushed even further to the fringes. Like Alexei. And like me.

They all want me to be scared. To be timid and soft. To whimper and cry when men touch me.

Only, I want the men to touch me. I want them to fuel my self-hatred. And I use them to do it. I want to use Alexei too. I want him to fuck me and use and degrade me like the trash that I am. Like the trash society always said I was. It would make me feel better. I crave that validation from him.

But when I look at Magda right now that isn't what I see in her eyes. It isn't shame, or frustration, or the inability to understand. It's the complete opposite of all of those things. It is love and acceptance.

My lip trembles, and I want to push her away. The way that I always do. Because hope is the most dangerous thing of all.

"Come here, child."

She pulls me against her and hugs me. And I don't know what to do. So I just let her. There is pressure behind my eyes, but I won't allow it to seep out. My throat aches from the years of repressed words and emotions I have not given voice to. The deep insecurities embedded in my DNA.

"He chose me because he knew he could only ever hate me," I tell her. "Because I remind him of what he doesn't want to remember."

"It isn't that simple," Magda tells me. "You are more alike than you know."

She takes me by the hand and leads me from the room. Downstairs to the sitting room. Where Alexei is sitting on the sofa, his back towards us. Glass of cognac in hand.

Magda shifts uncomfortably as though she is second guessing herself. And then she turns to me, her face severe.

"I am going to tell you something about Alexei," she says. "That you must never divulge to anyone outside of this house. Something that requires absolute trust and faith, Miss Talia. Because this information could hurt him if you ever expose it. Do you understand?"

"Then why tell me at all?" I ask.

"Because you need to know. And he is too ashamed to tell you himself. But perhaps it will make you see."

I remain quiet and watch as she makes a gesture with her hand.

"Call out to him."

"Why?"

I move my gaze over his figure on the sofa. Tall and strong, but desperately alone. His posture is defeated. Tired. He is not ten feet away from us, and still he has not turned.

"Alyoshka," Magda calls out.

Nothing. There's no response. No movement from him at all. It's as if we are not even in the room.

"You try," she tells me.

"Alexei," I call out.

No response. So I try again, louder.

"Alexei!"

Nothing.

Magda reaches down and pats my hand. "He isn't ignoring you, Miss Talia."

Her words leave the necessary unsaid. And I stare at the back of his head in confusion. How could I have not seen it?

"He reads lips?"

"He reads everything on your face," Magda answers. "But if you are very close to him, and you speak into his right ear, he can hear a little bit."

It makes sense now. The truth is so incredibly simple. Right in front of me all along.

Alexei cannot hear. This is why he keeps himself locked away in his house. He doesn't want anyone to know his secret. Because in the mafia, in his world, that secret would be a weakness.

And I suddenly find myself wondering if he sees himself as weak too. If this is why he chose me. Because we are both flawed and damaged.

"It will be a long evening for you," Magda tells me. "You should go upstairs and relax until the party starts."

I give Alexei one last glance before I nod and do as she says. "Okay."

Twenty-One

Alexei

By five o clock, all of the guests have arrived. Viktor and his most trusted Vory have come to dine with us tonight. In celebration of my marriage. This party includes Katya and Anatoly as well. Even Nikolai and my own father who dutifully ignores me the way he has always done.

I don't foresee a happy occasion, and the longer I wait for Talia to come down, the more my nerves agitate me. I don't know what her mood will be like this evening. If she will prove them all right by ignoring me too. Wearing the same flat expression I am now accustomed to. The same desire to end her life rather than be married to the likes of me.

I should have gone to her. Spoken to her after the incident. But my anger is too much. I cannot look at her without betraying how I feel. Like she has betrayed me.

Viktor is speaking to me when his eyes move behind me. And before I even look, I know it is her. I wait, wondering what version I will get this evening.

She appears by my side, and when I turn towards her, she is reaching up to kiss my cheek. The action surprises me, and Viktor does not miss it. It's only after a moment that I realize she is too short and I am too tall, so I bend to accommodate her.

Her lips are soft and warm against my skin, and absent of any anger or despondency that I've come to expect from her. When she pulls away, she threads her arm through mine and rests her pale fingers against the black of my sweater. She's wearing her wedding ring. As am I.

My eyes are moving over her, dressed in all black. It's the perfect accompaniment to her ghostly white skin and pale blonde hair. She looks like a haunted angel, eyes smoked in black and lips painted red. And right now, every pair of eyes in the room is on her.

"Good evening," she speaks to Viktor.

In my mind, I know I need to turn my attention back to him. To avoid making a fool of myself. Missing any cues in conversation. But I'm having difficulty tearing my eyes away from my wife, who… I don't seem to recognize at all.

There is a smile on her face as Viktor takes her free hand in his and greets her. She is tucked in close to my side as though she is my partner. As though it is both of us against all of them. When it has only ever been me.

There are so many questions in my mind, but I don't have time to consider them. She taps my arm and smiles, and I realize she's trying to get my attention.

I turn back to Viktor, whose eyes are moving between the two of us with a curious expression.

"You have done very well for yourself, Lyoshenka."

I can't tell if his words are genuine or not. When only last week he referred to her as a whore, now he can't seem to take his eyes off of her. I pull her closer on a nod, wrapping my arm around her waist, and he smiles.

"Tell me," Viktor speaks to Talia, "how married life is treating you."

When she glances up at me, there is genuine warmth in her eyes. I don't know where it came from, but I find myself wishing the room were empty now. Instead, I settle for placing my hand possessively on the back of her neck. Stroking the warm skin there and watching her as she answers.

"I would tell you that my husband is a perfect gentleman," she says. "But we both know that's a lie."

Viktor laughs, and when his eyes land on me, there is approval behind them. I pull Talia even closer still, grazing her cheek with my lips. She does not protest. In fact, she leans into me and gives a soft sigh of approval.

"You are happy though," Viktor remarks. "Yes?"

It's not a question, even though it is phrased like one. It is an observation. And right now, she does seem happy.

Talia looks to me, her eyes moving over my face when she replies.

"I am."

And then Viktor holds up his glass, reciting a classic Russian toast to our health and happiness.

Across the room, Katya's gaze finds mine. Hurt and anger fill her eyes as she moves them from me to Talia. I ignore her and focus my attention on Magda when she enters the room.

"Dinner is served."

We all move to the dining room, and Talia takes her place at my side.

Throughout dinner, I catch all of the men staring at her. Sergei and Nikolai included. When his gaze finds mine across the table, it is apologetic. And something else.

I don't allow him to introduce himself to her.

Dinner is a long affair. With toasts and blessings from all the notable members at the table. When Sergei's turn comes around, he mocks me by simply saying, to *my* good health.

Katya's eyes are on Talia throughout the whole evening, and Talia has taken notice of her as well. Beneath the table, her hand finds mine, and I move my attention to her.

She smiles at me, and it still disarms me.

I have half a notion to remove the sharp cutlery from her reach. Convinced she is deceiving me somehow.

But she plays her part well, never missing a beat when someone asks her a question. Every word out of her mouth is a lie of course, regarding our marriage. But only she and I know it.

When the plates have been removed and the men begin to scatter back into the sitting room, Anatoly stops me. He glances at Talia and smiles and then asks me in Russian to retrieve the information he needed on a local politician.

"I will look after your wife," he tells me. "While you retrieve it."

Instead, I call for Magda and instruct her to remain at Talia's side.

"I will be right back," I tell her. And with all of the eyes in the room on us, I lean down and kiss her as a husband should. Softly, on the cheek.

She smiles up at me, and I retreat upstairs to my office.

As I suspected, I am not in there for more than two minutes before Katya makes an appearance.

"Lyoshka," she greets me.

My eyes move over her tall figure, filling out the blue dress she has chosen to accentuate all of her best features in the way she always does. She has the body of a model, and the face of one too. The gem that many of the Vory covet, but do not have the position to attain.

At least not permanently. Though I'll never know how many she has been with besides myself and Nikolai. I was one of the few who had the rank she lusted after in a partner. Only, I did not have whatever else she needed.

I fell for her. And she made a mockery of me. And still, here she is, begging me back.

"When are you going to give up this ruse?" she questions, leaning against my desk and entrapping me into the space.

"There is no ruse, Katya." I pull the information I need from a file though it's clear to me Anatoly had only one intention upon sending me up here.

"This girl is not good enough for you," she tells me. "She is not family. Not bred for being a Vor's wife."

"She was not bred for that," I answer her. "That is why I married her."

The insult does not go unnoticed. Katya flinches, but quickly recovers.

"It is not too late," she tells me. "You can send her away and choose me instead. Tell me what I have to do Alexei. To win your forgiveness. Anything, and I will do it."

"I want nothing from you."

Her eyes move over me as she inches closer. So close that her leg brushes up against mine as she leans into my space, her perfume soaking the air around us. All calculated moves to get my attention. Katya is an expert of manipulation.

I was manipulated by her beauty and her words. But now, I feel nothing when I look upon her.

"It is only the chase that thrills you," I tell her. "You need to give up these fantasies of yours now and accept reality. Take up with Nikolai. You two should be very happy together."

She scoffs in my face as though I have burned her. "You know I can do no such thing. He is only a soldier. I am bred to be the wife of a high ranking Vor."

I meet her wrath with a shrug. "He was good enough for you to fuck. What is the difference?"

"It was a mistake," she utters. "Please…"

The desperation in her voice grates on me. I just want her gone.

A shadow falls over the doorway, and when I glance up, I find Talia staring back at me. Her eyes flick between Katya and I, questioning the narrow distance between us.

I reach out my hand in a gesture for her to come to me, pleading with my eyes that she will not misunderstand the situation.

She does, without hesitation. And once she is close enough, I pull her directly onto my lap, kissing her fiercely and possessively in front of Katya.

When I come back up for air, Talia is studying me, and Katya is barely able to conceal her disdain.

"Have you met my wife?" I ask her.

"No." Katya's lips curl into a false smile conceived from years of training. "I don't believe I have."

My hands move over Talia's body, pulling her closer to me. It isn't a calculated move on my part, but an instinctive one. Right now, she is pliable. Doing as I ask and playing the role of my wife as though she were born for it.

I like her like this.

I want to soak up every second of this mood while it lasts. Before I inevitably ruin it.

Talia reaches up and touches my face, kissing me softly before pulling away.

"Sorry," she murmurs to Katya. "We can't keep our hands off each other. Honeymoon phase."

"Enjoy it while it lasts," Katya replies.

"I intend to." Talia smiles up at her. "And on that note, would you mind?"

Katya remains in place, her jaw tense and her gaze burning into mine. Willing me to say otherwise.

"Shut the door when you go," I add.

She swears at me in Russian, and then she does as I ask.

Twenty-Two

Talia

I don't move from Alexei's lap when Katya has gone. Instead, I pull my dress up lewdly around my hips and lean back against his desk, allowing his eyes to rake over me.

He's watching me closely, waiting to see my next move. He doesn't understand my motives. I don't either. But seeing how much that woman wanted him makes me feel possessive. It makes me need him in a way that I shouldn't admit.

My hand reaches out to trail over his jaw. Strong and freshly shaved. Smooth. He is beautiful.

I can see why she wants him so much.

But that isn't what really bothers me.

"You wanted to make her jealous," I say.

"Yes."

"Because you loved her," I add.

"No," he answers.

"Liar."

My lips come down on his, and I kiss him hard. Alexei's hands roam the backs of my thighs all the way up to my ass. His hot palm slides into the back of my panties to cup my ass cheek, and then he pulls me down against his hardness.

"Do you want to fuck me and think of her?" I ask him.

"You'd like that," he answers. "Wouldn't you?"

"What does that mean?"

"You would use any excuse not to feel the way you do right now."

He's right. He's so right that it scares me. I feel something with him. Something more than the reckless behavior and the self-hatred.

I feel… safe with him. His house is my sanctuary. His body, my fortress. He is tall and strong and dangerous. And like Magda said, I believe that he will protect me.

That's the most dangerous belief I could ever have with a man.

I need to level the playing field. I need him to know that I know his secrets too.

"That's exactly what a hypocrite would say." I lean close and murmur into his right ear. "Lyoshka."

He freezes, his hands still on my ass, his head moving back to examine me. To question me with those pale blue eyes.

"I know," I tell him.

"And what have you to say about it?" he asks.

His jaw is taut, his eyes hard and appraising. I know instinctively this man could spot a lie if I ever dared to utter one. But I only ever have my honesty to give to him.

"I like it," I admit. "Because maybe that makes us even. Maybe that means it's you and me against the world."

He relaxes slightly, and his brows draw closer. I've surprised him with my answer. He expected something different.

Hatred? Disgust?

I can't quite figure it out. But Magda's words are ringing through my mind, loud and clear.

You are more alike than you know.

"How do you conceal it so well?" I ask. "How do you read lips without being obvious?"

"Like any skill, you perfect it by learning. Through practice."

I nod, and he continues to watch me. And explain.

"I don't catch everything that is spoken. I catch pieces, and I put them together in my head. Like a puzzle. Everyone is different. Some talk too fast, some mumble. Some cover their mouth, or look away. Some are easy to read. Some are hard. It isn't just about reading lips. Your face says a thousand things that your lips never will."

"What do you mean?"

His fingers come up to touch my chin. And then my brows. They trail over my face, examining me in a way he hasn't done before.

"It's a thousand micro expressions. The way your eyes contract and expand. The flutter of lashes. The involuntary hitch of a shoulder or a tick you didn't even know you made. There are so many emotions that go unnoticed because most are only used to listening to the words. But I learned to watch. And now I see everything."

It makes sense. How he's so observant. How he seems to anticipate my moves before I even know them myself sometimes.

"And what do you see in my face?" I ask him curiously.

"The pain you are too proud to admit you feel."

"That's rich. Coming from you."

"Is it?" he asks.

"Do you drink so much because you feel sorry for yourself? Or is it because of Katya?"

He doesn't reply. His grip on me is tight and unforgiving. I keep pushing him.

"Is that why we are married in name only? So you can fuck me and think of her?"

He kisses me again. Hard this time. All the while his fingers are pulling the zipper down the back of my dress. Freeing the material enough that he can shove it down and trap my arms at my sides, allowing the cool air to hit my breasts.

He pulls away and kisses at my throat, using his hand to grind my hips down onto his erection.

"I married you so that I can fuck you," he answers. "And think of you while I do it."

His mouth comes over my breast, and his fingers slip into my panties and then inside of me. Fucking me with his hand while I sit in his lap. I close my eyes and try to numb myself the way I usually do. To rid myself of the feelings he is provoking in me.

Lust. Desire. Want.

And worst of all… hope.

He squeezes my jaw tight in his hand and pauses, his voice tense when he speaks.

"You look at me," he orders. "You think of me. When your husband is fucking you."

I open my eyes and meet his. Dark and so hot I feel like he's burning right through my skin.

"You will only ever think of me," he orders again, harsher this time. "I want to invade your every thought."

I don't know if it's a command or a plea. So my honesty comes out again.

"You already do."

I jerk in his arms and his fingers move inside of me again. The party is still happening downstairs, but Alexei doesn't care. He takes his time. He doesn't allow my fucked up needs to hinder our progress, and he gives me exactly what I require. He nurtures my desire for pain by pulling my hair and dragging his teeth down my throat before sinking them into my shoulder. And when I relax in his arms, he heaves me up and sets me on the desk, tearing my panties away and splaying my legs apart. He holds my thighs beneath his palms, scooting me to the edge of the desk so that my ass hangs off.

I'm on display for him. Lewd and dirty. My dress bunched around my waist, my breasts on display and my legs spread wide. I wonder if he likes me like this. Filthy and wrong.

I don't have to wonder for long. He reaches for the cognac on his desk and opens it, pouring it down the front of my body and wetting my skin and my dress. My back arches and the liquid warms my skin as it slides down between my spread legs.

Alexei chases the liquid with his tongue, drinking it from my flesh. And yet I'm the one who is drunk off the combination. But there is still that part of me that feels the deep chasm of shame. He knows it, but he doesn't let me give in to it.

His eyes meet mine before he leans forward and buries his face in the exposed part of me. He eats me out on his desk. On top of his paperwork and while his guests are downstairs. He fucks me with his tongue and grunts out his approval as he devours me.

And there isn't anywhere else I could take my mind right now if I tried. He is the only place I want to be. In this moment. Watching him ruin me. Feeling the brutality of his grip on my ass, bruising my flesh and imprinting his mark on the deepest level of my psyche. The place where all of my fears and needs collide.

I come hard for him. And still, he doesn't stop. Until I beg him to be inside of me.

And then he's pulling me back into his lap. Freeing his zipper with his fingers and yanking my hand down in his to touch him. He wants me to need this. To need him. It must be his own fear that blinds him from seeing that his control over me is absolute. And that I do need it from him.

I leave no question in his mind. I cup the hot bulge beneath his briefs and run my fingers along his shaft. His eyes never leave mine.

Only when I free his cock completely and shift my hips to push him inside of me, do his eyes close briefly.

Once he's fully rooted, he grabs my face and forces me to look at him again.

"Mine."

Then he's fucking me. Using me. And thoroughly enjoying it. His hands guide my hips, and his lips sear my skin. Everywhere. He's kissing me everywhere. Sucking on me. Tasting me. Breathing his fire into me.

His brand of fucking is more intense than any other I've ever experienced. His eyes never leave my face. Watching for every slight tremble. It's intimate, and raw... being face to face like this. Skin to skin. Every time he gets close, he pauses or stops altogether just to kiss me. To touch me. To draw it out and soak as much pleasure as he can from the act itself. It scares me and sends a thrill through me.

And I feel like I need to ruin it.

"Do you like fucking your filthy whore wife?" I ask him.

He smiles up at me, and his cock swells inside of me. "I love fucking my wife," he answers.

He thrusts up inside of me harder, harder. "Now tell me how much you love it too."

"I like it," I admit.

"Do you like calling yourself a whore?" he asks. "Do you like to be degraded, my little Solnyshko?"

"Yes," I answer him honestly.

From him. I want that. I need it. To give myself permission to enjoy it. To let my mind be free.

"Then tell me you're my whore," he demands. "And the only thing you're good for is pleasing me."

"I'm your whore." I lean back against the desk so that my body is on display for him. "And the only thing I'm good for is pleasing you."

His lips find my ear, and the sounds of his ragged approval vibrates against my skin.

"Now tell me thank you," he demands. "For what I'm about to give you."

"What?" I ask.

He thrusts as deep as he can go and comes on an agonized groan, spilling himself inside of me. Only when his cock is empty and I am sagging against him do his lips find my ear and he answers.

"A baby."

Twenty-Three

Alexei

It is late when I get to the city.

Normally, Franco drives me. But now that Talia is at the house, I feel his services are best required there. Against his protests, I have driven myself to Slainte.

I needed this meeting to take place on the Irish's home ground. The lies are prepared to slip from my tongue when I greet Lachlan in the office. The way they have been ever since I brought Talia into my life.

He will have no choice but to understand. His alliance with the Vory will not be strained by one girl. I know this. And I am taking full advantage of it.

"Alexei." He shakes my hand as a sign of respect and then pours me a glass of cognac.

When he sits down across from me, we both make the usual toasts. And then the business begins.

"You have word on Mack's friend?"

"I do."

I finish the glass and meet his gaze.

"There is… a complication."

Lachlan frowns. "What sort of complication?"

"She was purchased by Arman Kassabian."

"I see."

I let the information settle on him. Arman is the Bulgarian weapons dealer that keeps a sizeable chunk of the global market in business. He also happens to be the supplier of the Irish and the Vory. It is a profitable business relationship to all of us. Lachlan will not start a war over one girl, or even lose his arms supply over one girl. This is just a fact of the mafia business. The steady supply of arms is the lifeblood of the Irish syndicate.

In the end, this is how I know the choice he will make. His loyalty is to his brotherhood. To the well-being of the organization. And a leader must always choose the organization over all else.

Lachlan knows me fairly well. As well as I allow anyone to. He is aware of my defect although I am not certain how he caught on to it. And yet, he has never shown me any disrespect or disloyalty. He trusts my judgment and does not question my abilities.

For this reason, I consider him a friend as well as an ally. Our pact makes good business sense, but he is the only one of the Irish I like to deal with.

"Have ye spoken with him?" Lachlan asks. "Is he prepared to part with her for a cost?"

I shake my head and keep my expression neutral. "He has an attachment to her. He is not willing to part with her on a permanent basis."

"What does that mean?" he demands.

"I have the girl in my possession now."

His eyes widen and then narrow. "For how long?"

"He parted with her as collateral on a shipment that went missing," I tell him.

He brushes his hands down his face and leans back in his chair. I can see the thoughts running through his mind. They are the same that initially went through my own. Getting the girl a new identity, sending her somewhere else. Telling Arman I lost my head and she was just a casualty of doing business.

"There is nowhere she will ever be safe from him," I tell Lachlan. "And even if she were…"

The words drift off, and a part of me feels guilt for speaking of Talia this way.

"Even if she were, what?" Lachlan asks.

"The girl is not in a good state of mind."

"I didn't guess she would be," he replies.

"She can't be on her own."

"We can't send her back to Arman."

"I have no intention to."

"Then what?" he asks.

"I have handled the situation in a way that is best for all concerned parties."

Lachlan's agitation is clear when he speaks. "Which is?"

"I have married the girl."

The room falls silent, and his eyes bore into mine, incredulous. He doesn't believe me. But he also knows I have never been one to joke. So he waits. And I do also. And after a time, it settles on him. This is serious.

"You married her," he repeats. "Without consulting me."

"I don't generally consult with those who hold no sway in my own decisions."

"This isn't just your decision," he grates. "Did she even want to marry you?"

Inwardly, I flinch.

I know it isn't a reference to my defect when it comes from Lachlan, but a part of me still believes that is what he is implying.

"I have fulfilled more than what I promised," I inform him as I stand. "I have retrieved the girl, and I have kept her safe. I have secured a future for her away from Arman. A simple thank you would do."

Lachlan sighs, and then nods. "Ye're right. You have my apologies, Alexei. I realize that this is something I can't ever repay ye for."

I move to leave, but he stops me.

"But I do have another favor to ask."

I glance at him and wait.

"Mack needs to know she's okay," he says. "She needs to hear it from Talia."

Twenty-Four

Talia

It snowed this morning.

And I convinced Magda to let me outside to see it. Her answer came only after she received permission from Alexei.

I know he's watching me from the window above. I saw his face when I laid down on the ground.

"Miss Talia," Magda chides me, but I ignore her.

I stare up at the sky and let the flakes fall onto my skin, even catching a few on my tongue. My arms and legs move to the sides, making a perfect snow angel. And then I get up and repeat the process four more times. When I am on my fifth, I open my eyes to meet ice cold blue.

Alexei.

"You made one too many," he remarks, as if he knows anything about my mind.

"No, it's exactly right."

His face hardens and he does not try to hide his disdain for my attitude. He has barely spoken to me since he fucked me two nights ago. Since he told me the worst thing he could have said to someone like me.

No, not even someone like me. Just me.

I'm as insane as my own mother was. I cannot be a mother. I will destroy everything I love. Just like she did.

I am poison.

I told Alexei as much in my panicked state. He disregarded it entirely. Instead, he kissed me and dressed me and brought me back down to the party, filled with his come and looking more like the girl who first arrived than the one who was supposed to be his wife.

The sight did nothing to sway Katya's determination. In fact, it only seemed to strengthen it. She is not willing to give him up, married or not.

Again, I wonder why he is not with her. He clearly loved her. She wanted to be his wife. Probably would have bore his children. And she is not nearly half as insane as I am.

When I look up at him now, hovering above me I almost tell him so. That he should rethink what he has done. But I can't bring myself to say the words.

It's just as well, because he stoops down to gather my chilled body into his arms, carrying me like a child back inside the house. I cling to him, letting his warmth surround me as he carries me up the stairs. He takes me straight into my bathroom and sets me on the counter, undressing me.

He walks to the shower and turns it on, testing the water on his palm while I watch. His head reaches above the glass doors, and I wonder what his own shower looks like.

"How tall are you?" I ask when he comes back to retrieve me.

He lifts me back into his arms and watches me while he speaks.

"Six feet six," he replies.

I nod, because it was close to what I had guessed. I only stand at five foot three, so there is always a large gap between us when I look up at him.

He takes me to the shower and sets me inside, and I stand beneath the hot spray, letting it soak into my muscles. After a few moments, the door opens again, and Alexei is behind me. Naked. Pulling my body into his while he kisses my neck.

Without further delay, one of his hands comes around my front and slides down my stomach, dipping between my thighs.

"I'm going to fuck you," he tells me.

"Okay."

"But first I want to play with you. Bend over and grab your ankles."

It isn't easy, but I do as he asks. And it feels vulnerable, in this position. Having his eyes on the most intimate part of me. His touch is soft at first. Feeling the wetness already between my legs from being in his proximity.

Always wet for him. Like the whore I like to tell him I am.

"You like it when I play with you like a toy?" he asks.

"Yes."

"I like it too," he tells me.

And then he spanks me. Three times on each side. So hard he has to grab my wrists to keep me from falling forward.

When he's done, he pulls me back into a standing position and slips his fingers between my parted thighs again. Testing my response to him. I'm alive for him. Ready for anything else he wants to give me.

He pulls my hand behind me to wrap it around his cock. And I'm stroking him while he fingers me. Neither of us facing each other. I am glad. Because right now, I don't want him to see the things he can see so well.

How scared I am. How vulnerable I feel. How the war raging on in my mind tells me I need more pain. Anything to escape the other feelings building inside of me. The feeling of trust and comfort and safety when I'm in his arms. They aren't real. They are like sand, always shifting beneath me.

"Please," I whisper, but I know he can't hear me.

Alexei doesn't need to hear me though. He knows me. Too well. I don't know how that's possible, but it's true.

He grabs hold of my hair in his fist and pulls my head back in a forceful grip so that I have to meet his gaze while his other hand moves up to pinch my nipple. I hiss and jerk against him and he repeats the process on the other side.

"You need to do better," he tells me. "I cannot always give you pain, my sweet. I don't want to spoil you."

Even as he says the words, I know he's a liar. He would give me anything that I asked for. So long as he is in control of it. He likes to control me just as much as I like him to.

He resumes his previous activities of fingering me while he kisses all over my shoulder and back while he holds me in place. I lean my head back against his shoulder and watch him watching me. His cock is sandwiched between my ass cheeks, hard and ready for me. His other hand is on my breast, kneading it before he reaches around to suck on it.

I come for him.

It doesn't even take me long this time. When my eyes open again, I meet his.

"What are you thinking about right now?" he asks.

"I'm wondering if you had my IUD removed," I give him an honest answer, and his reply is the same.

"I did."

"And I'm wondering if you're going to come inside of me again."

"I am."

"I can't get pregnant," I tell him.

"You will."

And that's the end of the conversation. Because now I'm pressed back up against the shower wall, my hips in his hands as he pushes his cock inside of me.

He lowers his head to within an inch of mine and hovers there, his eyes burning into mine.

"Mine."

"Yours," I whisper.

"Kiss me," he demands.

I do. I reach up and wrap my arms around his neck and kiss him. His tongue invades my mouth and seizes mine while his hips move in time to the masculine grunts erupting from his throat.

I wonder if he can hear them. Hear any of this.

When I come up for air, I find his right ear with my lips. And I kiss him there, and then stay, so he can hear my sounds. So he can hear what little I have to give him.

He swells inside of me. He's about to come. So he pauses again. Just sliding in and out of me in the slowest way.

His voice is thick and rough when he speaks. "Talk to me," he murmurs into my hair. "I want to hear your voice."

It's a vulnerable request for him. And I respect him for it.

I bring my lips closer to his ear, kissing him and then asking a vulnerable question of my own.

"Do you like your women insane?"

He pulls back just enough for me to see the smile on his face.

"Obviously," he replies.

And then he kisses me again.

"I like your insanity," I tell him. "And I like the way you fuck me. I like the way you make it all go away."

He pauses mid thrust and comes hard inside of me. Filling me once again. I close my eyes and shudder, terrified and… something else I can't explain.

When he moves back to stare at me, his expression is relaxed and determined.

"I'm going to fuck you every day."

He grabs my face and kisses me hard.

"And you won't ever remember anything else."

Twenty-Five

Talia

I expect him to leave me when he's done with me.

Because Alexei has his own issues. He tells me he won't love me. And I believe him. He will always keep me at arm's length.

Fucking me and loving me are two different things.

He loved Katya. And now he will never want to love anyone else again. Because she poisoned him somehow. And I can't fix him, just as he can't fix me.

We really are alike.

I watch him as he rifles through my closet. Through the racks of designer clothing that I haven't so much as touched. He's wearing nothing but his trousers, his back muscles stretching and expanding with every movement. His tattoos on full display.

Sometimes, I don't think they suit his personality.

I know he probably scares most. That is his intention. But I know the real Alexei. The recluse who remains in his home and plays chess and sits at his computer most of the day. The one who is quiet and reserved and honest.

He doesn't need to put on a show to be a threat. His body is strong, but I have no doubt it is his mind that is his most dangerous weapon of all.

He returns to me with a simple black sheath dress and holds it against my pale skin before nodding his approval.

"Black suits you."

He helps me to dress. The way he often takes care of me. I wonder why he does it. He knows I am capable. But here he is, dressing me. Stitching my wounds when I bleed. Showering me. Bringing me in from the cold.

They are little things. But nobody has ever done these things for me.

I can't look away from him, but I know that I need to. So when he retrieves a brush and starts in on my hair, I take it from his hands.

"I can do it myself."

He nods, but doesn't leave.

Only once I am finished do I learn his motives for lingering.

"There is something I need you to do."

"Okay."

I turn towards him, and his eyes meet mine. Sometimes, I still forget that he can't hear me. That I need to face him when I speak. But he just pretends, the way he does with everyone else.

"You won't like it," he adds.

"Tell me what it is."

"You need to speak to Mack."

"No."

My chest is tight. And there is pressure behind my eyes. Just the mention of her name brings an enormous wave of shame and guilt over me. She can't ever see me like this. She won't understand. And I will only disappoint her all over again. I keep touching the star on my hand. Hoping for the comfort, but it doesn't come. Because he's the one who is doing this to me. Bringing this up.

"She was married today," he tells me. "Consider it a wedding gift. Some peace of mind for a friend who is loyal to you."

"I know she is loyal," I snap at him. "Don't act like you know our relationship. Like you know anything about me, or her for that matter."

"I know enough," he tells me. "She did come to me, after all. She is the reason you are here now. Away from Arman."

I turn away because I don't want him to bear witness to the tears that are now spilling down my cheeks. But I know he knows they are there. He doesn't attempt to give me false comfort. Or come near me. Which I respect.

I know what I'm doing isn't fair. I know it's selfish.

But Mack won't be able to accept this. Accept what I've become.

She'll try to fix me.

Just like she's always done.

I was bad then, but now… the damage is irreparable.

I pace towards the window and tap on the bulletproof glass, gathering my thoughts. I know what I need to do. I know what the right thing is. But it doesn't make it any easier.

I turn and find Alexei, waiting for me to finish doing battle inside of my head.

"I'm not going back to Boston."

"You aren't," he agrees. "You are my wife now, Solnyshko. Which means I am responsible for your safety. And I will never ask you to do anything that puts you in harm's way."

His tone is low and serious. As if protecting me is more important to him than anything else. But it doesn't make sense. For a man who considers himself incapable of love. For the husband who is married to me in name only.

"Why?" I ask him. "Why does it mean so much to you?"

"Because you are my wife. And that is what husbands must do. They should put family above all else."

I tilt my head to the side and examine him, another piece of the puzzle that is Alexei falling into place.

"You mean the way that your father didn't?"

He blinks, startled by my response. And in that instant, I know I'm exactly right.

"Do not speak of things that you don't understand," he tells me. "And never mention my father again."

"So it's okay for you to push me into things that make me uncomfortable, but not the other way around? That seems fair."

"Life isn't fair, Solnyshko," he answers. "You know this better than anyone."

The room goes silent as we face off. My husband and I. This man that I'm only beginning to know. And yet, he reads me like no other. Perhaps it works both ways. Perhaps the damaged like us have a way of spotting that same wound in another.

And right now, I want to poke at his. To avoid the topic at hand.

"I don't even know who my father was," I volunteer. "None of us did. They were all different, but the same. Absent."

"I'm not going to discuss this with you," he answers tersely. "No matter what you volunteer. You forget these are things I already know about you."

"I haven't forgotten," I tell him. "But there's a difference between me telling you, and you reading it from a file."

"It makes no difference to me."

His words burn me, but I don't show it. I never show anyone they have the power to hurt me anymore.

"Why do you accept it so easily?" he asks, stalking closer to me. "Why do you not put up a fight when a man you don't even know tells you that you will be married? And you will live here in this house, with a stranger. And yet, you cannot even bring yourself to speak with the one person who knows you best?"

"Because she doesn't know me best," I answer quietly. "She doesn't know me at all."

I try to turn away, but he grabs my wrist and halts me.

"Why?"

I blink up at him, and I have the sudden urge to hate him again. He is such a hypocrite. Demanding these things of me. These answers. When he will not give me the same in return.

"How could she?" I ask him. "How can anyone, if they have not walked the same path? How can someone understand what it is like for you not to hear when they themselves have only ever had perfectly functioning ears?"

He doesn't answer. So I answer myself.

"They can't. They can't understand these things, and yet, they feel like they have the right to judge you for them. To ask you to change who you are. To fix what cannot be fixed."

I've given too much away, I realize, when I meet his gaze again… and find complete understanding staring back at me.

Alexei takes my hands in his and brushes his fingers over my palms. He can see now why I'm here. Why I didn't put up a fight. Because he accepted me as I am, from the moment he took me in. He never asked me to change. To pretend that I am normal. Or that I'm okay. Until now.

"You don't need to be fixed, Solnyshko," he tells me. "But you can't avoid your feelings forever. You believe that you would rather face death than your fears. But this is not the way it works."

"Why not?" I ask him. "You do."

"I am not avoiding anything," he lies boldly. "I have simply accepted what is."

"And so have I."

"No," he argues. "You haven't. You have simply numbed yourself."

He taps me on the head and then grips my chin between his fingers, tilting my face up so that he has complete access to my every emotion.

"It is a defense mechanism. The brain, is a wonderful thing. Can survive any trauma by doing this. But your traumas are over. It is time now to process them. To feel."

I swallow, and he takes me by the hand. Leading me down the hall to his office. I don't fight him. Because we both know the entire conversation was just my attempt at delaying the inevitable.

He sits down in his chair and then pulls me into his lap and drags the phone closer. He doesn't make me do anything. Anything at all.

He simply dials the number and hands me the phone.

"Simply tell her you are safe," he says. "And anything else you wish to say."

It rings for a long time. And every sound is like a jackhammer to my ears and my armor. I'm shaking in Alexei's arms, and he is rubbing my back in a soothing gesture. There are tears in my eyes. And then the muffled sound of someone answering.

"Hello?"

My lips are sticking together, and it takes me three attempts to get her name out.

"Mack?"

There's a long pause, and the guilt is stabbing at my heart. The one I swore I no longer had. She sounds so scared. So nervous that this is some sort of a sick joke. That it can't be real. And I know now, she thought I was dead. She thought I was lost forever.

Because I was too much of a coward to tell her otherwise. She deserves so much better than this. Than me. She deserves everything I could never be to her.

"Talia?"

"Yes," I whisper. "It's me."

"Are you okay?" she asks. "Please tell me you're okay."

"I'm okay," I answer. "I can't talk very long though."

"What do you mean?"

"I just…" My voice cracks, and I can barely speak. I'm going to break. Any second now. I'm going to break completely. And it isn't fair to Mack. I can't let her hear me cry. The best thing I can do for her is to let her believe I'm okay. The way she always wanted me to be. "I just wanted you to know that I'm okay. And that you shouldn't worry about me anymore."

"What do you mean don't worry about you?" she demands.

"I'm safe," I repeat. "And I'm not coming home."

"Talia…"

"I have to go, Mack," I tell her. "I just wanted to say congratulations on your wedding. And that I love you, and I miss you so much. But I'm okay now, and I have you to thank for that."

It's the last sentence I can manage to get out before my resolve breaks and I disconnect the line.

Twenty-Six

Alexei

"Arman has sent word on the shipments," Viktor informs me. "You will need to inform him soon."

"Of course." I nod my assent, but Viktor doubts my assurances.

It is one thing to doubt me, but to do it in front of the Vory is something new. Viktor has only ever shown me respect. But right now he is giving Sergei precisely what he wants. A reason to doubt me. To prove that I am not worthy of my title. Of my rank.

"This could very well get ugly," Viktor adds. "He may not wish to part with the girl."

"It is too late." I shrug. "It is done. She is my wife. He has no claim on her now. And he will be compensated accordingly. The choice is his. He can have his money and his life, or nothing at all."

"And what of our shipments?" Sergei asks.

"There are plenty of other suppliers."

"Not with his arsenal," he scoffs. "You full well know this."

"So then we take over his supply. Run his operation ourselves. It would not be the first time we have done so."

"What you are speaking of means going to war, Lyoshenka," Viktor replies.

"So we go to war then."

All of their eyes are on me. My father's disapproving gaze. And even after all of these years, it burns me. He still has the power to make me feel inadequate in his presence. Which is precisely what he wants. He wants me to doubt myself. To waver in front of these men and prove I am worthless.

But my resolve is steadfast on this matter. And that will not change.

"Going to war is an easy solution for you." Sergei doesn't attempt to hide his disdain for me. "When you have the brothers doing all of the dirty work for you."

I meet his gaze and hold it. "I am a Vor, too. You seem to forget."

His lips sneer and Nikolai steps up to place a hand on his shoulder before he says something he will regret. That will incriminate him and allow all of the others to know his dirty secret. That he is the father of a son who will never live up to Nikolai's standard. That he is the father of me.

"And I will be the first through the door," I add. "Should it come to a war."

Viktor steps beside me and places a hand on my shoulder, showing his support for me without speaking a word. It grates on Sergei, and his eyes linger on the connection for far too long.

That his defective son should rank higher than him in his own organization is something he will never accept. While he remains a captain—an Avtoritet—his rank will never go any higher. I am invaluable to Viktor. It should not come as a surprise to him. He set the bar for me when he cast me and my mother onto the street. When he set the course of her fate, he also set mine.

I was always destined to prove my worth. To serve as the constant reminder of what he did. Of how he had been wrong about me. And it gives me enormous pleasure to see that ugly twisted sneer on his face every time he looks my way.

"I do not believe that it will come down to that," Viktor states. "Arman knows better than to try to take on the Reds. There is only one reason a man would ever surround himself with so many weapons."

I meet my father's gaze and nod my agreement. "Because he is a little bitch."

His reply is filled with equal venom.

"I hope you are certain." He slaps Nikolai on the back and beams at him proudly. "Because I would not send my only son into battle for you, let alone your worthless whore wife."

What happens next is a complete loss of my self-control. I am used to the insults he directs towards me. But Talia is another matter altogether.

I don't realize what is happening until Viktor pulls me off him and calms me down. Nikolai helps Sergei to his feet, and he spits a bloodied tooth onto the floor while he glances over at me. His finger is shaking when he points in my direction.

"I am done with him, Viktor," he roars. "Enough is enough. I don't want to see him here again."

"You are right," Viktor states calmly. "Enough is enough. Everyone out."

The remaining Vory filter out of the room, leaving only Viktor and I on one side, and Nikolai and Sergei on the other.

When the door is shut and the room is silent, Viktor's gaze moves over Sergei. And while he has always maintained a cool manner, right now his disgust is obvious. And though it should not, as Viktor has always been loyal to me, it comes as a surprise.

I was out of line, hitting Sergei in a business meeting. Goading him in front of all the other Vory. But it is clear at this moment, it is not me who Viktor wishes to speak to.

"Tell me what you do for this brotherhood," he says to Sergei.

My father's gaze moves to him, and he replies. "Everything that is asked of me. I am only loyal to the Vory."

"It is correct that you do everything that is asked of you," Viktor answers. "But you are not loyal to the Vory. You are not loyal to the code of which we live by."

Sergei has the good sense to keep his mouth shut while Viktor goes on.

"You do not value family. And is that not one of our most important values?"

"I do value my son," my father answers.

"Ah, yes." Viktor moves his gaze from Nikolai to me. "But you have two sons. One which you have discarded and disowned. And left me to take on the role of a father figure in his life. Is this how you honor your family?"

The room falls silent, and I cannot meet my father's gaze. His shame.

We do not speak of this. Ever.

Even when I explained my situation to Viktor and was inducted into the brotherhood, we did not speak of it. We were all aware of the situation, but the topic has been avoided. Until now.

And it is clear to me, I am not the only one who wishes it to remain buried.

"And your wife?" Viktor goes on. "What of her? You made a mockery of her for all to see. Bringing your mistresses into your own home. To sleep in your marital bed? And then casting her out on the street with your son."

The temples in my head are aching. And I want Viktor to stop. But he is the pakhan. And neither Sergei or I would dare to question him right now. I know all of these things to be true. And speaking of them will not breach the divide between us. But Viktor seems to think it is necessary.

And as he is like a father to me, I trust his judgment.

"Now you come into my meeting and make a mockery of Lyoshenka for all to see? To offend his wife in front of the brothers? You are aware of the consequences for such actions. And if it were anyone else, you would not have done so."

It is true my father knows the consequences. This is why he remains unapologetic when he meets my gaze. He is aware there is no avoiding it now. And the only thing he has left is his pride, which he will not sacrifice at any cost.

"He is defective," Sergei replies. "Worthless. He is no son of mine."

Viktor reaches for his phone and taps out a message to one of his soldiers, the room silent while we wait for what comes next. After a few moments, a Boevik appears with the shears, passing them off to Viktor.

"Nikolai," Viktor says. "You will do the honors."

Nikolai glances at Sergei and receives his nod of approval. Then he takes the shears from Viktor and reaches for his hand.

"No," Viktor stops him. "Not the fingers."

Sergei tries to hide the fear on his face, but it's there. He meets Viktor's gaze, wordless, as he waits for his punishment. Even I am not breathing, and I know Nikolai is not either.

"An ear," Viktor says.

The room is quiet. For a long moment. But Nikolai does not delay any further, and Sergei does not protest.

I watch as my father tries to remain stoic while Nikolai cuts off his ear. It does not last for very long. Like the coward he is, the pain brings him to his knees. It is only Nikolai that I feel a small pang of regret for. This will certainly drive a wedge between them as Viktor intended.

But an order from the pakhan will never be questioned or ignored, by anyone. And Nikolai does not deserve my sympathies.

When the act is over, Viktor tosses Nikolai a handkerchief to stem the bleeding. And there is a sigh of relief from Sergei.

We all believe it to be over. The punishment for his offenses have been carried out, and he now knows never to speak ill of my wife again.

But Viktor is not finished.

"I am stripping you of your duties as Avtoritet," he announces. "And from here on out, you will take your orders as Boevik to Nikolai. Who I am promoting in your stead."

"You cannot be serious," Sergei bellows. "He is only a boy."

"He is twenty-five. And he conducts himself in the way that a Vor should."

Viktor catches my eye before he goes on. "And besides, you should be happy. He is your pride and joy, no?"

Twenty-Seven

Talia

Alexei comes in late.

I know, because I can't sleep in his absence.

Even though we are still worlds apart and will probably never trust each other, his being in the house is the only thing that makes me feel safe. Even though it shouldn't. Even though it's the most foolish thing I could do after Dmitri.

I hear him fumbling around in his office, and then a curse before the light comes on down the hall. I swing my legs over the bed and move towards him, like a beacon in the night.

I find him at his desk, pouring a glass of cognac, although it is apparent he has already had several. Only the lamp next to his desk is on, so the light is dim, but even still, I can tell something isn't right.

When his face comes into view, I see he has a split lip, and a bruise on his cheek.

I step inside and move towards him, only catching his attention when I'm directly in front of him.

"Go back to bed."

His voice is harsh and cold. I ignore it and round the desk, instead.

He is too wound up, so I don't chance sitting on his lap. Instead, I sit across from him, on the desk. Studying him, as he does the same.

"What do you want?" he demands.

Right now, I want to fix whatever is hurting him. But I don't know the way. Nobody has ever showed me. So I do the only thing I can to connect with him. The only way I know.

I lift my hips and discard my shorts while he watches, followed by my cami. And then I'm naked on his desk, spreading my legs for him to see me. My hand slides down between my thighs slowly, playing with myself while he watches.

The room is quiet, and I have every bit of his attention. Cognac long forgotten, he leans forward, just a little, his eyes moving over my body.

"You said you were going to fuck me every day," I tell him. "But you're a liar."

He's on me then. I've never seen him move so fast.

His body is pressing me down against the desk, one hand tangling in my hair and yanking my head to the side so he can kiss my throat. The other is fumbling with his belt and zipper. He frees his cock and then sinks inside of me.

There's a sigh of contentment, and then some angry muffled Russian against the skin of my throat. He fucks me into the desk and I get more of the same, wrapping my legs around him and letting him use me.

He fucks me hard. Punishing. But the war he is fighting is with himself.

I don't understand a single thing he's saying, but his message is clear in any language when he yanks me off the desk and sends me down onto my knees.

I take his cock in my mouth and he gags me with it. And then strokes my face in a tender gesture. I get more of the same. Harsh and then gentle. The words continue to flow from his mouth uninhibited, and I'd give anything to know what he was saying to me right now.

I feel him tensing. But he won't let himself come. He grabs my head to hold me in place, allowing himself time to pull back from the edge. And then he's yanking me up, flipping me over. Now my ass is hanging off the desk, and he's behind me.

"Don't move," he tells me.

I feel him disappear from the room, but only for a moment. When he comes back, there's a candle in his hand, which he sets on the desk beside me.

Anticipation and fear war inside of me.

But between them, somewhere in the middle, is the one thing I shouldn't feel.

Trust.

I can hear him shuffling through his drawers, and then the smell of butane combined with the catch of the lighter. The room is quiet and still when he leans down and kisses my back. Gentle and soft. Right between my shoulder blades.

"Mine."

It calms me when he says that. There is so much meaning behind that one word. So much promise. And against my better judgment, I relax for him. Gripping the edge of the desk beneath my palms and laying my face flat against the wood.

He picks up the candle with one hand and strokes my ass with the other.

On the opposite side of the wall, his shadow looms over me. His arm tilting. I close my eyes and breathe. The first drop of wax falls onto my skin and steals that same oxygen. The second hurts less. And the third is when I feel the rush of endorphins.

His palm slides down between my thighs to cup me and then

finger me. He alternates his movements from the dripping candle to the hand between my legs. Pleasure and pain. So much pleasure and so much pain. I come harder than I ever have this time. My back covered in heated welts when he drags his fingers down and pulls off the wax while he shoves his cock inside of me. And then he's fucking me again. His hips jarring against my ass. I have to grip the desk to keep myself in place.

I think he's going to come, but he doesn't. He flips me back over and lifts me into his arms, holding me close while he fucks me in the most intimate of positions. Face to face.

"I want to look at you," he tells me. "I need you to always see me."

He kisses me, and then he comes inside of me.

Then he lays me down on the desk and steps back.

"Stay like that," he tells me as he sits back down in the chair. "I want to look at you."

That's what he says. But I have a feeling that isn't the case at all. I have a feeling he put me in this position for a reason. Legs bent and knees up. He wants me to get pregnant. To have his baby. And yet, when he finishes with me here tonight, he will go to his room. And I, to mine. We will not have lingering conversation or touches because we are both afraid.

So I disobey him by sitting up and gathering up my clothes.

I can't bring myself to leave without a word, so I lift my fingers up to touch his bruised and swollen face.

"I hope you made them pay."

His eyes are tormented and filled with longing. For me.

But he does not act on it.

So I leave.

Twenty-Eight

Alexei

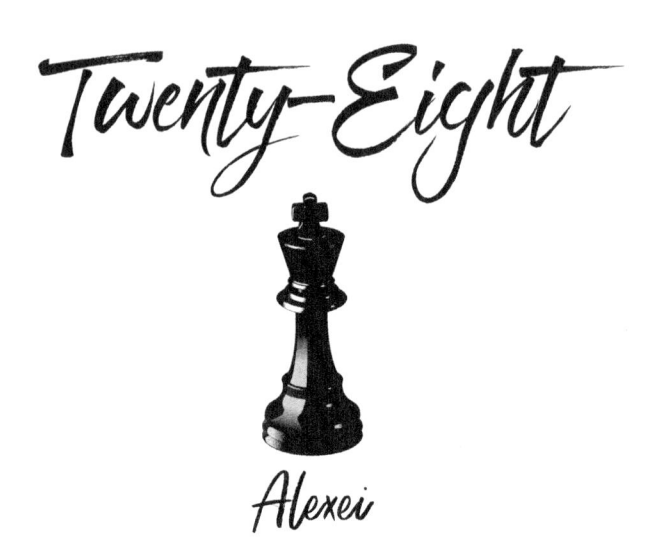

"Talia has made breakfast this morning," Magda announces cheerfully.

"She has?" I question, my lack of excitement clearly deflating hers.

She nods. "She is getting better."

"It always gets better before it gets worse," is my answer.

Magda frowns and then moves her attention to the reports I'm working on.

"You will eat together this morning," she tells me.

I cock my head to the side, and she smiles.

"You must, Alexei. You must reward her progress. It is the only way."

"My time and attention is not a reward."

"I think Talia would disagree."

I shift uncomfortably in my chair and glance out the window. The seasons have changed so quickly now that she's here. Tonight is the Christmas party. Which she will attend with me. And do her duties as my wife. And for this reason, I tell myself, I will go downstairs and indulge her this once.

I can't have her moods changing when I need her to play her part.

When I tell Magda this, she frowns.

I ignore it and file my papers away before going downstairs.

Talia is in the kitchen, just as Magda said. And in a good mood, just as Magda said. I turn to Magda, who is trailing behind me.

"You should not have left her alone in there," I warn.

Again, she frowns.

"It is not an act, Alyoshka." She shakes her head. "She is getting better."

"Until she finds a knife to set herself free."

I do not wait for Magda's response. Instead, I take a seat at the table, unsure what else to do. I usually dine in my office unless there is company. Magda delivers my meals, and I rarely give it any thought. But now, I feel uncomfortable. Out of place. Watching her move around the kitchen.

When she turns around and looks my way, there is flour on her nose and shirt. And some sort of batter tangled in her hair.

But also, a smile on her face.

I clear my throat to hide my own.

"Good, they are all ready now," Talia says. And then she delivers a heaping plate of fresh waffles to the table, followed by a bowl of Strawberries.

I reach for one waffle, and she stares at me. So I take another. Magda does the same, and we all eat in silence.

During the meal, I watch Talia carefully. Her good mood dissipates quickly. Magda glances at me, silently telling me to do something. But I don't know the answer. So we wait in stillness.

And eventually, Talia speaks. Trapped by old memories. Locked inside the darkness in her head.

"She made waffles that day," she says, as though she is just remembering.

She blinks up at me with glassy eyes. "I should have known, because she made waffles."

"Your mother?" I ask.

"Yes," she answers, her fork clattering to the plate. "She never cooked. She barely let us out of the room. I should have seen it."

"You couldn't have," I tell her from experience. "When someone is that far gone, they make you believe what they want. They fool everyone."

Both Magda and Talia are staring at me now, and I look away. Pushing my chair back, I reach for Talia's hand. She does not hesitate to give it to me. But the despondency has set in again, so she cannot walk. I lift her into my arms and rest her head on my shoulder while I carry her up the stairs.

I don't know what to do with her. How to help her. And it weighs on me.

I can't leave her alone, so I simply sit down with her and cradle her in my arms. She rests her face against my chest and relaxes. Her fingers move over the soft material of my sweater, sliding the material between her thumb and forefinger.

"I don't think I can do this," she says.

Live.

That's what she means by those whispered words.

"You can, and you will," I tell her.

She is quiet. Thinking dark thoughts. And I know that I need to coax them from her. I know that helping her means facing my own fears. That she will not recover. That I can't ever help her.

I reach for her fingers and place them over the star on her hand. And without further insistence, she moves them of her own accord. Into a rhythmic pattern. Tracing the lines and my name, over and over again.

"Tell me about your mother," I insist.

She meets my eyes, and hers are violent with emotion. More than I've ever seen in her before. It wants to break free, but she doesn't know how.

"Don't tell me what you think I want to hear," I encourage. "You have only ever been honest with me, Solynshko. So be honest now."

It takes her some time. Time to decide she trusts me. But that's exactly what it is when she looks up at me. And I know it is not easily given.

"I hardly knew her," she tells me. "She was a storm. And we just tried to survive the bad days until the sunlight broke through."

"You took care of your siblings," I reply.

"I was the oldest," is her answer. "She kept us locked away. During the bad times. In a room, together. We only had each other."

Her eyes drift up to the ceiling, and she finishes. "And now, it is just me."

I know what I need to tell her. The thing that is true, but I cannot bring myself to admit. That she has me. The words don't come. So I comfort her in the way that I can. With my hands. Combing through her hair. Clearing away the tangles from her face.

She likes this. She will never admit it. Just as I will not admit I enjoy doing it.

"Tell me what you think you should feel about your mother," I say.

This time, she answers without delay. "Sorry. I should feel sorry for her. Because she was sick."

"But what you really feel is anger," I reply.

She moves her gaze back to me. Examining me. Picking me apart. "Tell me about the woman in the bathtub."

"This is not about her," I deflect.

"It never is," she replies.

"You need to allow yourself to be angry, Solnyshko. Release that anger. On me, if you want. But you have to accept that it's there."

"But you don't," she says. "That's always the way it works with you."

"I'm trying to help you."

"By lying to me and yourself?" she sits up and stares at me, the anger I asked for rising to the surface. "You're such a fucking hypocrite. A selfish asshole."

She tries to get up. To leave me. But I hold her in place. My own anger coming out to play.

"Yes, and you are a psychotic bitch."

She tries to yank herself away, but again I don't let her. I grip her chin in my hands and force her to kiss me.

"But you're my psychotic bitch," I murmur against her. "And I am your selfish asshole."

Her resistance flees, and she places her hands on my face. Kissing me back. Stroking through my hair. But then she pulls away again, angry and hurt.

"They are just words, Solnyshko."

And then she says the thing I don't expect. The thing that guts me. Because it is the most vulnerable thing she's ever said.

"Not when they come from you. Not then they aren't."

Twenty-Nine

Talia

When Magda and I reach the bottom of the stairs, Alexei is waiting for me.

He is dressed as he always is. Gray trousers, black oxfords and a charcoal sweater stretched across his muscular frame. He is in the process of shrugging into his black coat and flat cap when he pauses to look up at me.

He takes a breath. And I feel a sense of relief pulsing through me.

The dress is one that he picked, Magda informed me. Not something I'd ever worn before. Black embroidered tulle with an exposed back. It's expensive and flashy. Alexei wants to show me off tonight. As his wife.

A part of me questioned if it was because Katya would be there. But the response from him now tells me otherwise.

He moves towards me as if he can't help himself. Magda smiles and steps to the side as his fingers find my cheek and skate down over my neck.

"You are so lovely, Solnyshko," he tells me.

I reach for his waist and touch him too. My hands against his warmth. And for a moment, we just look at each other. I want to believe that I'm not the only one who feels this pull between us, but I've been wrong before.

I've been so wrong.

My heart is beating too hard. Too fast. And I need to think of something else.

"What does it mean?" I ask.

"What?"

"Solnyshko?"

He pulls me closer still, his lips hovering over my ear. "It means little sun."

He kisses my ear and pulls away, resuming his activities of dressing for the outdoors. Once he has finished, he takes me by the hand and leads me from the door.

Franco is already outside where two separate cars are parked and waiting. He's examining one of them, checking underneath and all around it. I swallow and glance up at Alexei, who is already staring at me.

"It is okay," he tells me. "Just a routine safety check."

I nod, and he leads me to the car and deposits me in the passenger side. Then he kneels down beside me and captures my leg in his hand.

"Give me your foot," he tells me.

It is a strange request from him, but I don't argue. I stretch out my leg over his muscular thigh, my heel dangling in the cool evening air. He removes the shoe and does the unexpected. Dragging his fingers down the center, the most sensitive part, before he removes a switchblade from his pocket.

"You will want this tonight," he tells me. "But only a little bit."

How he can know this about me is unnerving. But he does. He sees my anxiety at the prospect of leaving this sanctuary.

"Only a little bit," he tells me as he drags the knife to the ball of my foot. "And only the first time, Solnyshko."

I nod, and he scratches the sensitive flesh with the blade. Not even to draw blood. But enough to sting. And then he leans down and presses his lips to the curve at the top of my foot.

I watch in fascination as he puts the heel back into place and directs me to press down onto the ball of my foot. Until I feel the pain that I will need at some point tonight.

"Good?" he asks.

I nod, and he puts the knife away before buckling me in and closing the door. He speaks with Franco for a few moments, and then climbs inside with me, the scent of him mixing with the rich leather interior. The headlights of the car behind us follows as we leave the house, and I know that Franco is coming too. Though why he is driving separately, I'm not entirely sure.

"I thought it would be more comfortable this way," Alexei answers my unspoken thought. "It is a long drive."

I nod and sink back in the seat, turning my attention towards him.

"It's not a good name for me," I tell him. "Solnyshko. It doesn't make any sense."

"It makes perfect sense to me."

That's the only answer I get before his hand is on my thigh. He glances at me, his eyes moving over me as his hand slides up. Further and further until it's between my legs.

"Pull your dress up," he instructs me. "I want to look at you."

I do as he asks because I always do with Alexei. I lift my hips and bring the dress up so the material falls around my waist, giving him full access to me.

He isn't shy about what he wants. He just takes. But with Alexei, it never feels like he is taking anything from me. But rather, giving instead.

His hand cups the matching lace thong and his thumb pushes the material against me. I don't make a sound, but my hips jerk and inside I'm begging him for more.

I like it when he touches me.

When he makes me forget. And makes me feel alive too. His hand on me is large. And I feel safe with him. He doesn't let me get away with anything. But he doesn't hurt me either.

"You are wet for me already," he says, his voice husky.

I don't reply, and he doesn't say anything else either. His fingers move the thong aside and slip inside of me. Casually playing with me while he drives. His eyes on the road, his forearm flexing as his hand moves inside of me.

My head falls back against the seat and my legs splay wider. The wife he dressed to look so classy right now looks anything but.

"Take your tits out," he says. "I want to see them."

I pull the material of the dress down over my shoulders, trapping my arms and forcing my breasts out. They are hard and aching when he reaches up to squeeze one in his palm, leaving me cold down below.

"Play with yourself while I watch," he tells me.

I try, but swiftly give up.

"It's better when you do it."

He smiles at me and returns his palm between my thighs, giving me exactly what I need.

"Your foot," he reminds me. "To give yourself the pain if you want."

I do. And it only takes a couple minutes before I'm feeling on edge. Unable to tear my eyes away from Alexei. The way his wedding ring gleams against the steering wheel on his left hand. He wears it proudly.

Sometimes it's still hard to accept that this man is my husband.

He's more than that.

He's my savior. My unwilling hero. And the thing that is most dangerous of all.

My hope.

"Be a good girl and come for me, yes?"

I do.

I come hard for him. And he pulls his fingers from me and sucks them into his mouth before placing his hand back on the steering wheel.

The car is quiet, except for my loud breathing as I come down from the high. He doesn't speak. Or say anything else. Ask for anything else.

But I want to give it to him regardless.

I unbuckle and balance my knees on my seat, leaning over into his space. I kiss his throat and jaw, and then briefly, his lips when he turns into me.

My hand is fumbling with his zipper. His belt. I get them undone, and lower my head towards his groin. When I pull his cock free and get him into my mouth, Alexei grips the back of my head with his right hand, pushing me down further.

He drives, and I suck him off. My head bobbing up and down in his lap with the guidance of his hand. The insistence. He groans and then comes in my mouth.

"Swallow it all, Solnyshko," he tells me.

My throat works around his cock, doing exactly as he orders. And only then does he release his hold on me, his fingers stroking over my face.

"Good girl."

I put him back together, zipping him up and buckling his belt. And then linger in his space to kiss him on his throat once more. It's a stupid thing to do. And it's too much.

"Buckle yourself in," he orders.

I move back to my side of the car, putting myself back together and buckling the seat belt. When I stare out the window, my throat is clogged, and I don't know why.

Alexei's hand finds mine, his warmth enveloping and surprising me.

"You are the perfect wife," he tells me. "Perfect for me, Solnyshko."

I look at him and nod.

I don't know if it's an insult or a compliment.

Thirty

Talia

The Christmas party is held at what can only be described as a compound. Every car is checked at the gate, and every guest vetted before they enter.

And in that moment, I realize that my life here with Alexei is not so different from how I lived at Arman's. Only now, the same security measures that felt like a vice grip around my neck feel safe.

Alexei parks the car and tells me to wait, coming around to open my door for me. He is old fashioned in these ways. A man who values tradition. It is a rare quality. And for the briefest of moments, when he takes my arm in his, I feel a flash of pride from the idea of being at his side tonight.

We are greeted at the door by several men I do not recognize, nor understand. They speak in their native tongue, except for when Alexei makes introductions. Even then, they barely glance at me, except to nod and congratulate me on my nuptials. A sign of respect, I think. For Alexei.

It makes me curious. Exactly what his position in the organization is. I don't even know what he does. But when I look up at him, looking down at me, I don't care either.

He keeps me safe. He protects me.

He saved me.

Even now, in this room full of his own friends, he shields me with his body. Keeping me pulled close to his side and ready to destroy anyone who dares to enter my orbit.

We sit down to dinner within minutes of our arrival. A feast consisting of breads and pies, borscht and fresh fruit and nuts throughout the meal. Alexei keeps his arm across the back of my chair while we eat, sheltering me while he carries on conversation with the man across from us.

Viktor.

The same voice that called me a whore.

From his position at the table, I can see he is important. The most important man here tonight. He is served first, and nobody eats until he has taken the first bite. These men respect him. Alexei respects him. But I still can't bring myself to truly respect him. So I keep my attention diverted to my plate and the food until the meal is over.

After a round of drinks is served, music starts to play from the other room, and the guests begin to migrate in that direction.

"You must take your new bride for a spin, Lyoshenka," Viktor says.

Alexei looks uncomfortable with the suggestion. But still, he nods. And then he takes me by the hand, leading me into the other room.

"One dance?"

It sounds like a question, but already, he's positioning my body close to his. Our right hands clasped together, his left on my lower back. Which we quickly discover isn't going to work due to the height difference.

But Alexei is not one to let something like that stop him. So he kneels down and places my hands on his shoulders while he removes my heels. When he stands up again, the distance between us is even further, and I look up at him with questioning eyes.

"On my feet," he instructs as he lifts me up and deposits my feet onto his shoes.

"Now wrap your arms around my waist."

I do.

"Good girl," he tells me.

And then we're off. Dancing slowly, my cheek pressed against his warm chest. I don't have to do anything but hold on, and we quickly garner the attention of some of the other couples around the floor. Some are laughing, jesting about his size.

But Katya is definitely not.

And when I see her standing next to another man, his eyes cold and lasered in on me, it makes me tense. He has been to our house before. To celebrate our marriage. But he did not speak to me. And right now, it looks as though he hates me.

Katya whispers something in his ear, and he brings his drink to his lips.

"Do not pay them any attention." Alexei's voice cuts through my thoughts, his fingers turning my gaze up to him.

Our eyes lock, and it's easy enough to forget them as he asked. Because I'm captivated by the man holding me in his arms right now. Staring down at me with what feels like genuine emotion.

His eyes are warm, and it warms me too.

And then he does something unexpected. He leans down and kisses me. Not to put on a show. But because he wants to. It's soft and tender, and I can feel him hardening against me as our bodies move in tandem.

I stretch up to meet his lips, which soon move to my throat. And for a moment, we both seem to forget that we're in the middle of a party. That anyone else exists outside of us.

Until Viktor's voice cuts through the haze and he slaps Alexei on the back.

Alexei reluctantly pulls his mouth from me and positions me in front of his body, his arms wrapped around my waist while he speaks with Viktor in Russian.

More than a few times during the conversation, Viktor's gaze moves to me, and it's obvious that I'm the topic at hand. But the disgust he felt for me before isn't there, in his eyes. It's something else. It's warmth, and what looks to me like sincere happiness. It confuses me.

"It is time for the men to talk business," he says in English. "Why don't you send your little dove off to mingle, Lyoshenka."

I tense against him, and he turns me in his arms.

"You will spend time with the other women tonight," he says with a small shrug. "Tradition. The men in this room, the women over there."

I follow the direction of his nod and my fingers move over the star on my hand.

"Don't worry," he says. "I have someone I'd like you to meet. I think you will be more… compatible with her."

I don't know what he means by that. But as he leads me in the direction of the women, all of their eyes on me, I feel like a lamb being led to slaughter.

They are looking at me as if I don't belong. The same way Katya looks at me when she sees me with Alexei. As if I don't deserve the man on my arm.

And they are probably right.

"Tanaka," he calls out.

A girl around my age looks up at us from her chair where she is sitting alone. Not speaking with anyone around her. She is beautiful. With raven hair and amber eyes, and a reserved smile as her attention moves from Alexei to me.

I give her my own reserved smile before Alexei grasps my shoulders and smooths his palms down my arms in what can only be a comforting gesture.

"You will be just fine, Solnyshko," he tells me. "You have your star, yes?"

I touch it and nod.

"I'll be just a few short steps away if you need anything."

"Okay."

He waits until I am seated beside Tanaka and gives me one last glance, as though he too is hesitant to leave me. But he does.

And then it's just Tanaka and I, in somewhat awkward silence for a few moments before she speaks.

"I don't fit in here either," she tells me.

"What do you mean?" I ask.

When I look at her, I can't tell if she knows my background. But she seems to see me. And recognize something in me that she too is familiar with.

"I am simply collateral," she tells me. "My father owes a large debt, and I am in Nikolai's charge until he comes through with it."

"Oh," is my only reply.

I don't want to feel sorry for her because sympathy is what gets you in trouble. But the more I examine her, the more I don't think it is sympathy she needs anyway.

"When do you think that will be?" I ask her.

She shakes her head. "Never. My father cannot pay."

The words leave my mouth before I can stop them. "So what will happen to you?"

She sighs and then glances across the room. A flicker of something moves through her eyes when her gaze lands on Nikolai. Who is currently speaking to Katya, her hand on his arm like she owns him. It takes me a moment to read the emotion in Tanaka's eyes. She has feelings for him. For her captor.

"Whatever Nikolai decides," she says, tearing her gaze away.

I feel the need to comfort her. But I don't have the right words.

"I was collateral too," I blurt.

She looks at me and smiles. "Yes, I know."

"You do?"

"I overheard Nikolai mention you."

"Oh."

The conversation dies off for a moment, and when I look around, I see more than a few questioning gazes being directed our way.

"Don't worry," Tanaka says. "You will get used to it. They don't like you because they will never be you."

"I don't understand," I tell her.

"Your husband." She nods to the other room. "He is the ah… councilor to Viktor. He outranks their husbands in every way. Which means that you do also."

"Oh."

My mouth is dry, and I seem to have lost all conversational skills. Tanaka is kind though, and she just continues to talk, seemingly glad to have company.

"They are very traditional," she says. "You will be starting a family soon, yes?"

I wring my hands in my lap. "That is what Alexei says."

Except, family isn't what Alexei and I have. It is an arrangement. Which I can never forget. Even when I glance at him across the room and find him looking back at me, a slight tilt to his lips.

"He is handsome," Tanaka remarks. "You are lucky. Nikolai speaks very highly of him."

"He does?"

I find that odd since I noticed the tension between the two on the last occasion. Alexei never even introduced us.

"He does." Tanaka nods. "I do find it strange though. How similar they look in some regards. Don't you?"

I can't read her expression. But I don't think she finds it strange at all. I think she's trying to tell me something.

But then the man in question is at her side, speaking to her in Russian. By all outward appearances, he seems indifferent to her. But his focus on her lingers a little too long for that to be true. And it breathes hope into me. That Tanaka will not be lost to this world that seems to have trapped her too.

"Talia." Nikolai bows in my direction. "I haven't had a chance to properly introduce myself."

I'm not sure what to do. If I'm supposed to rise to meet him. Or shake his hand. Or any of the protocols, really. But Nikolai puts my worries at ease when he kneels so that he is on the same level as Tanaka and I.

He has a friendly smile on his face. But his voice is low and serious when he speaks.

"I need to speak with you," he says.

I look at Tanaka, her gaze reassuring and steady. As though she trusts Nikolai implicitly. And I should do the same. It eases my discomfort a little as he presses on.

"Alexei will not listen to me," he says. "He won't speak with me. But I know he will listen to you."

I shift in my seat and simply nod.

"Sergei is not going to let this go. Neither is Katya, for that matter. You should both be careful."

"Nikolai…" Tanaka's voice cuts him off, and then a shadow falls over us.

Alexei.

His gaze is fixed on Nikolai, who stands up to face him. Angry words pass between them, both of their hands gesturing in a way that signals a long history of bad blood between them.

Only when Nikolai's shoulders fall in defeat, does Alexei turn to me. Gripping me by the arm and yanking me from the chair. Scolding me like a child for all to see.

"You are my wife," he hisses into my ear. "You can no longer conduct yourself the way you did at Arman's."

His words are like acid to my insides.

"You mean like a whore?" I pull back to look at him.

His eyes are cold, filled with accusation and anger. No trace of the man who kissed me on the dance floor only thirty minutes ago.

"Yes, that's exactly what I mean," he answers.

My throat is clogged, and there are tears threatening to spill over. I don't want him to see me cry. I don't want him to see that he has that power over me. The power to hurt me.

"Go to the wash room and compose yourself," he demands. "And when you come back, perhaps you can make it through the rest of the evening with better judgment."

Tanaka stands up, her voice soft and quiet when she speaks. "I will accompany her."

"You will not," Alexei barks. "She must learn how to conduct herself at these events."

And then he releases me from his grip, leaving the tears to spill down my face as I make my walk of shame down the hall and to the bathroom.

I lock myself in and cry for twenty minutes. I have not cried so much in as long as I can remember. Because I know now that all my bravado has been for nothing. Alexei does have the power to hurt me. Just as I do him.

But it will not change a thing.

I am still only his wife. And he is only my husband. And he will never let those feelings prosper. Because he is stronger than I am. And the weakness I swore I would never have is staring me right in the face again.

I am falling for a man who is using me.

Who will only ever use me.

When all of my tears have run dry, and the acceptance of my

reality has settled upon me, I move to the mirror and glance at my reflection. But I can't look at her. I can't look at that girl right now.

The door opens behind me, and it confuses me. I thought I locked it.

"Sorry," I murmur, without opening my eyes. "I'll be out of here in just a moment."

Strong hands come around my waist and pull me back into a hard body. I sigh and relax in those arms. And then blurt something honest and vulnerable.

"I'm sorry if I hurt you. Embarrassed you."

"Hurt me?" dark laughter echoes through the cavernous bathroom, and dread crawls through my veins. "It has been some time, but I don't recall you ever hurting me, Talia."

My heart throttles against my chest. And I'm frozen. I don't want to look. But I have to. Because that voice is the one from my nightmares. The one who betrayed me worse than any other before him. The one who changed my life forever and destroyed the last hope of human decency that I harbored.

"Dmitri."

The word is like sandpaper on my tongue.

He kisses my neck, his breath hot on my skin. "Yes. Did you miss me?"

I open my eyes, and the room spins. But I can only focus on him. His reflection in the mirror. His body behind me, trapping me. With nowhere to go.

"Arman misses you," he tells me, his fingers moving over my body like he still has that right.

And I'm too numb to move. To think. To do anything but let him. I wasn't prepared for this. I've never been prepared for this.

"He wants you back."

My legs wobble, and he tightens his grip on me to keep me upright. But he doesn't stop talking. It doesn't even faze him.

"You are just as beautiful as I remember." He presses his nose into my hair and inhales, and my stomach roils at the sight of him touching me again. "Perhaps we could spend some time together before I must return you. I did always enjoy your company."

And this is the thing that snaps me out of my frozen horror. I turn around and shove him away from me, and to my surprise, he does not argue. He simply laughs and moves towards the door, giving me one last lingering glance.

"Your new lover plays chess, yes?" he asks.

I don't reply. But he already knows.

"Perhaps you should remind him that it is never wise to leave the queen unprotected, little one. En Prise, as the French like to say."

He reaches for the door, and I crumple against the wall.

"Deliver that message for me, Talia," he tells me. "And I will see you soon. Very soon."

And then he's gone.

Thirty-One

Talia

I move through the hall in a daze. Adrenaline flooding my veins and making every shadow appear as a threat.

I have only one target in mind. I need to get to him. My safety.

Alexei.

I stumble into the room full of women, and they all stare at me in shock and disgust. My face is swollen. My mascara running. The whore that they all believe me to be. The imperfect match for Alexei.

I don't care.

I only know that I need him. Right now. In this moment. And I haven't needed anyone for a long time.

But when I find him across the room, it is not me he is thinking of. With Katya at his side, her hand on his arm as she smiles up at him with her beautiful and perfect smile. His attention is on her too. With no concern for me.

And just like Dmitri, I realize he has fooled me too.

Because this man is not my safety.

He is just like the rest of them. Only worse. Because I thought he might be real. I thought for a moment, he could have cared.

My knees buckle, and I collapse. Tanaka rushes over to me, swiftly followed by Nikolai. He glances around the room, worried. And then he sees what I saw too. Alexei and Katya together. And he makes a decision.

"Come." He lifts me up in his arms and gestures for Tanaka to follow.

They take me down the hall and set me on a chaise. Tanaka sits beside me, taking my hand in hers while Nikolai kneels in front of me again.

They both ask me what is wrong, but I can't answer. I can't even look at them.

"Get Alexei," Nikolai instructs Tanaka.

She squeezes my hand and then does as he bids. More tears spill down my cheeks while we wait in the silence.

Nikolai is kind. He does not press me for answers. He simply remains at my side, a comforting presence. Until Alexei is storming down the hall, and Nikolai rises to meet him.

More angry words fly between them, and so do one of Alexei's fists as he tries to take a swing at him. It is Tanaka who intervenes, speaking to them calmly in Russian.

They are all looking at me now, but Alexei still has not calmed. He speaks to Nikolai again, something that sounds like a threat. But Nikolai looks to me, and replies in English.

"Do what you must. I was comforting her. As you should have been. Instead of playing this game you continue to play."

Alexei is quiet, his gaze moving to me and back to Nikolai.

"If you wish to punish someone, Lyoshka, then it needs to be me. Not her. She has done nothing wrong, and yet you treat her as if…"

"Do not tell me how to conduct myself. This is my marriage. My business."

"I am not telling you as a Vor," Nikolai replies quietly. "I am telling you as your brother. This is not the man that I know."

The room falls completely silent as his words settle over everyone. Even Alexei seems shocked by his admission although I cannot understand why. Why they don't want anyone to know they are brothers. Which would make Sergei—the same man Nikolai warned me about—Alexei's father.

Footsteps echo down the hall, and soon, Katya has joined in on my public shame and humiliation. Her eyes move over me, and she gives me a false sympathetic smile.

"Your wife looks ill," she says under the guise of being helpful. "You must allow my maid to watch over her so you can come back and enjoy the party, Lyoshka."

He glances at her and back to me. And there is a flicker of shame and remorse on his face as he shakes his head. He doesn't meet Nikolai's gaze again as he comes to lift me into his arms.

"I am taking her home."

"But you can't," Katya insists. "There is still so much more to come. I have worked so hard on the planning…"

"My wife is more important than your party." He meets her gaze and then moves towards the door. "She is the most important woman in my life."

Thirty-Two

Alexei

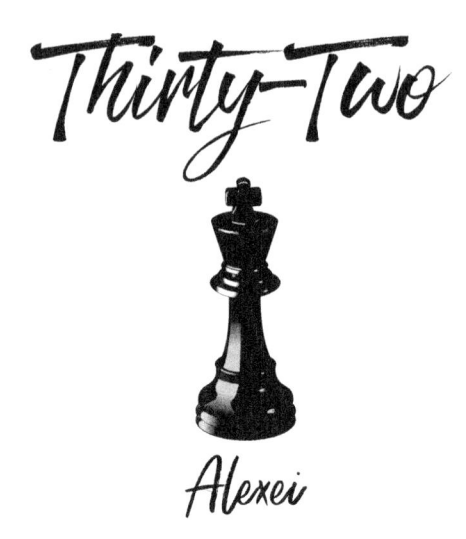

"What have you done?" Magda demands from her position across my desk. "She is wrecked again."

I toss back the rest of my cognac and meet her eyes. "You knew that would happen. It was only a matter of time."

She turns to leave, the frustration evident on her face. But then she pauses at the door and points a shaky finger at me.

"This is not the man I raised you to be, Alyoshka. This is not you."

When she leaves, I move to pour another glass of drink. But she reappears before I can finish, and surprises me by grabbing the bottle from my hands.

"In case I did not make it clear. You need to go to her. Now. You need to fix this."

This time, when she leaves, she takes the bottle with her. I don't argue.

It has been a day. I have not spoken to Talia. Not fixed anything the way that I should.

Because everything Nikolai said was correct. It should have been me there to comfort her. Instead, I was the cause of those tears. He believes it is a game to me. That I do not care for her and simply wish to make Katya jealous.

When I went to Katya that night, it was with one intention in mind. To embarrass Talia the way she had done to me. With Nikolai.

It was too soon. To take her to that party. To expect so much from her.

To believe that I could trust her with Nikolai. It still burns me.

I want another drink. But since Magda has taken it, I have only one choice.

I walk down the hall and into her room. She is on the bed, curled on her side. Awake, but despondent. As though not a day has passed since her arrival. She has retreated to the identity she knows. The one that she believes will protect her. But it cannot protect her from me.

I am angry with her, still. And I want to claim her.

It's exactly what I set out to do when I reach for her ankle and pull her slight body towards me on the bed. I spread her legs apart and lay myself between them, pressing her into the mattress as my fingers grab her face.

"You need to give me a baby," I demand of her. "You need to take my come inside of you every day until you are swollen with my child."

She meets my gaze, and there is nothing on her face. No emotion. No expression at all.

"I don't want you."

She could have said anything to me. Anything at all. Except for those words.

The effect is immediate, and I cannot contain the honest emotion on my face. I move off of her, and she flinches. Her hand reaches out to me, but it is too late. I am already gone.

I move downstairs and lock myself in the gym with a fresh bottle of cognac. I take to the bag, directing my aggression towards the leather. But it does not temper the feeling inside of me.

Neither does the drink, this time.

And when I glance in the mirror, it is my father's voice I hear.

He is defective. And I do not want him. I don't want either of you.

For all the days of my life, I will never forget the vacant expression on my mother's face when he cast us out. And when I look in the mirror now, it is that same vacant expression staring back at me.

I tried to fix what I had done. With crayons and paper and gifts that promised her things I could not deliver at the age of ten. But that I someday would.

I did not get the chance.

I do not want your gifts, Lyoshka. I want nothing from you. You are my greatest shame.

My fist sails into the mirror. Over and over again. The blood pouring down my arm only serves to remind me of her too. Of that day. Of the last gift I tried to give her. Which she rejected. And then bowed out of my life completely.

The door opens, and when I look up, I am not surprised to find Franco standing there. He is always watching me. Looking out for me.

I don't know why.

I don't know what I ever did to earn his loyalty, besides paying off his debts in exchange for a job. One which, he returns to faithfully. Every day, he is by my side. Looking out for me.

He sighs at the sight before him although it is not a shock to him. This is not the first time my temper has bested me. The first time the memories have come back.

But this time is worse. Because it involves her.

Franco shuts the door behind him and retrieves the first aid kit from a cabinet by the door. I watch through bleary eyes as he stitches me up and then helps me stumble upstairs to my room to pass out. Which is exactly what I do when my head hits the pillow.

A warm hand moves over my arm, rousing me from my sleep.

When I open my eyes, I'm not sure if it is an angel or devil I see.

"You're hurt," she says, her fingers tracing over the stitches on my swollen hand.

I pull her closer, wrapping my arm around her waist and trapping her body against mine.

"What are you doing in my bed?"

"I don't want to sleep alone tonight," she says.

Her eyes flutter shut as though it pains her to admit it. I know the feeling well.

She is still angry with me, and I with her. But I need to be inside of her. I need her to…

I just need her.

It hits me hard. And I swallow. My fingers move up to touch her face.

"You are my wife," I tell her. "You should not be speaking with Nikolai unless I am present. You should not be speaking with him at all."

She looks up at me, and my hope that those words would serve as an explanation for my behavior dissipates quickly.

Her eyes are glassy. Vulnerable. And soft.

"You let him touch me," she whispers. "You didn't protect me from him. Your star didn't protect me either, and you promised."

My hand shakes with the force of my anger as I examine her, digesting her words. "Nikolai touched you?"

"No." She blinks up at me. "Dmitri did."

I am certain I misunderstood her. Misread her lips somehow. But as I examine her, I know that is not the case.

Dmitri is Russian, but he is not a Vor. He could only be considered an associate, at best. He had no business being at that party. I only know of him from my research when I was searching for Talia. But I need her to confirm it. To confirm what it is I believe to be true.

"He sold you."

Her fingers dig into my arms, clinging to me. "I thought he was my boyfriend," she admits. "I thought… and you promised this would protect me."

The words die off, and only her pain remains. She is touching my name. Gutting me with her words. My failure.

"Tell me what he did. At the party."

"He found me in the bathroom," she answers. "He said he would retrieve me for Arman. Soon."

My rage cannot be contained. I am holding her too tight, but she does not protest. She does not say a word even when I have drawn breath and calmed myself.

"That is all you ever had to say, my sweet."

I reach for her hand and place it on my chest. Over the very star tattoo that makes me who I am. I hope she will understand that by swearing on it, my words mean everything. My honor. My loyalty.

She has it.

"Do you feel that?" I ask her.

My heart beats beneath her palm, my chest expanding with every breath. She feels it like a child, with soft fingers that flutter over my skin in the same rhythm.

"Yes," she answers.

"As long as there is breath in me, as long as my heart beats, I will protect you, Solnyshko. You will remain by my side for all the days of my life. And even after my death, you will have others watching out for you. This, I can assure you."

She blinks up at me with worried eyes. "You can't die."

I don't argue with her. She does not yet understand the Vory way. That these words are my promise to her. That death is not something to fear, but to be honored.

She fears losing me.

And right now, nothing else matters. I know there is only one thing to do. Now that she has confirmed it. I know what must be done.

But first, I must repent my sins. I must make her forgive me for the things I always said I wouldn't do. That I would never be like my father. The way I was with her that night.

I failed her.

She is right. I promised to protect her. And instead, I have shamed her. And left her vulnerable while I was blinded by my anger.

"I will never allow that to happen again," I assure her as my lips meet hers. "I am sorry, Solnyshko. I am sorry that I failed you."

She cups my face in her palms and kisses me. Hungry. Needy. Just as I am for her.

I roll her onto her back and quickly dispose of her clothing. Leaving her naked and exposed and vulnerable only to me. The way that she should be.

I kiss my way down her body, murmuring my apologies as I go.

"You should be worshipped every day," I tell her. "And I am sorry that you have not been."

When I reach the apex of her thighs, she opens for me without being asked. My woman is shy and sad and sometimes broken, but she is open for me. Still willing to give me a chance. I thank her, and then I bury my face between her legs. Eating her out. Tasting her. Fucking her with my tongue and grinding her hips onto my face.

"Today you will come just like this," I tell her. "Give in to me, my angel. Allow me to pleasure you without any pain."

I know I don't deserve to ask this of her right now, but I want this of her right now. And she gives in to me, just as I ask. She relaxes and simply feels, for once. Without any shame. When she comes, it is cathartic for both of us. The pleasure she needed that I was able to give to her. And then her eyes are on me. Pleading at the same time her mouth does.

"I want you, Lyoshka."

Those words are exactly what I need from her. And it should bother me that she knows that. That she has seen this part of me. But when I bury my cock deep inside of her, it doesn't bother me at all.

She is so wet for me. So pliable to me. She allows me to take her as I please. To suck on her throat and wrap her legs around me and let me all the way in.

I like that. I like it very much.

But I want even more from her.

I pick her up and adjust our position so that we are both sitting upright. She is in my lap. On my cock. Taking me as deep as it will go. Her hands are on my shoulders, and then in my hair as I watch her. Fucking her face to face. So close I won't miss any of her expressions. Her sighs or the flutter of her lashes.

"Let me hear your voice," I tell her.

She pulls me closer, her lips finding my ear. Her teeth grazing it as her hot breath hardens my cock to the point of unbearable pain.

"I want you," she tells me again. "I want you too much, Alexei."

"Lyoshka," I grunt. "That is what you call me."

"Lyoshka," she murmurs into my ear. "You have the power to destroy me."

"I won't," I assure her, but I know it is a lie.

She doesn't argue. She kisses my throat and I fuck her hard and deep. Her body contracting around mine. Sucking me in and squeezing my cock.

It is too much. And I come inside of her, thinking about her pregnant with my child. I want to start a family with her. And I am impatient with that desire.

I won't admit the reasons why. To myself or to her.

"Come." I lay her down and position my body beside hers, patting my chest. "Lay with me."

She curls into my side and rests her face against the place where my heart beats. Her finger tapping out the rhythm on my skin. My other arm curls around her body and I kiss her forehead.

"You will sleep in my bed from now on, Solynshko. My wife should be in my bed every night."

Thirty-Three

Talia

I am woken by Alexei's arm wrapping around my waist as he slips his cock inside of me from behind.

He takes me twice this morning. Kissing my throat and murmuring things in Russian. And once he is sated, he leaves me in bed to rest while he showers.

Magda pokes her head in the door, and when she sees me in his bed, a smile lights up her face.

"Miss Talia," she says. "I was looking for you."

She seems happy. And I feel uncomfortable. There is hope in her eyes. So much hope.

"I have breakfast for you. Would you like to take it in here?"

My eyes move around the room, filled with Alexei's things. It still feels too unfamiliar, so I shake my head.

"In my room is fine."

She nods and disappears down the hall, just as Alexei re-enters with a towel wrapped around his waist. There are still droplets of water on his skin and hair as he turns and rifles through his closet. I watch the muscles of his back expand and admire his frame.

Beautiful. Strong. Solid.

When he turns, he catches me looking. It does not seem to faze him as he removes his towel and reveals his plump cock, hanging heavy down his leg.

He is pure male.

It makes me curious all over again. Why he is with me. He could have any woman he wanted. But he does not act that way. There is nothing arrogant about him.

He is simply a force of calm. A flash of pale blue in the otherwise dark and tumultuous storm of my life.

I watch him put on his briefs, the muscles of his thighs contracting as he snaps the waist band into place.

"Tell me what you are thinking," he says.

"I was wondering why you didn't marry Katya."

My question makes his brows draw together. I expect evasion. But I don't receive it.

"She slept with my brother," is his honest reply.

"Nikolai."

The jerk of his chin is his answer.

I digest those words and watch him put on his trousers, followed by another charcoal gray sweater. And then a shoulder holster.

"Nikolai said that she wouldn't give this up," I tell him. "That she wouldn't give you up."

"She has no choice." Alexei dismisses the thought with a wave of his hand. "She won't cause trouble."

"How can you be sure?"

He meets my gaze, his words carrying a hint of threat as he speaks. "Because she would die if the truth were revealed. You never betray a Vor."

"Do you think that I would betray you?" I ask. "Is that why you didn't want me speaking to Nikolai?"

He turns away from me and shrugs into his jacket and flat cap. A sure sign that he is leaving somewhere, which I don't like.

"I will provide you with a good life, Talia," he says quietly. "Anything you wish, it will be yours. You will have my children. You will be happy. But you must never betray me."

And there it is.

He doesn't trust me. I wonder if he ever will.

I don't give him my assurances because I know they would not do any good. Just as his assurances can only placate my worries for mere moments until the memories come back. Replacing everything present with the poisonous past.

Alexei comes to say goodbye. He sits beside me on the bed, stroking my face in his hands the way he often does. I don't want him to go.

"What about Sergei?"

This time, my question angers him. And he goes cold, his fingers falling away.

I regret asking.

"What of Sergei?"

"Nikolai said to be careful of him too."

"Nikolai has a big mouth, and should not be concerning you with these things. He should have come to me."

"He said you wouldn't listen."

"And he was right. Everything he has to say is nonsense, Solnyshko. You have nothing to fear. I said I would protect you. So leave the worrying to me, yes?"

"Okay."

"I have to go handle some business," he tells me. "It might take me a couple days. But I want you in my bed when I return."

"Okay," I say again.

"Wear something nice for me," he says, his eyes moving over me as he reaches down to adjust the bulge in his trousers. "Something silk. And black."

This time, it is me who reaches up to touch his face. I bring my lips to his, and he returns the sentiment by cupping the back of my head and devouring my mouth with his.

When he pulls away, my lips are swollen and aching for him all over again.

"You be a good girl." He kisses me on the forehead and then moves to the door. "I will return soon."

Alexei is gone for three days, instead of two.

I used my Mac to order a few silk chemises in his requested color. With overnight shipping, they arrived the next day. But that wasn't the only thing I ordered.

Magda of course saw the pregnancy tests when she opened the box and inspected the contents before allowing me to have it. And she has already checked in on me three times this morning, her subtlety failing her horribly.

"Everything alright, Miss Talia?" she asks me as I look up from my book.

"I haven't taken the tests yet, Magda," I answer.

She frowns. "Maybe you should."

I know that I should. But I'm scared.

"I will wait with you," she volunteers. "If that helps."

I know she isn't going to let this go. So I give up reading and stand up. Magda is practically hopping from foot to foot while my stomach is churning.

She takes me by the hand and leads me towards the bathroom. Where I have left the tests laid out and ready.

"I will wait over here," she tells me as she sits on her usual chair.

I grab three of the sticks and go about my business before

setting them on the sink and washing my hands. Magda checks her watch, and then she meets my gaze.

"Why is it so important?" I ask. "Why does he want this…?"

I leave the words 'with me' out of that question, though that's what I'm really asking.

"It is the Vory way," Magda answers. "Marriage and family are very important. This is the tradition. And Alexei is thirty-five now. He is ready to start a family."

The rest of the time passes in silence while I process Magda's words. Alexei is twelve years older than me. But it does not feel that way. It feels as though we are so similar, sometimes. Except where tradition is concerned.

I never planned to have children of my own.

I always worried that my mother's insanity had infected my own mind. Which it clearly has. These are the thoughts that eat at me while the time ticks down, determining my fate.

I am bound to destroy anything I love.

"Miss Talia?"

I blink, and Magda is before me, leading me over to the chair.

"You've gone pale as a sheet," she says.

"I can't be a mother," I tell her. "I will ruin them. My mind… it's infected."

She kneels before me and takes my hands in hers. "Why? Because your mother's was?"

She knows too. I don't know why this surprises me, but it does.

"Do you think Alyoshka is infected too?" she asks.

"What do you mean?"

She is quiet for a moment, contemplative.

"Did you know that I have raised him since he was a boy?" she asks.

I didn't know that. "Why?"

"Because his own father rejected him after his illness. He was born as beautiful as he is now and almost taken away by meningitis as a child. But he is a survivor. Like you. His father did not see it that way though. He could only see him as defective when he lost his hearing. And he cast both his mother and Alexei out."

My heart longs for him, in this moment. To hug him. To touch him. But I am fascinated by Magda's words, and desperate for more. She gives them to me.

"He believes he is destined to destroy everything he touches as well, Miss Talia. But we both know this is not true."

"The woman in the bathtub?" I ask.

Her gaze moves to the floor, pain flickering across her face. "His mother. She blamed him for what happened too. And left him to suffer her actions for all of eternity."

"Is that why he picked me?" I ask.

"He relates to you," she says. "But he picked you long before he ever knew your story. He picked you from the moment he saw your face in that photo. The one your friend brought here, asking for his help. He saw something in you, Miss Talia. The same thing I see when I look at you too."

"What?" I ask.

"He saw life." She smiles. "He saw the sun breaking through the dark clouds."

I don't see how that's possible, but I don't argue with Magda. Just as Alexei said to me before when I inquired about the name he calls me. Little sun. He told me it makes perfect sense to him.

Could he really see me that way?

I don't know.

"He is a good man." Magda pats my hand and rises to her feet. "He will do right by you, Miss Talia. He will do everything for you. But you must give him time. And be patient."

She moves towards the sink and then looks back at me. "Are you ready?"

I nod. And I am grateful for her presence. I am grateful for this sweet woman who raised Alexei and cares for me too. Even though I don't deserve it.

She has been so kind and good to me. And I want to hug her. To thank her. If I knew how.

She glances at the tests and then brings a trembling hand to her face. When she looks at me, her eyes are brimming with tears and she cannot contain her smile.

"I knew it," she says as she holds up one of the tests for me to see. "You have brought life back into this house."

Thirty-Four

Talia

When Alexei returns, it is late.

And I am in his bed. Wearing a silk chemise for him as he requested. But he does not join me.

He sits beside me instead, waking me with a gentle touch to my face. "Solnyshko."

I move my face into his palm and kiss his fingers.

And then he's pulling me from the bed and into his lap, his fingers sliding over the silk material with a groan.

"You have been waiting for me?"

I lean into his right ear to answer in the darkness. "Yes."

He grabs me around the waist and grinds me down onto his hardening cock beneath the trousers, his hand tangling in my hair.

"I am going to take you often tonight," he tells me.

My response is to kiss his neck, wrapping my arms around him and absorbing everything that is Alexei. His scent, his sounds, his breath on my skin. I want what he promises so darkly.

My hand moves between us, finding his zipper and pulling it down. I stroke his heated bulge through the cotton of his briefs, and his mouth finds my breast over the silk nightgown. He sucks the material and my flesh into his mouth while I fondle his heavy cock in my hand.

"This time will be quick," he tells me as he reaches down to retrieve his cock. "I just need to come inside of you. I want you to smell like me. Only of me."

I lean back in his grip when his other palm slides up my thighs, bunching the material of the chemise around my waist and giving him access to what he wants.

He doesn't wait or explain any further. He just slides inside of me and fucks me right there on his lap, both of us on the edge of the bed.

I can't see his face. I can only hear his voice in the darkness when he tells me how good I feel. How he has missed my body.

"You won't come now," he tells me. "Save it for later. You will need it."

I don't know what that means. But I just hold onto him. My arms wrapped around his neck as he fucks me quick and with only one goal in mind.

He comes inside of me, his cock pulsing for what feels like minutes as he fills me with his warmth. His voice is calm as his lips move over the column of my throat, and his body is relaxed now.

He squeezes my ass in his hands and rocks me against his pelvis a few more times, drawing it out even as he softens inside of me.

"Now, I have something to show you," he tells me. "And then I will reward you with what you need, my lovely Solnyshko."

He pulls out of me and zips himself back up before readjusting my chemise. His come drips down my thigh and he stands me up, wrapping something around me. A silk robe, I realize.

He takes my hand in his, warm and strong and solid.

"Come with me."

And I do.

Ghost

I have never been to this part of the house.

The basement.

It is cold and vacant. Stone walls and a simple cement floor. Alexei's oxfords echo off the cavernous walls while my bare feet absorb the cold of every step beside him.

His arm is wrapped around me in a protective manner. Warming me and keeping me close by his side. We stop at another steel door. He taps on it and turns to me.

I cock my head to the side and examine him. He looks odd. A strange mixture of excitement, pride, and nerves on his face.

"I don't want you to be afraid, Solnyshko," he tells me. "Remember, I am here. And I will destroy anyone who ever tries to hurt you. That means in your past as well."

His words make me nervous, and I cling to his hand. But he still doesn't move. His other hand comes up and untangles my hair, opening my face to him.

"I want you to know the level of my devotion to you," he states. "I don't ever want you to question it. The things I have and will continue to do to protect you. To avenge you. They are dark things. But that darkness is my burden to carry, and it always will be."

His voice is so impassioned. So filled with strength that there is no question in my mind he means what he says.

"Show me," I tell him.

He reaches for the door, his grip on me firm. Anchoring me to his body as he leads me inside. Until I freeze at the sight before me.

I'm in shock, I think.

But even after I blink several times, the image in my eyes does not change.

It is Dmitri.

Bound, gagged, and naked on a wooden sawhorse. There is a man behind him. A big man. Huge. His shirt is off, and all he wears is a pair of leather pants. But the room reeks of sex and sweat, and it is obvious what has taken place in here already.

"Talia," Alexei's voice cuts through my thoughts. "This is Boris. He will be seeing to Dmitri during his stay here."

His words from the corridor outside make sense to me with shocking clarity. He is avenging me. He is going to make Dmitri suffer for what he did to me.

I wait for my mind to tell me that this is wrong. Or sick. Or that I shouldn't feel any enjoyment when I look at Dmitri, knowing what awaits him.

But none of those things happen.

I do feel enjoyment. I feel some sense of justice. The scales finally being tipped back in my favor if only a little.

He is the reason I have no trust. No hope. He is the reason I am dirty and ashamed. Touched by men who had no right to. The reason I struggle to look in the mirror most days. He handed me to Arman on a silver platter and made me wish I was dead every day.

So it should not surprise me when my lips tilt into a smile, but it does surprise Alexei. And relieves him.

"Go," he tells me. "Say whatever you would like to say to him. This is the last time you will ever see his face, Solnyshko."

I move to step away, and Alexei hesitates to let me go. And it is only then that I realize he is struggling with this too, in his own way. Knowing that Dmitri has had me before. There is a possessive gleam in his eyes as they move over my body. My body that is filled with his come and his child inside of me, which he does not yet know. My skin, that smells of him. And my face, which no doubt does little to hide my swollen lips from his kisses or tangled hair from our romp.

He has marked me as his own. As though to rub it in Dmitri's face.

As if he would ever care.

He sold me.

Ruined me.

And Alexei is putting me back together. Piece by piece.

I stretch up on my tiptoes and kiss him on the lips. And then I give him the thing that he needs.

"Come with me," I tell him. "I need you with me."

My words set his worries free, and he takes charge, leading me in front of Dmitri so that I can meet his eyes. His cold, lifeless eyes.

They were never that way before. That is how he tricked me. He was so good at making me believe.

But not now. The horror of his experience is only just beginning, and it is written on his face for me to see. I savor that. I soak it all in, and I smile right at him.

Even if Boris used him a hundred times over, it would not equal the torment this man has caused me. But it does not matter. Because I have peace, now. And so there is only one thing I have to say to him. The same thing he said to me when I discovered he had sold me.

I lean forward so that I'm right in his face. My eyes unmistakable in the truth that I feel nothing for this man anymore.

"You better get used to it, kitten," I mock him. "The pain is going to be your new best friend."

His eyes plead with me, even though the gag in his mouth prevents him from speaking.

But there is no mercy to be found here.

Not with me, and certainly not with Alexei.

He makes a gesture to Boris, who moves behind Dmitri again. Unzipping his pants as he steps between Dmitri's spread thighs.

"Enjoy yourself, Boris," Alexei tells him. "He's yours to play with for the week."

Thirty-Five

Alexei

My beautiful Solnyshko.

The moment we are back into the corridor, I cannot contain myself.

I kiss her. And touch her. Pulling her body into mine.

So brave. So vicious.

I am harder for her than I have ever been. She knows this. And she climbs up my body and into my arms. So small and vulnerable and mine.

"You feel safe with me," I tell her.

"Yes," she answers.

I groan. Because I want her to. Even if it's wrong. Even if I am defective. She does not see that when she looks up at me. She does not care. She only sees my body around hers, sheltering her. The blood I spill for her. She does not see anything else.

"I want your pussy wrapped around my cock," I demand. "Right now."

Her arms come around my shoulders and hold me tight as I unzip my pants and she wraps her legs around me. She is soaked for me.

Soaked in lust and want for me. Soaked in the thrill of Dmitri's blood which will soon coat my basement floor.

She is a siren. A filthy angel. But only for me.

She will only ever have me.

I tell her so as I thrust up inside of her, possessed by my madness for her. The door behind us is not all the way shut. And I know she can hear Dmitri's cries.

She is getting off on it. His pain and her pleasure.

I finger her and fuck her at the same time. Playing with her tits. Rubbing her body all over me.

"Come for me," I tell her. "Come, so that he can hear you being fucked by me. So that he will know who you belong to when he dies."

She moans into my right ear. The sound is distorted. But there. It vibrates down my spine and all the way into my cock. She thrashes in my arms, crying out as the orgasm rips through her body.

So beautiful. So violent.

So perfect for me. This damaged angel.

"Lyoshka," she whines into my ear.

"I know what you need," I tell her.

I thrust harder, faster. "And I will give it to you."

I come inside of her again. Balls deep, stuffing her full of my come.

It has not sated me at all. And already, I want to take her again. I want Dmitri to hear her cries all night long as she bounces on my cock and I fill her with everything I have to give.

These are the thoughts going through my mind when I pulse inside of her, emptying every last drop.

"What about Arman?" she asks. "When will he die?"

I blink at her, and struggle to come up with a lie. She will not understand.

"Is my little sun so bloodthirsty already?" I ask.

"Yes," she answers without hesitation. "I want him dead too."

She looks so hopeful, and it is in this moment that I realize, I will have to kill Arman. Despite Viktor's wishes. I will have to find a way. To please my wife. To keep my word to her. To avenge what was done to her.

"He will take longer," I answer her with a kiss. "But he will die too, Solnyshko."

She smiles, looking at me like I am her hero. The way nobody has ever looked at me before. And then she speaks. And everything changes.

"I'm pregnant, Lyoshka."

Thirty-Six

Talia

He pulls back to look at me, his grip taut on my chin.

"What?"

"I'm pregnant," I repeat.

Relief flashes through his eyes, and I swear that I can see the weight of his worries floating away into the distance.

"That is good," he tells me in a dazed tone. "Such a good girl."

He kisses me and then strokes my face.

"This will change everything."

And that's when I see it. Behind his relief, I see his true motive. And for a split second, there is a stab of betrayal at the realization.

"You did this so I wouldn't hurt myself."

He looks up at me and lies right to my face. "I want a family, Solnyshko. It is time."

"But you also believed that this would fix things," I press. "That it would fix me somehow."

"You are going to be an excellent mother," he tells me. "I have no doubts."

"How can you not have doubts?" I argue. "This doesn't fix my broken mind, Alexei. It only means you have bought a lifetime of certainty. Because you know now that I wouldn't do anything. But what if you're wrong? What if I…"

I can't get the words out. *What if I'm insane? What if I hurt the people I love too?*

"You are not your mother," he answers. "You are nothing like her. You are so much stronger."

"You didn't know her."

"I don't need to. I know you."

"Hardly," I reply, wiggling my way out of his arms.

I'm angry at him. And I don't know why. I can't sort out my emotions anymore. It's been so long since I felt real emotions. Besides numbness and pain. This is something else.

All I can think of is that he did this with one intention in mind. It wasn't because he wanted to start a family… with me. It was because he married me and I'm broken and he needed to fix that and so this was his solution.

"It wouldn't matter," I say stupidly. As though I didn't already know this. "This was your plan."

He doesn't deny it. "I told you I wanted a family."

But he doesn't say the words I need to hear. I've been so confused, thinking that maybe this meant something to him.

"How will this work?" I ask.

"What do you mean?"

"I mean… it's an arrangement to you. It's not like this is a normal marriage. So how will it work?"

"I provide for you," he answers. "And you will be a mother and wife."

He doesn't get it. And I'm not even sure what I need him to say. But I need there to be… more. It's hope again. Niggling at me. Telling me that I should be able to have it all. But that was never true.

"I don't even know what you do," I blurt. "On the computers all day."

"I run gambling operations for the Vory," he answers. "And the Irish as well."

"So what does that mean?" I ask. "It's illegal. You could get caught. What happens then?"

"I will never get caught," he scoffs and actually looks insulted. "I am the Ghost."

His answer doesn't reassure me, so he tries to.

"I am the best at what I do, Talia. This is why I am invaluable to Viktor. To the Vory. There is nobody else with my skill set. I can assure you of this."

I do believe him. I've seen him work. And I know there is something dangerously genius in that brain of his. But it's all settling in on me. What I've done.

I've married into the mafia. Signed a contract that I can't take back. And now I'm having his baby. This man who has also given his assurances that he could never love me. I didn't think I would want it. But now… I fear that he is right. That it will never happen.

And I will be lost to him. To this world.

"You spend all day in your office," I tell him. "Drinking. Working. Playing chess. Is that going to change?"

His brows draw together. "I will help with the baby," he answers. "It will be our child, Talia. Shared responsibility."

I swallow, tapping my fingers against my thigh. He doesn't get it.

"And will we eat dinner together? Go on vacations together? Watch movies, play games…"

Now he is the one who is getting uptight. Every word makes his posture more rigid.

"I don't know," he answers. "I am a busy man."

"Right." I take a breath and gather my thoughts. "So it will be like it is now. I'll stay in my room all day. You'll stay in your office.

At night you will fuck me, and we will have a child together, who we share responsibility for."

He seems confused by my anger. "Is this not what we agreed on? I don't understand, Solnyshko, what is upsetting you so."

"I don't either." I stare up at the ceiling and rub my temples. "You wanted me to get better. And maybe I have. But you haven't changed."

"Why would I change?" he asks, finally getting the point. "This arrangement works for us. It is less messy. No emotions, no feelings. We can both be happy."

"Right."

Only, I'm not anymore.

Maybe that's not fair. Maybe I'm too fucked up and my hopes are too high.

Alexei seems agitated. Anxious to get back upstairs and pour himself another drink. Hole himself away in his office with only his thoughts to keep him company.

"No," I agree with him. "I think you're right. I think it's best this way."

He nods, content. Relieved. Relieved that I'm asking for nothing from him in this way. That we can carry on as we have been. As though nothing will change. Or has changed.

But everything has changed.

"It's probably best if I stay in my room," I tell him. "To keep things the way you want them. Less messy."

He frowns, but doesn't argue.

"It's for the best," I repeat again.

Thirty-Seven

Alexei

"What have you done now?" Magda asks me after she sets down my breakfast.

"I don't know what you mean," I answer, turning my attention back to the computer.

She taps on my desk to let me know she is not through.

"You have not spent any time with Talia in over two weeks. She is slipping, Lyoshka. Slipping back into her sadness."

"She wants things I cannot give her."

"That is ridiculous," Magda replies. "You are supposed to give her everything. She is pregnant. Now is the time when she needs you most."

"I have done everything I can for her. I have scheduled doctor's appointments. Ensured she is eating the best food. I have given her free rein to decorate the nursery any way she likes. What else can I do?"

"Perhaps pull your head out of your ass," Magda suggests.

I blink at her, sure I misread her. But I did not.

Magda has never spoken to me that way. Not since I was a young boy in her care.

"You have a dinner party this evening," she reminds me. "It is supposed to be a celebration. What excuses will you give for the frown on your wife's face?"

Perhaps the same as my own since she has not allowed me to touch her since that night. She has made excuses of not feeling well, and I did not press. After the second time, I did not bother returning to her room at all. She has not come to me either. And we are at an impasse.

I am irritable already. And Magda is not helping matters.

"She will get over it," I tell Magda in an effort to appease her. "It's just hormones."

She curses me in Russian. And then says the thing which she knows will affect me the most.

"I am disappointed in you, Alyoshka. And I'm beginning to think that you are not up to the task of marriage. Or fatherhood for that matter."

"That is enough." I slam my hand on my desk. "You will not speak to me that way."

"I will speak to you any way that I choose," she replies. "I am not one of your Vory. I am the woman who raised you. And if you cannot share your heart with Talia, then how on earth do you ever intend to share it with your own child?"

With those words hanging between us, she leaves.

Talia is in her room when I step inside. Dressed for the party. In a designer dress and heels. Just as a Vor's wife should be.

She looks lovely. And miserable.

I can hardly even look at her. Look at what I've done to her all over again.

"You are beautiful," I tell her.

When I kiss her on the forehead, there is no reply. She nods and meets my gaze.

"Is it time?"

"Yes."

I want to stop her when she moves towards the door. I want to make her smile again. I want to tell her that I'll cut out Arman's heart and give it to her on a silver platter, if it would make her smile again.

But that isn't what she wants right now.

She wants a piece of me. She wants more than I offered her. She is changing the rules of the game halfway through.

I reach for her arm and halt her, and she looks up at me with a blank expression.

"Don't worry," she says. "I won't embarrass you tonight."

Her words cut me. And she does not give me any time to make amends. I don't blame her. But when we move downstairs, I'm on edge. I like to feel as though we are a team. Like before. But now we are as separate as two people can be.

Just as I told her I wanted.

Magda has already greeted our guests when we reach the bottom. A close party of the other Vory and their family members. Everyone is here to celebrate my wife's pregnancy. Including Sergei and Katya.

It is ridiculous, considering the sour expressions on their faces when I see them. But it is tradition. Viktor is very traditional in this regard. Every season, every change... there is a party.

"Lyoshenka." He greets me with a firm handshake. "What is this frown on your face? Have you heard the news already?"

I blink at him, unclear what he is referring to.

He pulls me aside and ensures we have privacy while the other guests congratulate Talia.

"Tonight is a celebration," he says. "I don't want to dampen the mood."

"Just tell me what it is Viktor," I insist. "I won't relax otherwise."

"We have a complication," he announces. "Arman is stateside. With both shipments and an additional for our troubles."

"He wants Talia back," I state.

Viktor nods, and we both fall silent.

This is a complication. I was supposed to have more time to plan. To corner him so that he has no choice but to agree to my terms. But Arman is greedy. Impatient. He must have worked overtime to get these shipments to us.

"I will meet with him tomorrow and offer him a settlement," I tell Viktor.

He shakes his head. "I already tried to cut a deal with him, Lyoshenka. He isn't willing to part with her."

"You did this without me?" I ask.

"I did not want to trouble you with it."

"You mean you did not want me to kill him."

"You can't," Viktor answers me. "We need his supply."

"And he cannot have Talia. She is my wife now. It is done. She is protected by Vory code. By me. Arman has no choice but to accept it."

"Yes, well…" Viktor sighs. "We will figure something out, Lyoshenka. We always do. But for now, you must give me your word that you will be patient and not do anything rash."

Viktor knows me well. He knows I want Arman dead. But he is right. I must be patient. I must bide my time. He does not want to risk our arms shipments. But Arman will die. When he does, it will look like an accident. Or as though it is at the hands of another party.

As much as Viktor claims to put the Vory first, I know he would do the same if it were his own wife. So I simply give him a nod, and he squeezes my shoulder.

"Come," he says. "Now we must celebrate."

Thirty-Eight

Talia

Tanaka is here with Nikolai. And I am glad.

She is probably the only woman at this party who is actually happy for me. The only woman who does not wear a fake smile for me.

"How are you?" she hugs me, and it is a warm embrace.

"I am well," I answer her.

Her eyes move over my face, and her smile fades. "You can't fool me with that act."

"The better question is how are you?" My eyes move across the room, to Nikolai. "Any news on your father?"

"No," she sighs. "But Nikolai is taking good care of me."

Right now, it appears as though he is trying to fend off more of Katya's advances though. When Tanaka turns, she dismisses the interaction with a wave of her hand.

"That is just Katya," she says. "She is desperate for a high ranking husband and now that Nikolai has been promoted, she has her target set on him."

"Does it not worry you?" I ask.

"Why should it?" she replies. "My fate will be written one way or another. I have no say in it. This is the Vory way."

"I suppose it is," I answer her, knowing she is right.

"I was raised in this world," she tells me. "It does not bother me so much. It must appear strange to you though. All of these arranged marriages. Women as payment. Collateral. We are simply pieces on a board in the game of men."

"But you have feelings for Nikolai?" I ask.

She glances down at her shoes, and for just a moment, her cool demeanor crumbles.

"My feelings don't matter. I will accept whoever they choose for me. They are all good and decent men, despite their outdated practices. You will never find a husband who holds his wife in higher regard than a Vor does."

The way she speaks makes it sound so simple. She has accepted her circumstances without a fight. The way I accepted mine when I came here. How has so much changed since then?

"You are one of the lucky ones," Tanaka tells me, her eyes moving behind me as she leans in. "Your husband can't take his eyes off of you."

"Only because he fears I will pounce on Nikolai or one of the others the moment he has his back turned."

Tanaka laughs and it lightens the mood. "It is in their nature to be possessive. But that is not why he can't take his eyes off of you. He cares for you."

I don't argue with her, and I try to forget she mentioned it at all.

"What do you do?" I ask. "At Nikolai's?"

"Probably the same thing you do here," she answers. "Flit around the house all day and keep myself occupied."

I nod, and the man in question steps up beside her, finally evading Katya it seems. I don't know the protocol for such things, especially in Tanaka's situation, but I decide to make a bold suggestion.

"Will you let me borrow Tanaka?" I ask. "For a day? She can help me decorate the nursery."

My suggestion pleases and surprises Nikolai.

"Of course." He nods.

His gaze moves to her, and they seem to be under each other's spell for a brief moment. My heart aches.

And then Magda announces dinner.

It is a long affair. With a lot of different toasts, some in English, a lot in Russian. I don't understand all of the sentiments, but I appreciate them.

Alexei is at my side, taking them all with a respectful nod. Until it is Sergei's turn. He toasts to the baby's good health. But the tone of his voice suggests otherwise.

And I realize this is a dig at Alexei. At his hearing.

And I don't understand this man. This father. The one who has made it so difficult for Alexei to allow himself to care about anyone or anything. I realize this is why he must keep himself locked in his house. Away from the world and people like Sergei.

His father tossed him away like trash. Told him that he was defective. Even here now, beside me with all these men who respect him, he is not comfortable. I wonder if he still feels that way. I wonder if he is afraid like me. Afraid to let me in, for fear I will do the same. Like his mother. And like Katya too.

The present distance between my husband and I is immeasurable, but I lessen it by reaching for his hand beneath the table. A silent show of solidarity. That he is not alone in this world. That even if he can't ever love me, I understand him. And I am loyal to him.

His fingers close around mine, warm and strong. He accepts what I offer him, and I think he is grateful for it.

And then Nikolai takes it upon himself to interrupt his father, standing up to make his own toast. When he meets Alexei's gaze, there is remorse in his. It is clear how much Nikolai respects his brother, even if he has not shown it in the past.

I wonder if Alexei can see that. If he can see how much Nikolai admires him. How much so many of these men at the table admire him. Or if he can only ever see that his own father doesn't.

"To new beginnings." Nikolai raises his glass. "I know you will both make great parents. This child is blessed already. Like with everything he does, I have no doubt Lyoshka will lead by example. Setting the bar high for all other Vory who enter fatherhood after him. And to Talia. He could not have picked a woman better suited than you to take this journey with. I wish you both the best."

He glances at Sergei, who is grinding his jaw with the false smile he wears.

"To my family," Nikolai finishes.

The rest of the table toasts, and Alexei shifts in his chair beside me. It has not escaped my attention that he's hardly touched his beloved cognac tonight. And I wonder why.

Once Magda has cleared the table, we all move back to the sitting room. And Alexei does not allow me to leave his side for the rest of the evening. Instead, he pulls me directly into his lap and carries on a conversation with several of the other men while he touches me.

At first, it is innocent. A stroke of his palm on my arm. A kiss of his lips on my neck. His fingers brush over the brand on my hand. His name and his star. A not so subtle reminder for both of us who I belong to. He touches it often when we're in the company of others. I think it's a comfort to him knowing that it's there.

It's a comfort to me too.

My body shivers for him, and longs for him too. It has been too long since he touched me. But he did not return to me after my last rejection. And now he can't seem to control himself, even in the room full of company. Where he knows I will not reject him.

I wonder if this is why he's doing it.

But he has to feel it. Feel my body coming alive for him.

My dress is flared at the waist, with a large skirt. Alexei takes full advantage of this by sliding his hand beneath the material and squeezing my ass in his palm. He finds the material of my thong, pulling it up in the back so that it rides against my front.

I shift my weight on top of him and feel his own discomfort beneath me. His free hand comes around my front, wrapping around my waist and pulling me back against his chest.

The conversation around us continues, and Alexei speaks when appropriate, even as his hand moves between my thighs. His voice deepens slightly when he feels the wetness there. And then his fingers are inside of me. Playing with me while he talks with his friends.

It is so dirty and filthy and wrong. And I love it.

I love that he's doing this with me.

But then he stops and pulls his fingers out of me abruptly, wiping them on my leg. He makes some sort of excuse in Russian, and then lifts me off his lap, still half dazed as he takes my hand in his.

He leads me into the kitchen and promptly sets me up on the counter where anyone could walk in and see us. And then he kneels before me and puts his head up my skirt, yanking my ass towards him and eating me out.

I come hard after only a few minutes without any pain. This pleases Alexei.

"Your husband is hard for you," he tells me. "It is your job to take care of that."

"I want to take care of that," I answer him.

"And I want to spank you for denying me," he replies as his fingers brush over my face. "But you would enjoy that too much."

It's true, so I don't argue with him on that.

"Now open your legs for me," he demands. "Your legs should always be open for me."

I spread them as far as I can to let him in. And he rewards me with his cock, inside of me. Fucking me in the kitchen while our guests continue to drink in the other room. He seems to have an affinity for this. I recall the same thing happening in his office the last time they were here.

He assaults my lips and wrecks my hair that Magda worked so hard on. I wreck his too, with my own fingers.

And then something catches my attention over his shoulder.

Katya.

She is watching him fuck me. And she is angry.

I meet her gaze and hold it while Alexei thrusts into me.

"He treats you like the whore you are," she tells me, knowing full well he can't hear her.

"And he loves every second of it," I reply.

My words alert Alexei to someone else's presence. He glances over his shoulder at Katya and does not bother to acknowledge her. Instead he grabs my hips and pulls me as deep as my body will take him. Coming inside of me with the same simple word he always gives me.

"Mine."

And then he kisses me. Tenderly. Passionately.

I don't know when Katya left. Only that she did at some point. But I still worry about her. Worry that even my pregnancy is not an obstacle for her. She still considers Alexei on the market.

"Why is she always at these parties?" I ask him.

"She is Anatoly's daughter," he answers. "Do not worry about her, Solnyshko. It is only you that I want."

"That isn't what I'm worried about," I tell him.

"She is harmless," he says, trying to put me at ease.

But I don't think she is. I saw the look in her eyes tonight. Like I was nothing more than trash that needed to be disposed of.

Alexei doesn't allow me to breathe any more life into my worries.

"You will sleep in my bed tonight," he orders. "It has been far too long since I've been inside of my wife."

When I look up into his pale blue eyes, I can't deny him.

"Okay, Lyoshka."

Thirty-Nine

Talia

When all of the guests have gone, Alexei and I retire to his room for the evening.

There is no question what he wants when he grabs me around the waist and hauls my body against his, kissing me roughly.

I come up for air when he starts in on my throat, grazing the skin with his teeth.

"You did not have very much to drink tonight," I remark.

The vibrations of my voice alert him that I've spoken, but it is clear he missed it. So when his eyes find mine, I repeat it once more.

"I drink as much as any other Vor," he tells me. "But it displeases you, no?"

"What does it matter?" I ask him.

"I want my wife to be happy," he answers sincerely. "And perhaps you are right. I should be focused on other things now."

What other things, he doesn't say.

But his phone starts beeping and vibrating across the room, and doesn't stop, even as he continues to maul me. I tap him on the arm to get his attention.

"Your phone is going off."

"Ignore it," he answers me with another kiss.

But it doesn't stop. And after another full minute, he finally turns to check it. And then he frowns. I see him bring up the security system on the house. The same cameras he has in his office.

He pockets the phone and returns to me with a completely different demeanor than only a moment ago. This is Alexei, the Vor.

"There is nothing to be concerned about," he tells me in a calm voice. "But we have an unexpected guest. I'm going to see what he wants."

He kisses me on the cheek and grips my chin. "I am locking the door behind me."

I nod, but I'm curious who is here. And I don't really want him to go. But I know that he has to. He moves to his closet and grabs his holster and gun, shrugging it on before he locks the door behind him.

And I wait. Moving towards the window to see if I can get a glimpse of anything from up here.

There's a car parked in front of the house. Franco is already outside, and it looks like he's arguing with someone. But it's too dark to see what's going on.

So I walk around Alexei's room and examine his things to keep my mind occupied. The furnishings are sturdy and well made. In his closet, I find much of the same as he always wears. An assortment of gray and black trousers, sweaters, button downs, and suede jackets. At least five pairs of oxfords, and several different flat caps.

The man finds something he likes and sticks with it.

I bring one of his undershirts that is draped over the cupboard to my nose and inhale. It smells of him. Oak and cloves. I have an urge to take off my dress and put it on. But with the unexpected company downstairs, I decide to wait.

Which turns out for the best. Because a few moments later, I hear voices in the outside hall. On the same floor. One of the accents is familiar and unmistakably Irish. It makes me curious, but I can't peek outside.

So I wait. And walk around the room some more. On Alexei's dresser, I find a cracked chess piece. I've often seen him playing with it in his office when he is contemplating something. Staring at it as he moves his fingers over the ridges. It is old. And no doubt it holds some sort of memory for him.

I wonder what it is.

The door opens, and I quickly set it aside. Alexei's eyes find mine, and he steps inside.

"No need to worry, my sweet. It is an acquaintance. He is wounded, but Franco is tending to him. I will be as well."

"Okay."

"You should get some sleep," he tells me. "Keep the bed warm for me."

I nod, and he comes to kiss me on the lips again. It confuses me, how he can be so sweet. So thoughtful at times. How he can look at me the way he is right now. Like he doesn't want to leave.

"I want you naked," he tells me. "When I return."

"I thought you said to get some sleep." I smile up at him.

"I will wake you." He shrugs. "You'll have plenty of sleep until then. Now I must go, Solnyshko."

He kisses me again and then leaves. I wait until his footsteps have retreated down the hall, and then I peek through the door. And I am surprised to see two familiar faces here.

Sasha and Rory.

One of the men from the Irish syndicate who owned the club I worked at. And one of the dancers too. It seems odd to me that they are here. And I feel the strangest pull to go to them. To inquire about Mack.

But my fear keeps me rooted in place.

In my head, I tell myself that she is happy now. That she is better off. That she would never in a million years be able to accept what I've done. Even if she herself married the man she swore was an awful human based solely on her judgment of his reputation.

I want to know why she married him. If she has changed so radically since I knew her. If she is okay. And if she is genuinely happy.

But I am terrified to let her see me.

She will see right through my act. She will tell me the hard truths as she always does. That Alexei does not love me and he never will. That I am stupid for allowing myself to carry his child.

She will judge me.

And as much as I love Mack, I cannot handle that right now.

It is while I am lost in these thoughts that the door shuts down the hall, and I realize too late that Sasha is walking in my direction.

I shut the door and sit on the bed, hoping she didn't see me. But I know she did.

And it isn't a minute later that the door creaks open.

Her eyes go wide when she sees me. And all of my defenses go up, preparing for battle.

"Talia?"

I don't reply. My mouth is dry and I'm dizzy. I feel like she can see all of the wrong and bad parts of me. All of the things that happened while I was gone. And I understand now why I felt safe with Alexei from the beginning. Because he didn't know me before.

But Sasha did. And she can see that I'm not the same. That I'm broken and damaged and… wrong.

"Do you remember me?" she asks.

My heart is beating too fast. Too loud. My palms are clammy. And the memories are swirling around in my brain. My last days at the club. How I was so happy when Dmitri came to see me. How excited I was for our time in Mexico.

I don't want to remember. And she is bringing it all back. This girl who used to know me.

"Of course I remember you," I snap. "I'm not brain dead."

"Everyone thinks you're dead," she says. "You do know that, right?"

I want to tell her I am dead. That as far as anyone who knew me in my old life goes, I no longer exist. But I don't. I can't get the words out. I can't stop thinking about Mack. Because I know she's thinking about her too. I can see it in her eyes. It's ripping me apart. I want to ask her so many things. I want to ask if Mack is really happy. If she hates me. But I don't.

I shrug. That's it. That's all I've got.

"Do you realize what this has done to Mack?" she asks me. "She's been sick over this whole situation for months. Do you have any idea what she went through to try to get you back?"

The guilt weighs heavy on me. But it's too soon. I can't deal with this now. I'm not ready to face that part of my life again.

"I don't want to go back there."

"Okay…" She sighs. "But can't you call her? Let her know you're alright?"

"She won't understand," I try to explain. "Mack has never understood. She'll want the girl back that she lost. But I'm not her anymore. I'll never be her again."

"So you're just going to let her think you're dead?" she demands. "She was your best friend."

She was. And I care for her. I know my actions don't show it. That Sasha can't understand it. But how can I explain it when I don't understand it myself?

"I'm going to tell her," she says. "She's my friend too. And I can't let her go on thinking that you're dead when you're not. It isn't right."

"Do what you have to," is my reply.

Sasha edges back towards the door, and I breathe a little at seeing her retreat. At seeing my past ebb away and preserving my safe little bubble where the present cannot collide with it.

"Are you okay here?" she asks. "Are you safe?"

"Yes. Alexei is very good to me. I don't want to leave him."

"Okay," she says. "Would you like my number though? Just in case?"

I shake my head.

And she walks out the door.

Forty

Alexei

Ronan is patched up and officially on the mend.

He's going to be alright, the doctor tells us. She is on the Vory payroll, and her services are available only to us. Which means late hours and sometimes odd locations. But she is one of the best.

Those services don't usually extend to our Irish alliance as well. Especially not the man who took it upon himself to shoot at Franco and I in the not too distant past.

He is still slightly delirious as the drugs wear off, but he has the coherence to say what he needs to.

"Thank you," he tells me. "I know I do not deserve such a kindness from ye."

"You can thank your girlfriend," is my reply.

I never could stand to see a woman cry. His woman loves him deeply. And it earns him a little of the respect that he lost from me. But nothing in this life comes for free, and both Ronan and I are aware of this.

"I'll need you to do something for me, once you've healed."

"What do ye need?"

I turn to Franco and speak to him in Russian, asking him to retrieve the information I've been keeping on Arman. He is here in the states, staying in a posh hotel while he awaits the return of Talia. He's going to be waiting a little longer.

Franco returns with the file a moment later and hands it to Rory. But it is Ronan who will carry this out. This is his specialty.

"These are the locations of two warehouses where he is holding our shipments. I need you to hit them and make it look like an Italian job."

He raises a brow at me, and I shrug. "Or someone else. Whatever you choose, so long as it is not one of us. There can be no doubts."

"I will sort it out," Ronan gives me his assurances. "Two days maximum."

It's a reach, considering his current state, but I don't argue with him. I just need it done, and it can't have any implications that it was connected to the Vory in any way. Arman will look like a fool again, and it will buy me more time. More time to study his operations and find the best way to make him disappear without raising questions.

"Would ye mind terribly if we crashed here for a wee bit?" Rory asks. "We've caught some heat back in Boston."

I don't particularly care to have them roaming my house. This is why I live so far from everyone else. Because they don't visit as often and leave me to my solitude. But now that we have an alliance with them, it is my duty to be hospitable.

Before I can even give them an answer, Ronan takes it upon himself to add another reason. One he knows I can't turn down.

"Sasha is having my baby. We need a safe place for her to stay."

"You can have the third floor," I tell him. "But you'll need to use the back entrance when you come and go. And stay off this level. I have my own pregnant wife to worry about, and we like our privacy."

Ronan is surprised by my words, but I don't give him any further explanation. I am anxious to get to my bed. To be inside of Talia.

I move to the door, and Rory follows.

I leave them to their business and move down the hall to my room.

Talia is asleep. Her blonde hair spread like a halo across my black pillow. She looks beautiful. And when I lift the covers and see her naked, my cock is painfully hard.

But I don't wake her when I climb in behind her. Instead, I simply pull her against my body, breathing in her scent and soaking up her warmth. She sighs a contented sigh and nuzzles in closer to me.

And that's exactly how we fall asleep.

Forty-One

Talia

Life with Alexei is a pattern.
Never a straight line. Always a series of highs and lows as we get to know each other. Discover more of each other.

I learn new things about him every day.

Everything he does is done with precision. Carefully considered and weighed out before he decides. A simple trip from his home often takes him several days to prepare.

I know it is because the world has been a cold and cruel place to him. He doesn't like to feel vulnerable. But he is. He is especially vulnerable when he leaves the house. Always worrying that his secret will be discovered.

His mind must be switched on all the time. He muttered to me once, under his breath, that I had become a distraction for him at the dinner parties. It worries him. But he likes it too.

I like being his distraction.

Which is why I often find myself in his office, in the middle of the day, like I am right now. He likes the way I look on the outside. And he accepts that I'm a whole lot of fucked up on the inside.

But I make myself pretty for him. Every day. In these designer clothes that don't belong on the likes of me. And then he dirties me up with his eyes and his hands and his cock.

When he sees me today though, he seems distracted by something else. And I don't like it at all. I want to be the center of his world. I want to be so much more than his wife in name and his fuck toy in the bedroom. Want is a dangerous thing.

Still, I walk around behind him and touch his shoulders. He tilts his head back against the chair to look up at me, and I lean down and kiss him. My fingers move over the sensitive flesh of his neck, hoping to infuse myself with some of the cologne he wears.

I like to smell of him. I like to rub my body all over him.

"You are teaching me bad habits, Solnyshko," he tells me.

"How so?" I ask innocently.

He turns around and tugs me into his lap, burying his face in my neck and inhaling me. I try to kiss him. To get him going because I know he won't stop once I do. But he doesn't let me get that far. He grabs my hands and keeps them trapped between us. Then he wraps his arms around my waist and pulls me against his chest.

And then he just looks at me. For too long.

This is the thing I don't like. And I've noticed it happening more and more lately. It is intimate, having someone's eyes on you with no intention of doing anything other than looking. Seeing you.

"I want you," I tell him.

His hand crawls up my back and reaches for my hair, tangling it in his fist and pulling it tight so that I can't move my head.

"You want me to do dirty things to you," he says.

"Yes."

"What if I just want to look at you?" he asks.

"I don't like it," I answer.

"I don't care," he replies.

It's obvious he's going to do whatever he wants. So I just wait, trying to hide by burying my face against his chest. He plays with my hair, and even though he is hard for me, he doesn't do anything else.

It confuses me. This type of intimacy from him. One minute he wants all of me. And the next, he backs away. Never letting himself get too close. I just try not to think about it. But when he holds me like this, it's hard not to. To ask him things that I shouldn't even be thinking.

Like if he cares.

Like if there will ever be more.

Instead, I ask him other things. Questions that give me small pieces of him. The only thing I can ever really have. Stolen moments. Pieces of his life and his heart. That's all he has to offer. And I don't have anything to offer him. Except for my broken thoughts and demented soul, stitched together by my frequent bouts of insanity.

"Magda thinks that we are alike," I tell him on a whim.

He is quiet, contemplative. His eyes moving over my face again. His hands holding me close.

"Do you agree?"

"Yes," he answers.

He doesn't elaborate, and I can tell he doesn't want to. So I ask him something else.

"Can you teach me something in sign language?"

He blinks at me, and this makes him smile. "I do not know sign language," he tells me. "So no, probably not."

"Oh. Well shouldn't you though?"

He just shrugs. "I never learned. I was young when I lost my hearing. The circumstances did not allow for learning. So I learned the only way I could."

"To read people."

He nods, and I touch his face.

"I wish I could read you sometimes."

"All you ever have to do is ask me," he says.

I want to. We both know that I want to. But I don't. Because I am scared. And I think, Alexei is too.

"I kind of like it," I tell him instead. "That we touch each other to communicate. You touch me a lot."

"I like it too," he admits.

But he doesn't have to tell me. I feel how much he likes it beneath my ass on his lap. The biggest turn on between us is him knowing that I accept him and me knowing the same.

"It's strange," I tell him honestly.

"What is?" he asks.

"That you can't hear," I answer. "And yet, you are the only person who has ever really listened to me."

"I will always see you, Solnyshko," he tells me. "Always."

"You make me feel," I whisper.

The words are both an accusation and a confession.

But Alexei does not retreat or shy away. If anything, he indulges in me further and I know the time for cuddling and intimacy is now over. He lifts up my dress and discards it, leaving me in only a bra and panties. But like they often do now, his hands move to my belly first.

"How is my baby?" he asks.

"Big," I tell him. "Like his father already."

Alexei smiles at me. And it's beautiful, that smile of his.

"I think it's a boy too," he answers. "I would like that."

And then he kisses me. It's soft and sweet for about two minutes before he gets to the good stuff. The really good stuff. His hands all over me. Sliding in and cupping my breasts beneath the lace of my bra. And in my panties. His fingers inside of me.

The entire time, his mouth is on mine. We kiss a lot. And I like it. I might even love it. Sometimes, it's a slow burn. And sometimes, like right now, I'm consumed by the madness of it altogether. I feel it happening. The falling. Falling for him.

I know what he says. That he doesn't care. But this isn't just fucking anymore. This is him, whispering something in my ear and me providing anything he asks. We both get off on it. Any man can fuck me. But Alexei fucks my mind. My heart. My soul.

He lights me up and burns me down.

Every single time.

I want to tell him so, right now. I want to be honest. But inside, I know I need to push those thoughts away.

"Be dirty with me," I tell him.

"Get down on your knees," is his reply.

I do. He grabs a handful of my hair and rubs my face against the heat beneath his trousers. My fingers dig into his thighs and my breath quickens as he unbuckles himself.

"Be a good girl," he says as he grips his cock in his palm. "And beg for it."

This is new. And I like it. I like it even more when I look up and see him anxious for me to say the words. To tell him how much I want him. And in his eyes, I can see how much he wants to believe it. I will make him believe. Because it's true.

"Lyoshka," I tell him as I reach out and take his cock in my hand. "You are my husband. You belong to me. And nobody else. You can't ever do this with anyone else."

"I am a Vor," he answers. "I will do what I like."

I glare at him, and his eyes fire with satisfaction.

"Now quit pouting and suck my cock."

I do. I push him all the way into the back of my throat and he groans. Hard. He loves it, but he can't bring himself to admit how much.

"Do better," he goads me.

I do even better. I suck him so hard he nearly blows his load in the first few minutes. But I know Alexei would never allow that to happen. So instead, he grabs me by the hair and yanks me up.

"Do you feel the need to please me?" he asks.

I feel vulnerable under his scrutiny. He already knows the answer. I don't know why he makes me say it.

"Yes," I whisper. "I want to please you."

He brings his lips to my ear and murmurs between kisses. "You always do, Solnyshko."

I tip my head back and allow him access to my throat, which he kisses tenderly.

"Please me now," he directs me. "By bending over the desk and spreading your legs for me."

I do what he says. He pulls aside my panties and fingers me while his other hand comes down on my ass. Hard. I make a noise, and I know he can't hear it, but he feels how much I like this. How much I like him like this.

He smacks me again on the other ass cheek, and then pulls them apart roughly with his hand, kneading the flesh beneath his fingers. And then he backs away, leaving me cold and annoyed.

"Sit on the desk and play with yourself," he tells me. "I want to watch."

When I turn around again, he's in his chair. Stroking his cock slowly and deliberately. Watching as I do what he says.

"Make yourself come," he says. "And do it fast. Or I'm not going to fuck you."

Again, I'm doing what he asks. Like a puppet. Like he owns me. But when I look at him, I know he does.

I hate it when he does this. When he takes away what I want from him the most. It isn't the same when I have to do it myself. But I make myself come anyway, just watching him stroke himself.

"Now fuck me," I beg him.

"Give me three reasons," he answers. "Tell me what you've done to deserve it."

"Because you like it," I tell him. "And I'll make you come."

"I could come like this," he says.

"But you like it better inside of me."

He smiles.

"And what else?"

"I'll let you work for the rest of the day without distracting you."

He makes me wait for an answer. But his eyes are on me. And I know he's going to give in. He just likes to torment me. Make me beg for this. For him.

"Come here," he tells me finally. "And sit on my cock."

I do it. Without an ounce of remorse or shame. He watches and then instructs me to ride him. Which I also do. His hands remain at his sides, his eyes closed, and it frustrates me.

"You aren't touching me," I speak into his right ear. "Or looking at me."

"Did you want me to?" he asks. "Or do you want the master fucking his slave?"

And I know now that he's trying to prove a point. About my remark earlier.

He tangles my hair in his fist and draws me closer, his mouth so close to mine I can almost taste him.

"I will look at my wife whenever I please," he tells me. "And don't ever tell me otherwise, Solnyshko. You will be intimate with me. And you will never hide from me."

His words are harsh, but his kiss is soft. And he gives me what I need. His hands on my body. His warmth and his sounds and his pleasure. He comes inside of me on a sigh, and remains there for a long time, holding me in his arms.

Neither one of us moves, and I know something is changing between us. Evolving. Growing. But I'm afraid to ask what it is. And Alexei doesn't mention it either.

He simply holds me.

And for right now, it is enough.

Forty-Two

Talia

Two months have come and passed. Our guests have gone, and I am grateful. Apart from the noise I would hear upstairs, I didn't see much of them. But whatever was happening ended up occupying a lot of Alexei's time. I'm happy to have the house back to just the four of us.

Alexei and I, Franco and Magda. And soon another little Nikolaev. It's surreal.

I had a scan this morning, and I am farther along than either of us suspected. Alexei sat through the whole process, quiet and steadfast at my side. We are having a boy. And when he found out, he smiled.

It was a beautiful thing.

The intensity between us is changing every day. The barriers dissolving more and more. And the question always lingering in the back of my mind. That maybe this time is different. That maybe this time, I can trust.

Alexei's days are still his own. Spent working in his office. But at night, we dine together. And go to bed together. And he holds me. Sometimes it's about sex. But sometimes, it's just about us.

The sadness has slowly ebbed away over time. It does not disappear completely. It never does. There are still bad days. Days when the memories haunt me. When the pain feels unforgiving and relentless. But I am learning how to process it.

Changing old patterns and thoughts does not come easily. I still struggle with my deep-rooted fears every day. I worry that this is just a dream. And that soon, I will wake up at Arman's again.

Alexei has not brought him up. Nor have I.

For now, I am giving him something that I swore I would never give again. My trust.

I am trusting him not to destroy me. I am trusting that if I work hard on my own demons, so will he. Because we have no choice. We have to be better than we were. For our child. And for ourselves.

I spend my days fighting. Fighting to overcome my fears and learning the things that I never had a chance to. Magda teaches me something every day. She teaches me how to cook, to sew, and even how to sing Russian lullabies.

I'm slowly learning the language. So that I can communicate with Alexei in that way. As well as our baby, who will speak both languages.

I spend time with Tanaka, at least once a week. She seems sad at times, locked inside of her own head. She does not speak about her and Nikolai. I only know that when she is here with me, she is happy. We have become close friends.

And more and more, I think about Mack.

I think about seeing her. And hoping that there is still some chance to recover our friendship too.

Soon, I think.

I will contact her soon.

My life has completely changed in so little time. I went from having nothing, to having everything. And it scares me almost all of the time. I think of my baby and wonder what Alexei will be like with his son. I know he will be a good father. But I also know he is nervous. He worries about letting us down.

I see that fear bloom more as my belly grows larger. I see it when he spends time in the nursery, examining the things I bought. And often, I see it late at night. When he is inside of me and looking into my eyes.

I don't try to reassure him. Because like me, Alexei needs to figure this out on his own. My words will not ease his worries, just as his words won't always ease mine.

Today, when I pass by his office, he is staring at the chess board on his desk. But Franco is nowhere to be found. Only Alexei, deep in his own thoughts.

I watch him for a while, in the silence. In his element, his brain working in a way that I will never understand. I watch the way his eyes calculate all of the moves, his hand brushing over his jaw. He is so incredibly handsome. My heart is beating too hard, too fast. I ache for him in ways that are not familiar to me. I ache for his words, his touches, his eyes on me.

When I have those things, nothing else in the world exists. He always leaves me longing for more.

"You could say hello," Franco says from behind me.

I startle at his presence, curious how long he was standing there. Watching me, watching my husband.

"Why don't you join us," he suggests. "Somebody besides me should see the man's chess skills."

I hesitate, but Franco ushers me inside before I can come up with any excuses. When Alexei sees me, he gives me a curious look.

I was bored this morning, so I spent extra time playing around with my makeup. Smoking my eyes and trying out a new lipstick.

"You look different," he notes.

I boldly take a seat on his desk and swing my legs off the side, meeting his gaze. "And you like it."

He smiles, and so does Franco. And then they turn their attention to the game that never seems to end.

"Franco tells me you have some mad skills," I note.

Alexei waves off the suggestion. "He always lets me win."

"I never let you do anything," Franco grunts.

"Can you teach me?" I ask.

Alexei seems surprised by my request. He reaches for my calf and feathers his fingers over my skin, tickling and massaging me.

"I cannot teach you, but you can learn."

"What does that mean?"

"Just watch, Solnyshko."

So I do. But I keep getting distracted from the game by the man playing it. His hand is still on my leg, my feet now resting on his thighs.

Alexei is giving and caring and warm. But he is also his own island. He does not accept these things from anybody else.

"What about that one?" I ask him, pointing at the cracked chess piece sitting atop his desk. The one that I know has absolutely nothing to do with this game and everything to do with something else.

He looks at the piece and then back to me. Franco keeps his focus on the game, and I'm glad.

"That is from the first time I ever beat my father at the game," he tells me. "Or rather, the first time I ever allowed myself to."

I reach out for it hesitantly, examining it between my fingers. It is odd that he has kept it all these years. But it is significant to him.

"Why?" I ask.

"My mother told me I should always allow him to win," Alexei answers. "And I did. Until he told me I was not a worthy opponent."

"It's cracked," I remark.

"It is," he replies.

There is nothing else said, but it answers my question. Alexei's father was enraged by this. And for some reason, it pleases him. I suspect that Sergei has always been insecure over his son. But I also suspect it has nothing to do with his hearing and everything to do with his intelligence.

Like me, Alexei had to adapt to the world he was born in. And I have no doubt he is always the smartest man in the room. Calculating his moves like he does on the chess board. Standing with his back towards a wall so he never misses a cue in conversation. His eyes working overtime to assess everyone in his orbit. Trying to appear as though he is normal.

But this man is nowhere near normal.

He is a genius in a room full of cavemen. Highly adapted and overqualified for everything he does. And yet he slums it with his Vory brethren and a wife like me, feeling as though he will never fit in. And maybe it's selfish of me, but I hope he never does. I hope he never realizes how much better he could do than the likes of me.

Franco's phone rings, interrupting the game. He speaks in short and precise sentences, giving Alexei a nod before he steps outside.

"How long do you think he'll be gone for?" I ask.

"Not long enough for what you have in mind," Alexei answers, wheeling his chair closer.

"You mean what you have in mind," I retort. "Pervert."

I reach for his hand that rests on my thigh. With an empty space reserved for another tattoo. One he has not added yet. An idea strikes me as I grab a pen from his desk. One that will probably reveal too much. But I do it anyway. And he lets me.

Pressing the ink to his skin, I write my name in that space. The one I feel like I have a claim on.

"When do you get my name carved in your skin?" I ask.

"Soon," he answers. "If that is what you wish."

I have an opportunity here. To be vulnerable. Or to keep my armor in place.

I did not think I could ever choose vulnerable again. But I do.

"I would like that," I tell him.

He wraps his arms around me and presses his face against my belly, peppering it with little kisses. My hands move through his hair, mussing it up before he pulls my face down to kiss him.

"Lyoshka," I murmur against his lips.

"Yes, my sweet?"

"You are so hot."

He smiles at me.

"I don't think I ever tell you," I continue. "But you're hot, and you should know it."

He grabs my chin and his eyes flick from my mouth to meet my gaze.

"Solnyshko," he says sincerely. "You terrify me."

I swallow, and he kisses me softly.

"I know," I tell him. "Because you terrify me too."

Forty-Three

Alexei

Just as I do every month on the 3rd, I arrive at a Vory owned club for the usual meeting. The meeting where we discuss numbers and operations and anything else that Viktor adds to the agenda.

And just as I do every month, I set up the flash drive in the computer downstairs and prepare the projector.

This is the way things are always done. The same routine I have performed as long as I have been Sovietnik.

And then we drink. Always for about thirty minutes or so until all of the Vory have arrived. We discuss business and ask after the other's family members.

It is the way things are always done.

Only, this evening is different.

This evening, I am betrayed.

When Viktor calls the meeting to order, he directs one of the Boeviks to operate the presentation as he always does. I take my seat beside him, prepared to discuss the details of our gambling operations.

What I am not prepared for is what comes up on the computer.

"What is this, Lyoshenka?" Viktor asks.

I stare at the video in confusion. It is from my own home. A video I have not seen before. From a low quality camera placed somewhere in my own sitting room.

I am on the couch. And Talia and Magda are behind me, near the stairs. Magda is telling her something. And it looks like Talia is calling out to me, but I can't be sure. I don't turn around, and Talia's face fills with confusion as she tries again.

"Turn it off," I demand.

The Boevik is fumbling with the computer, removing the flash drive, but the film doesn't stop.

Viktor is rigid beside me, and I know that my worst fear is confirmed.

Someone has just made a mockery of me in front of all the other Vory. Someone has announced my defect for all of them to see.

Instinctively, my eyes move to Sergei.

Viktor stands up beside me. Yelling something.

When I glance back at the screen, I'm moving across the room myself before I can make sense of what I'm seeing.

Images of Talia. Strung out and being fucked by other men.

And then one last single slide appears before I tear the computer from the table myself.

How does it feel to know your beloved Sovietnik is deaf and married to a whore?

I smash it against the wall. Until nothing but pieces remain. Viktor clears the room, but not before I see all of their eyes on me. Questioning me. Doubting me.

The rage inside of me cannot be contained.

I smash my fist through the wall four times before Viktor shakes me out of it.

"Let's go to the control room," he tells me. "We will check the security cameras."

I'm walking with him, but my thoughts are elsewhere.

"Nobody is allowed to leave this building," Viktor tells Nikolai before he shuts the door.

He waits while I go through the footage myself. But there is nothing. I cannot see anyone touch the computer from the time I installed the flash drive, no matter how many times I go back over it.

And then Viktor asks the question that is already at the back of my mind.

"Did you bring this flash drive from home?"

"She does not have access to these files," I tell him. "And she has no reason to do this."

"Are you certain of that?" he asks.

I nod.

But inwardly, I am questioning it. Doubting her. It would not be the first time I have misjudged someone so wrongly.

"Those photos are from her time as a slave," Viktor notes. "Most likely Arman's own security system. Perhaps we should start with him."

"Yes, perhaps," I agree.

"The only problem," he amends, "is that Arman has never been in your house."

His truth is too difficult to acknowledge. I'm still not willing to accept it myself. So I retrieve the hard drive from the computer. Setting out to prove him wrong.

Viktor is silent while I work. Contemplative.

There is no evidence the computer has been tampered with. And the flash drive is one of my own. Only, it does not contain the information I transferred this morning.

When Viktor sees the realization on my face, he grips my shoulder in a show of support.

"Perhaps her relationship with Arman was not as it seemed," he states. "There is no way you could have known, Lyoshenka."

I want to defend her. To argue that he is wrong. But there is no evidence to support that statement. And I know what comes next.

"You must face your Vory brothers," Viktor tells me. "You always knew it might come to this."

"I did," I acknowledge.

Keeping my defect from them was a risk I was willing to take. Now that I am exposed, I will pay the consequences of my lie.

"Come," Viktor says. "Let's get it over with. So you can go home."

The men are waiting for us in the basement. Solemn and drinking quietly amongst themselves. It is not the same atmosphere as when I arrived. They, too, know what must be done. As a high ranking Vor, keeping a secret like this from them is considered a betrayal. And punishment must be doled out. If they do not give it, they themselves appear weak.

I strip my shirt over my head and toss it aside, gladly taking the drink that Viktor hands me next. There is not a word spoken in the room. When the drink is finished, I turn to Viktor. And as with everything else we do, he is the first to perform the honor of punching me in the gut.

He does not hold back. The pakhan must never show weakness. And his punch nearly doubles me over. But I take another drink, and then each of the men take a turn. Punching my face. My chest. My back. Even Sergei. Which is the worst of them all.

He takes pleasure in it. And he gets me twice.

When the ritual is finished, Viktor calls a Boevik over to add a fresh tattoo to my body. One that means I have betrayed them, but have earned my way back in with honor.

There is no honor though. Lying on the floor, bloodied and exposed for all of the Vory to see me for what I am.

The rage is building inside of me. The rationalizing no longer valid. There is only one explanation. One person that I have brought into my home. That I trusted. And she was the only one who could have done this.

"Lyoshenka." Viktor kneels down in front of me, squeezing my shoulder. "Franco is waiting outside. Time for you to go home."

I sit up and meet his gaze, as well as the rest of the men in the room around me. The men who respected me. Who trusted my judgment and my abilities.

Now, they hold questions in their eyes.

"Go," Viktor says again. "Take the footage with you, if you'd like. I will continue to do what I can on my end."

I have gone through the footage on my security system from last night and this morning. But I cannot find the proof I need. I cannot find the evidence of her betrayal. It should bring me relief. But it does not. I need the proof.

I need what I know is true. That this has all been a game to her. That none of it was real. That she played me.

I find her computer in her room. And on that computer, I find the photos from the slideshow. The photos from Arman.

It is right there in front of me. But still I question it. Question her motives. It feels too easy. Something about this isn't right.

But I realize, when I look at the tattoo of my dishonor, that is just what I want to believe.

I am tearing the sitting room apart when Talia comes downstairs.

It is two am. And she wore the black silk nightdress as I requested.

My beautiful fucking liar.

My traitor.

She is gutting me with her innocence. The way she looks at me right now. So soft and sweet, and yet so fucking ruthless.

When she sees the anger on my face, she takes a step near me. I hold up my hand and tell her to stop.

"Where is it?" I demand.

"Where is what?" she asks, so innocently.

I am shaking with my rage. With my betrayal. The things I have done for her. I have lied to Viktor. Risked the other Vory to retrieve her. I have protected her as I said I would. Avenged her, as I promised. And now here she stands, refusing to own up to the truth. Just as Katya did before her.

I believed them different, but they are the same.

I can't even look at her.

"Where is the camera?"

"Alexei?" she stares at me as though she is confused. "Are you drunk?"

"No. For once, my mind is perfectly clear. Are you proud of yourself?" I ask. "You must be. You fooled me better than even Katya."

"What are you talking about?" she asks again.

"You do know I have cameras in every room of this house," I tell her. "I will find it. And will you still deny it then?"

"I have no clue what you're talking about," she answers.

Magda appears at the bottom of the stairs, followed by Franco a moment after. They are all staring at my disheveled state, the broken remnants of decorations on the floor.

"Take her up to the third floor," I demand of Franco. "Set her up in a room there."

"What are you doing, Alexei?" Talia demands.

"I don't want to see your face," is my reply. "I want nothing more from you."

Magda attempts to protest as well, but I turn away. And continue on my mission. Breaking and shredding every possible hiding place.

By the time Franco returns twenty minutes later, I have run out of places to search.

"Mr. Nikolaev?"

"The camera was in this room," I tell him. "Recording my private affairs."

"And you still believe it was Talia?" he asks.

He seems doubtful. Just as I know Magda will be. Their faith in her feels like another betrayal.

"I want all of her belongings sent upstairs," I demand. "This evening. I don't want anything left behind. She is to stay on that level from now on. You can inform both of them."

He doesn't argue.

So I walk upstairs to my office and settle in at my desk for the evening. The security system in the house only stores recordings for up to a month.

But I have no intention of leaving this room again until I've gone through every last recording.

Forty-Four

Talia

It has been two weeks since I've last seen Alexei.

I still don't know what happened.

The doors are locked, and I am now a prisoner of the third floor. I have no computer. No communication with anyone besides Magda, who seems tired and drawn every time I see her.

At first, I thought it was a misunderstanding. That Alexei was drunk and confused.

But now, I don't know what to think anymore.

I'm trying to stay positive. But every day, my belly grows bigger, and my heart grows smaller.

I gave him my trust.

And he's destroying me.

This morning, when the door opens, I am expecting Magda with my breakfast. But instead, it is Alexei.

My heart stutters in my chest, and I grip the arms of the chair I'm sitting in as he walks closer. He has my computer in his hands. But that isn't what has my attention.

It's his face.

Closed off. Completely devoid of any emotion for me.

He pauses at least two feet away from me and thrusts the computer onto the table beside me.

"I have recovered these files," he tells me. "From an email you received. Do you still deny it?"

I glance at the screen, genuinely horrified by the sight before me.

The photos are of me. But I don't remember them. I was too drugged. Too fucked up.

I turn away and feel the urge to retch. Alexei is watching me closely, devoid of any sympathy whatsoever.

"Why are you showing me these?" I ask.

"You were the one that received them. You were the one, always asking if I liked fucking my whore wife. So this is what you wanted? You wanted them to know it too. Why continue to deny it?"

"Lyoshka." I stand up and take a tentative step forward. "Tell me what's going on."

"Do not come near me," he says.

I feel like I've been slapped. My hands are trembling, and I am no longer able to contain the emotion that I've been holding back for the last two weeks as his eyes move over me.

"I want to know why," he tells me. "Why did you do it?"

"Do what?" I ask again.

"Make a mockery of your husband," he replies.

I take another step towards him, pleading. "Whatever has happened, you are wrong. I would never hurt you, Lyoshka. Please. I am begging you…"

For a brief moment, there is confliction in his eyes. He wants to believe me, but his past won't let him.

"You are having my child," he cuts me off. "But I want nothing more to do with you until then."

"No." I shake my head in between the painful sobs that are now wracking my body. "You are wrong, Lyoshka. Please… I love you."

He's on me then. His fingers squeezing my face between them in a harsh and painful grip, his eyes filled with wrath. He can't see past it. He can't see past his hatred. It's consuming him, and I am powerless to stop it. I don't understand. How can he not see that he is my whole world?

"Don't ever say that again. Don't ever lie to my face, Solnyshko. If you were anyone else, you would already be dead."

He releases me and walks back to the door.

And with the sound of the lock, so cuts the cord tethering us together.

Forty-Five

Alexei

I have not seen my wife in two months, with the exception of the cameras I sometimes watch her on.

Her betrayal is worse than any other.

I thought with time, she would relent. But she will not admit to what she has done. And even now, it hurts to look at her.

She is due in two months. And then, I don't know what will happen.

My rage is consuming me. Threatening the life I have built for myself within the Vory. Threatening my relationship with Franco, Magda, and even Viktor.

I have not left my house since the incident.

I have studied everything. Watched the tapes of us together over and over again. Looking for signs. Looking for her hatred.

I still can't see it.

And that is what burns me the most. How she continues to fool me when the only logical answer is there on her computer. I have not yet informed Viktor of what I found there. I still can't make sense of it myself. She could barely operate the computer when she got it. At least, that's what Magda said.

Another lie.

I have gone through everything. Credit card purchases. I cannot figure out how she got the camera. I believe that Sergei has gotten to her.

It is what makes the most sense. He wants to destroy me, and she is all too willing to help. I don't know how she did it. I only know that everything points to her. And I have learned for the last time never to trust anyone.

There has been no word on Arman. After Ronan hit his shipments, he returned to Bulgaria. And now, only in a few short hours time, I will be on my way there myself. Because I can no longer go another day without the answers. Without the truth.

Magda appears at my door, setting down my dinner. For the last month, she has not uttered a word to me either. But it is better this way.

I don't expect anything from her this evening, so I am surprised when she tries again.

"She is not doing well, Alyoshka," she tells me. "I am concerned for her."

"You only have one job, Magda," I answer. "Keep her alive and healthy."

She opens her mouth to protest, but I cut her off. "I am busy."

And so she leaves.

Leaves me to my misery. My cognac. And my plans.

Tomorrow, Arman will die at my hands.

And I will have my answers.

Why he sent her those photos. What they hoped to accomplish.

Franco taps on my desk and interrupts my thoughts. When I look up, Nikolai is beside him.

"What do you want?"

"Franco called me," he says. "And I am here to accompany you to Bulgaria."

"No."

"If you don't allow me to travel with you, then I will travel on my own. Either way, I am going."

"This is not sanctioned by Viktor," I tell him.

"I don't care," he replies. "Let me redeem myself, Lyoshka. You cannot do this alone. You know that."

"I am deaf. But I have no problems ripping a man's heart out. This I can assure you."

"Yes," he answers. "But first you have to get past the guards."

"Alexei," Franco cuts in. "Please. Be reasonable about this one thing. Going alone is a death sentence."

For once in my life, I don't care.

But I think of my unborn son upstairs. And it guts me to imagine him growing up without a father. It is the only reason I give my nod of approval.

"I don't want Talia in this house while I'm away," I tell Franco. "Not with Magda. You will need to take her to Viktor's compound, where she can be watched."

When he gives me a curious glance, I polish off the rest of the cognac in my glass.

"I want eyes on her every minute of the day. To ensure my son's safety, of course."

Forty-Six

Talia

The sadness is back.

Choking me. Suffocating me.

I miss him. I can still feel his hands on my skin. His breath on my lips. His taste. It's haunting me.

I need him. But he isn't here.

"Miss Talia?"

I blink, and when I look up, Magda is hovering over me. A sad smile on her face.

"You need to come downstairs," she tells me.

"Why?"

"Alexei has gone for a few days, and he would like you to stay somewhere where he knows you will be safe."

Her words feel like a lie.

Because Alexei no longer cares.

He ruined me. Just as he promised he would.

I don't have the will to argue anymore. I only have the energy to take each day as it comes. Each hour. And each second.

My hand is on my stomach, protective, as Magda guides me downstairs.

The house is empty. Lonely. And it no longer feels like my safe haven, but like the prison it now is.

"Why won't he just let me go?" I ask Magda. "Let me go back to Boston."

She seems surprised by my words, and then sad.

"You are married," she answers. "Having a baby together. Things will get better. You must give it time."

"Don't say that." I pause on the stairs. "Don't lie to me, Magda. You can't keep trying to give me hope when you know…"

My voice grows too emotional to speak, and Magda pulls me in for a hug. Tears spill down my cheeks, and she tries her best to comfort me.

"I am so sorry this has happened," she tells me. "I don't know how to fix it. I don't. I have tried. And I cannot get through to him. Franco has tried. You have tried. He is so angry. So jaded. He has never been able to trust."

"Magda," Franco's voice interrupts the moment. "I am sorry, but we must go now."

"What about you?" I ask her. "Aren't you coming?"

"No." She shakes her head. "Franco will return and we will keep the house running as we always do. But you will be safe with Viktor. His family will take good care of you. It is the safest place for you when Alexei is out of the country."

I nod, and she gives me one last hug before leading me outside.

There is a convoy of cars awaiting us. Three different SUVs.

Either for my protection, or to ensure I don't escape.

I would be lying if I said that the thought hasn't crossed my mind in the last two months. I want to run. I want to forget I ever knew him. Ever felt his touch.

Because I cannot bear a lifetime of this pain.

I just can't.

Franco takes me by the arm and leads me to the SUV positioned in the middle. Once I am buckled in and secured, he climbs into the driver's seat.

All three cars pull out of the driveway, leaving the lights of the house behind. I can't help but look back at it with a foreboding sense of alarm.

It feels as though I will never return, and I don't know why that scares me so much.

The drive is quiet. And since I know it is long, I settle in to the seat and keep myself occupied with the constant stream of thoughts running through my mind.

I want to know where Alexei is. What he's doing. And who he's with.

The last thought is the one that hurts the most.

I have no idea what he's been doing all this time. I'd like to believe that he wouldn't ever betray me in that way, but then again, I wanted to believe a lot of things that just simply weren't true.

"Do you care for Alexei?" Franco's voice breaks through the silence, surprising me.

"Yes," I answer without hesitation.

"He cares for you too," Franco replies. "But you must understand, it is easier to believe the worst in people. Easier to believe than having blind faith."

"I don't even know what happened," I tell him. "I don't know how to fix it."

"He will have answers soon," Franco says. "He will come back and..."

He slams on the brakes and his voice halts abruptly.

I look up just in time to see a flash of color exploding into the night sky ahead of us while the ground vibrates beneath of us. My ears are ringing, and time seems to slow down as the car comes to a halt.

I am vaguely aware that Franco is yelling at me, but it's distorted. Only when he reaches over and shoves me from the car, do I understand him.

"Run."

The two second delay feels like a lifetime as I stumble from the car in my confusion. I'm doing what he says, even as I glance back over my shoulder and look for him.

But he isn't getting out of the car. He's driving it in reverse, crashing into the SUV behind him. And then in one horrifying second, they are both gone.

Another flash of fiery orange, another vibration. A chunk of metal slices into my leg and the force of it knocks me to my knees.

I'm frozen in horror, looking back at the mass of metal skeletons lining the road. Nothing more than a fiery ball of flames.

"Franco?" I cry out. "Franco?"

But he isn't there.

Because there's nothing left of the car but pieces.

And the horrifying realization of what just happened washes over me as I gasp for breath. He kept driving. To save me. To keep the blasts away from me.

Fear and grief swell inside of me as I glance around the highway. I am alone. And I am bleeding from the leg. I'm in shock. But the only thing I can focus on is that someone tried to kill us. All of us.

My first instinct is to run. To move on autopilot.

I don't know where I am. I don't know anything.

The only thing I know is that I have to keep going. And so I do.

I move into the brush along the side of the road, using it for cover. Only then do I slow to a walk. At some point, I hear sirens in the distance. But I don't trust them. So I keep moving.

I walk for hours. Until the road meets the freeway and I'm a safe enough distance from the crash. Until I can't walk anymore. Until I'm nearly doubled over in pain. And I have no other choice.

I move up into view and watch for passing cars.

A woman in a sedan pulls up beside me, frowning when she sees my pregnant belly and the blood on my leg.

"Honey, are you okay?"

"I need a ride," I tell her.

She ushers me inside the car, and I don't hesitate.

I'm exhausted, terrified, and heartbroken.

Franco.

His name brings tears to my eyes as the woman in the driver's seat pulls back onto the road.

"Where are you headed?" she asks. "It looks like you need a doctor."

"No," I tell her. "I'm okay."

There's only one place I can think to go. The one place where my past and present will finally collide.

"Can you just take me to Slainte?" I direct her. "In Boston?"

Forty-Seven

Alexei

Arman's guards let me in without protest when I tell them I'm here to discuss Talia.

Nikolai glances at me, the same question in his own eyes as we exit the car. I expected more of a fight. But the guards did not seem tense. Or even ready for a fight.

"It is what he wants," I tell Nikolai. "Don't be fooled by the accommodation."

But even as we are greeted at the door by another guard, something feels off. This is Arman's head of security. And even he does not seem particularly bothered by my presence.

Perhaps they believe me weak, now that they are aware of my secret. That I pose no threat at all to them. Or perhaps they believe that I would not be foolish enough to walk in here with only one other man and attempt anything.

But they are wrong, on both counts.

Arman is sitting at his dining table as he always is. Stuffing his face full of food and drink.

"Mr. Nikolaev." He greets me as though we are old friends.

What he really sees when he looks at me is dollar signs. Money. The thing that makes the world go round. The thing that keeps his table bountiful and fresh slaves in his basement whenever his heart desires.

"Good evening, Arman," I greet him in an equally friendly manner.

His eyes move to Nikolai, but I don't bother to introduce them.

"I am here to discuss the return of your cherished slave," I announce. "And also, my friend would like to see what other merchandise you have available."

"Of course, of course." He wipes his hands and stands up from the table. "I will show you the catalog of my current inventory."

"I don't mean arms," I interrupt him. "I mean women."

"Oh." He blinks in surprise.

Arman won't want to part with another slave. But it's the cost of doing business. I know he will show us the one he values least. Most likely the one who took Talia's place when we left.

And I also know, she will be kept in the basement. Away from his guards.

"Now that you mention it," he says. "I have something I believe you will like."

He leads the way downstairs, and he doesn't ask his guard to follow. Again, I can feel Nikolai's eyes on me. Something about this is not right.

Arman is not acting suspiciously at all. He trusts himself alone in my presence. And even I am beginning to question his behavior.

When he opens the door to the cell, I do not even glance at the slave. My hands come around his throat from behind, cutting off his air supply.

"Keep her quiet," I tell Nikolai.

He moves towards the girl in the corner who looks so much like

Talia when I first discovered her. I meet her terrified gaze as I choke Arman and realize that perhaps I am mistaken. This girl still feels. Talia did not. Perhaps that should have been my first sign.

Arman struggles in my arms, but it is futile. He is stout and old and not trained to protect himself. And the anger swelling inside of me is driving my control now.

I remove the knife from the sheath under my jacket and plunge it into his gut twice.

He crumples to the floor, gasping for breath as I kneel beside him. I dig the tip of the knife into his forehead until it hits bone.

"Tell me why you sent her those photos," I demand. "Did she ask you for them?"

He stares up at me, and the shock and confusion on his face is genuine. It produces a sinking feeling inside of me.

But I know I am not wrong. I could not have been so wrong.

Talia has betrayed me, and I am determined to find out why. To prove it once and for all. I will pursue this belief to hell and back until I have my answers. My proof. When Arman does not answer me, I flay open his cheek.

He is bleeding from the gut, and it will not be long until he is dead.

"Time is running out," I press.

"I don't know what you are talking about," he sputters. "Please…"

"Please?" I mock him. "Did Talia ever ask you please?"

His eyes are answer enough. And I don't know why it matters to me. This is not for the purpose of avenging her. I have to remind myself of that when I look at him.

"I did not send her any pictures."

I sigh and retrieve my phone from my pocket. There are a number of missed calls from Viktor, which I ignore as I pull up the evidence.

And then I show Arman, flipping through the grainy photos, watching him carefully.

Again, his eyes register shock and disbelief, and my stomach turns.

"You sent these to her."

"Those must be from her training," he says. "Before I purchased her."

It sounds like a question. And I can see the question in his eyes. But I don't want to see it. Because that means I was wrong.

I slice open his other cheek and then dig the knife into his throat. "Answer me."

"I swear to you," he says. "It was not me. Dmitri. You need to speak with Dmitri."

I grab him by the shirt and slam him down into the cement, my arms shaking from the force of my rage. "Dmitri is already dead."

"I swear," he gasps. "You have my word. He and his men did the training. And then they sold them. That is all I know."

The gears are spinning in my brain. But none of this makes sense. Dmitri could not have sent her those photos. He was already dead. Arman can see I am doubting him. And he still believes I will be merciful. That I would allow him a chance to live.

He is wrong.

"He had a business relationship with some of the Vory," Arman tells me in a last effort to save his skin. "I don't know who. But that's how he found Talia in the first place."

"I need a name," I tell him.

"I don't have one," he pleads.

"Then you are no longer of use to me."

I stab him in the neck this time. Blood sputters from his mouth, and he bleeds out in a matter of seconds. And the only thing I can think of… is how much my Solynshko would have liked to see this.

Forty-Eight

Talia

Slainte is exactly the way I remember it. Only, it feels different somehow.

Like a lifetime ago.

Like a different person that walked these floors.

I keep my head down and aim straight for the back office, hoping to find Lachlan. But what I find is more. More than I am ready for. But something I can no longer avoid.

Mack is with him. And she is pregnant.

When she sees me, she nearly collapses from the shock.

I can only imagine what I must look like right now. After hours of walking in the brush. My arms and legs are scratched, and I am bleeding from a cut on my leg still.

I can't find the words to tell them what happened yet. So I say the only thing I can.

"Get me out of here."

They took me to a safe house. One of their own, which Lachlan assured me that nobody else is aware of. It is small, but safe. And lonely, even sitting here with my oldest friend.

I am showered and dressed in fresh clothes, the cut on my leg stitched and cleaned.

And Mack is staring at me. Waiting for an explanation.

We are in the kitchen, sitting at the table. Things have never been so tense between us, and I can barely bring myself to look at her.

"Have you heard anything?" I ask Lachlan.

"I've spoken to Viktor," he answers. "Alexei is fine. They are returning from Bulgaria today. He does not know anything yet, and I did not mention it."

"And Magda?" I ask.

"She is fine also."

I tap my fingers against the wood of the kitchen table as silence descends over us. I don't know what else to do. What else to say.

"Viktor thinks you are dead," Lachlan tells me. "He will tell Alexei soon."

My throat feels like it's closing in on me. There are tears in my eyes when I look at Lachlan.

"Is that what you want?" he asks.

"I don't know," I release a shaky sob. "I don't know what I want. I need to think."

Lachlan sighs and looks to Mack. Who is still staring at me like she doesn't know me. And she's right. I'm a completely different person than I was before. And I can see that even though she knows better than to say anything right now, the betrayal is there in her eyes.

She keeps glancing at my pregnant belly, silently judging me.

I hate this. I hate how stilted everything is between us. But I can't deal with that right now. I can only focus on the seconds. The minutes. Think of what I need to do. Of what's best for me and my baby. I don't want to leave Alexei.

I love him. I love him so much.

But I can't return to that house. Be a prisoner on the third floor. I can't live like that. With his coldness. His distance. He made me feel just so that he could destroy me all over again. He promised to protect me. But there is no protecting me from himself. From the fears that rule his life and his beliefs. He doesn't trust me.

He doesn't love me.

"Alexei is a mate and an ally," Lachlan informs me. "And he has been good to me. But you are Mack's mate. And Mack is my wife. So I'm telling you now. This is your chance to get out of this situation if you want it. Probably the only chance you are ever going to get."

I nod, because I know he's right. But I can't stop crying. It's freaking Mack out. Because I never cried before. But now, I'm a mess.

Just as she always said I was. And I always tried to prove so hard that I wasn't.

I don't care anymore. I don't care if she thinks me weak. My heart is broken. Destroyed. And I have to make a life altering decision. One that will hurt us both, no matter what I decide. I don't want Alexei to think I'm dead, but I know Lachlan is right. He won't let me go any other way.

This isn't what I wanted.

At all.

But this is my reality. And I need to think of what's best for me. For once in my life. And for the baby. Which deserves to have his father in his life. Alexei would be a good father.

But if he knew, then that would mean sacrificing myself. The rest of my life living with a man who hates me.

"I can't win," I tell them both. "No matter what I decide, I can't win."

"Then you never should have married him," Mack replies.

I look up at her, and so does Lachlan. Her voice is cold. Angry. Bitter.

"You should have come to me."

"You wouldn't have understood," I tell her. "And you can't fix everything for me, Mack. You can't fix me."

"Those are just the same old excuses, Tal. Complete bullshit."

"Mack," Lachlan's voice is warm and soft when he speaks with her. Filled with real love. It chokes me up even more. "Now is not the time."

"I know it's not the frigging time," Mack replies. "But Jesus, Talia. What the hell are you thinking right now? Of course you can't go back there. Look at you. You're a goddamn mess. For once in your life, think. Fucking think about this baby that you're bringing into the world. About what's best for him."

And I don't know why, but I laugh. Because maybe this is what I need. My anger. Maybe Mack is doing me a favor by picking a fight with me right now.

"So let me get this straight," I reply. "You can marry into the mob, but I can't? How does that work exactly?"

"My husband isn't an abusive asshole," she states. "Look at you. Look at what he did to you. You can barely hold it together."

"You don't know him," I snap. "So why don't you… for once in your life… quit judging everyone else around you, huh? I was like this long before Alexei ever came into my life. If anything, he put me back together."

I don't mention that he broke me too. Because they can both see it. But Mack is determined to argue.

"I'm not judging you, I'm stating a fact. You always assumed the worst of me, Tal. But all I've ever done was try to protect you."

"No, all you've ever done is try to get me to be exactly like you," I yell at her. "To think like you. Act like you. Do as Mack would do with all her high morals and bullshit. You are such a fucking hypocrite."

She blinks at me, stunned, but I'm not finished. It's time we got this out, once and for all.

"You pride yourself on your loyalty to your friends, but you don't even know them."

"I know you better than anyone," she snaps.

"No, you don't. You refused to listen to me. When I tried to tell you the dark things about myself. You just didn't want to accept them as a part of me. But that isn't the way life works, Mack. You have to accept the bad in people too. Like Scarlett. Like me."

"What does Scarlett have to do with this?"

"You don't even know what she does!" I shout. "When she's out at night."

"She sells her body," she replies. "Everybody fucking knows it."

"Except she doesn't." I look at her and shake my head. "Not at all."

Mack is stunned, and Lachlan seems uncomfortable with this conversation, but keeps his mouth shut. I've always appreciated that about him. That he lets someone speak their piece. And that for once, someone isn't looking at me like I'm completely crazy.

"She's a trick roller," I tell Mack. "She doesn't fuck men. She robs them. Because it gives her some of the power back that she lost. But you couldn't ever understand that."

"I could…" Mack sputters, but the words die off.

"No you couldn't," I tell her. "Because you aren't like us, Mack. I'm sorry, but you're not. You're stronger. And you haven't walked our path. But you judge us for it. You do."

"I don't judge," she whispers.

And then tears spring to her eyes, and I feel guilty for saying it. But it needed to be said.

"You do."

"Okay, maybe a little, but only because I want what's best for my friends."

"But you can't shame them into it, Mack. You can't force people to change. To cope with everything the way that you do. People are different. They all deal with things differently. You need to understand that."

"It's my fault, isn't it?" Tears spill down her cheeks when she looks at me. "I pushed you into it. That trip with Dmitri. Because the last time I saw you… we argued."

"You didn't push me into it." I shake my head. "I would have gone regardless."

"But if I hadn't been so pushy. So… judgy. And then I asked Alexei to save you."

"Mack."

I'm crying too, so it's the only word I can get out. We both stand up and close the distance between us. Healing all of the hurt and anger with a single hug.

I cry in her arms, and she holds me. And I don't know how long we stand there like that, but I only know that a piece of my heart feels like it isn't dead anymore. Like this is exactly where I need to be right now.

It takes me over an hour to say the words. To accept what it is that I need to do.

That I will need to hurt Alexei to protect myself.

And that I will hate myself for it.

But I don't see any other choice.

"I want to stay here," I tell Lachlan with a shaky voice. "I'm going to stay here."

Forty-Nine

Alexei

"Viktor keeps calling," Nikolai tells me from the passenger seat of the car.

"Ignore it. I will deal with him later."

"I don't think it's about Arman," he tells me.

He keeps scrolling through his phone, checking through messages and missed calls. And when he tenses beside me, I know something is wrong.

I pull over to the side of the road and give him my full attention. We are an hour from home. I just want to get back to the house. To figure out this mess. To ask Talia who sent her the photos again.

I'm clinging to that, because it's all I can do to continue down this path I have set out for myself. She has betrayed me. I could not have been so wrong about that. That is the only acceptable thing for me to believe.

But then Nikolai turns to me, and his face is pale. Worried. He's holding up his phone, and Viktor is already on the line, through a video chat.

I'm not prepared for what he is about to say, so I delay the inevitable. My mind is turning, my hands clenched at my sides.

"I will come to speak with you this evening," I tell Viktor. "To explain my actions. And to retrieve Talia."

"Lyoshenka."

His face is full of emotion. Something that Viktor rarely ever shows. But it's there now. And it's triggering the emotion inside of me too. Something I do not like. Something I try to avoid at all costs.

He isn't angry. And he should be angry with me. He knows I have gone against his orders. Killing Arman was an unsanctioned act. He should be discussing his punishment with me. Instead, he is showing clear pity for me.

"What is it?"

My stomach drops out and I die inside before I even read his words.

"Talia is dead."

The basement floor is coated in blood.

Corpses, stacked in the corner.

My hands, itching for more.

For all out war.

But Viktor is beside me, talking of nonsense. Telling me to keep a rational head.

"Those trucks were delivered from your house," I remind him. "Someone has betrayed us."

"Yes," he agrees. "But you have killed the men responsible for delivering them. Now we must wait. Be patient."

"I have no patience left," is my reply. "My wife is dead. My unborn son, dead. Franco, dead. And you ask me for patience?"

"We will right these wrongs," he assures me. "In time. When

we have discovered the traitor. There will be no mercy for him, Lyoshenka. None. But you must be patient."

"I have waited too long already," I answer. "There isn't even a body for me to bury…"

The words die off, and I take a breath. I cannot think about that right now. Think about my Solnyshko that way. In my mind, she is still up on the third floor. Where I left her. Where she is beautiful and perfect and mine, even when I break her heart. When I destroy her as I always knew I would.

There is only one way for me to go on. The only way that I know. And it's written in blood.

I turn to Nikolai, who is watching the conversation, but remains carefully quiet.

"What of Dmitri's men? The trainers?" I ask him.

He does not look to Viktor for permission to speak. He simply nods. "I have their location."

I move towards the door, gesturing for him to follow. Viktor tries to halt me with a hand on my shoulder.

"Lyoshenka, you must stop this."

"I will," I assure him. "When I have killed them all."

A hand on my arm shakes me from my blackness, and when I blink up, Magda is there. My head is pounding, and I feel the urge to retch from the amount of liquor inside of my system.

I want her to go away. I want everything to fucking go away.

"Alyoshka," she says. "You need to eat something. It has been two days."

No. It has been a month. A month since I died. Since everything just… stopped. I have spilled more blood in this time than in my entire career as a Vor. And I will continue to do so.

To honor her memory in the only way I can.

"Nikolai is here to see you," Magda tells me.

"Send him away."

"Too late." He steps into view. "And I have something I believe you will want to see."

My eyes move to the disk in his hand. And it is the only thing that fires a spark inside of me. Vengeance. It is the only thing that keeps me living from one day to the next. The kill. The destruction. The war I have waged on the animals who touched her. Who ever even thought of hurting her.

Magda leaves us to our privacy and I rouse the computer from its slumber, bringing up screen after screen on the wall. They are all filled with images of her. Of us.

I have replayed that video of her last day a thousand times over. The walk down the stairs. The way she paused and cried and Magda comforted her for the pain I had inflicted.

I never even said goodbye to her.

I allowed my anger to consume me. To consume her too.

She trusted me to protect her. And I did what I always said I wouldn't. I failed her.

I close my eyes and feel Nikolai's hand on my shoulder. I am too weak to turn him away, even if I should. He has been here often, in the days since. Checking on me.

But there is nothing new to report.

Life goes on. The Vory business goes on. Only I cannot go on.

I feel her numbness now. Her pain. It haunts me in her stead. My Solnyshko. The sun has gone from my life, and only darkness remains.

I am crying, I realize.

I don't even attempt to hide it from Nikolai. He doesn't say anything. He just takes over, bringing up the video on the screen. The same video I have also looked at a thousand times over. From that day at the meeting.

The day when all of this began.

"I had Mischa take a look at it," Nikolai tells me.

And then he brings the cursor to a time stamp on the screen and clicks it. I watch as he slows down the video, and only then do I see it.

And I cannot believe I didn't see it before.

That my anger had blinded me so badly from the truth.

"It's on a time loop," Nikolai answers my thoughts. "Whoever it was knew what they were doing. And they were fast. They came prepared."

"How long?" I ask.

"Thirty seconds, maximum. You couldn't have noticed it, Lyoshka. It was very well edited."

My body falls back against my chair as all of my worst fears are confirmed. Talia had nothing to do with the video. But someone wanted it to appear that way. Someone close to me. Who knew I would not trust her. Or believe her.

Someone who wanted to rip us apart.

"There is something else," Nikolai tells me as he takes a seat across from me.

"What is it?"

"Katya's guard mentioned that she visited a security store a few months back. He didn't know what she purchased, but found the trip to be out of character for her."

"Then we need to talk to her." I rise to my feet, even though I am still too drunk to make it down the stairs.

"I already tried." Nikolai shakes his head. "But she was found dead this morning, Lyoshka. Hanging from the rafter in her ceiling."

I blink at him as I process his words. Katya is dead. And someone is trying to cover their tracks. Talia told me. She told me she didn't think it was over. And she was right. I didn't listen to her. I didn't listen to Nikolai.

"She wasn't working alone," Nikolai says. "Someone is cleaning up loose ends. Katya is not smart enough to set up that slide show and she was not in the building that day. I believe it is one of the Vory."

I look at him from across my desk, and the name that has haunted me all my life is the only one that comes to mind. Nikolai knows what I am thinking before I even say it. His face is drawn, and I know he believes it to be true as well.

"Sergei."

Fifty

Alexei

The Vory has our own enforcers. Our own hitmen.

But none as skilled in the art of human suffering as the Irish Reaper. Ronan Fitzpatrick.

He is in my basement now, with Sergei.

While Viktor, Nikolai, and I watch from the camera in my office. I am feeling restless. Eager. It is all I can do to remain seated and have patience. But it is better this way. Because I have no control left. I would kill him in the first two minutes, and that would not do.

"You will end him," Viktor assures me. "That is your right to do so, Lyoshenka. But you must be patient."

I expected a fight from Nikolai. But I did not get one. Instead, he sits beside me. Watching as carefully as I. In my mind, I wonder if he has hope. Hope that we are wrong, and that our father did not do this. That he will somehow live.

But that is not the case.

It is evident when he finally breaks. Ronan has made him suffer past the point of all reason and strength. His mind can no longer withstand the pain.

"It was me."

Those three little words burst from his mouth and ignite the darkness that has always burned inside of me. Because of him. For him.

This man who refused to acknowledge me as a son.

My own father murdered my wife and unborn child in cold blood. Exposed me to the other Vory as weak. And destroyed my life.

Both Viktor and Nikolai are waiting for me to get up. To rush downstairs and finish the job. But I am frozen by my grief all over again.

"Perhaps we should do it together," Nikolai offers. "It would hurt him more if I were to help."

His words are true enough. Something that would have felt bitter to me before is now just an honest truth that I can no longer deny.

Sergei only ever had love for Nikolai. Everyone else in his life was disposable. Myself. My mother. Even his mistresses. Nikolai's mother disappeared years ago, and nobody knows what happened to her.

To have the only thing he ever valued participate in his destruction would be difficult for Sergei. I believed that I would never trust Nikolai again. That he could never make amends for what he did to me.

But as I rise up and he walks by my side to kill our father, I am grateful for his presence.

The basement is cold, with a persistent stench of copper and Sergei's sweat.

When his sons enter the room and meet his gaze, there is a flash of betrayal as I had hoped.

But it is not for me. His eyes linger on Nikolai, assessing his intentions.

Sergei has lived by the Vory codes for most of his life. He already knows death will come. There is no doubt he accepts that as fact. But he believes that because he is a Vor, he will receive an honorable death.

He is wrong.

Already, his toenails and fingers have been removed. He has been water boarded repeatedly by Ronan Fitzpatrick and brought back to life several times already with shock paddles. His eyes are cloudy and his pulse is no doubt weak.

But it isn't over. Not even close.

"Talia's death was quick," I tell him when I step forward. "But I can assure you that yours won't be."

I make a gesture to Ronan and he hands over the small black case. My fingers itch to open it. To touch the thing that will cause him pain unlike he's ever known.

But instead, I hand it to my brother.

"You can do the honors," I tell Nikolai.

It is difficult to relinquish this moment. But I know that Nikolai is right. This is what will hurt Sergei the most. His face is solemn but not repentant as he retrieves the syringe from the case. And under Ronan's guidance, he injects the special blend of snake venom into Sergei's arm.

It only takes a few moments for the effects to kick in.

Sergei begins to convulse on the table and foam at the mouth as the neurotoxins take over his body. When the paralysis sets in and his bulging eyes find mine, I lean over him so that there can be no misunderstandings between us.

"It is only the beginning."

And then beside him, I take my seat. A spectator to his last and final hours.

There will be no violence or bloodshed from my hands today. By all outward appearances, it could even be considered a gentle death. But the pain that Sergei will feel as the venom attacks his nervous system is anything but gentle.

It is a balm to my soul, watching him suffer. And yet it means nothing at all. I will still be forced to go on. Without Talia. Knowing what I've done. Knowing that I failed her. That I am no better than Sergei himself.

And the only satisfaction I will have in the end is that my father is dead too.

"How long will it take?" Viktor asks as he sits down beside me.

I did not expect him to watch. But it should not surprise me. Even after all I have done, Viktor still regards me as a son. As one of his own.

"It could be hours," I answer.

Beside me, the Reaper and Nikolai also take their seats.

And then we wait. The only sounds to break the intermittent silence are those of Sergei's tortured groans and the shaking of the table beneath him.

It is a short event. Shorter than I had hoped.

Just as I always suspected, Sergei was weak. But this knowledge does not give me any satisfaction.

Because in this house, and in my life, the sun no longer rises.

Fifty-One

Talia

"How is he?" I ask Lachlan.

He does not reply for some time. And it annoys me. I keep touching the star on my hand, and he is watching me with curious eyes. But guarded too.

"Talia, you must realize that it would be out of character for me to call him so often. He is not taking calls, anyway."

I tap at the table again. And Mack's watching me, but she keeps her lips zipped on the subject.

"But you said he's a friend. Wouldn't normal protocol be to go visit him?"

Again, Lachlan remains silent. And I realize he's hiding something from me.

"What is it?" I ask.

He looks up at me and frowns.

"I have been to visit him," he answers finally. "He's as well as you could expect him to be."

"Oh."

I need more. I'm desperate for more. But Lachlan simply sighs.

"His father was responsible for the car bombs," he tells me. "And he is dead now. Arman too."

"Good," I reply. "That's good."

They both look at me, and I shrug.

"I don't mourn the loss of them," I answer. "Alexei deserved better for a father than Sergei."

"Yes, well," Lachlan replies, "It wasn't just them. Katya's dead too. And a whole host of any other men that ever touched you."

I blink.

And my heart aches at the thought of Alexei on his murderous rampage. I can only hope that it has given him what he needs. Some peace.

But I doubt it.

His father had always been the root of his issues. And Katya didn't help.

They were the reason he did not trust me. The reason he told me he could never love me. And he was right.

I blink back tears, and Lachlan meets my watery gaze.

"I know you care about him," he tells me. "But you need to make a decision, Talia. You need to decide if you can move on from this. Without him. Because I can't keep going back there."

The pain on Lachlan's face guts me. Because he is hurting for Alexei. But still, he is loyal to me. I cup my face in my hands and try to pull myself together. I know he's right. That none of this is fair to anyone.

But I still don't know what to do.

I don't know anything.

So I do what I've always done. The thing I do best.

I avoid it altogether.

Fifty-Two

Talia

Mack has had her baby.

A little girl.

They named her Keeva Crow. And she is the most beautiful thing I have ever seen. When I get a chance to hold her, it scares and thrills me.

And I think of Alexei. Again.

Lachlan was there for Mack every step of the way. He was in the delivery room, coaching her through the delivery and cutting the cord. Kissing her forehead and holding his daughter for the first time with blinding love.

It makes me ache.

I won't have that. I will go through it alone, just as I always have been.

Mack says she will be there with me, but it's not the same. It's just not the same.

I keep telling myself that I have more time to prepare. That by the time that I go into labor, I will be stronger. That I will be mentally prepared.

Only, that isn't true.

Because my water breaks two weeks early when I'm alone in my bed. I'm fumbling for my cell phone when Lachlan's guard comes in to check on me.

He's young, and his name is Conor. He's been staying at the safe house with me, watching over me. And right now, I've never been so grateful for his presence.

"Everything good?" he asks.

His eyes widen when I flip off the covers and he sees the bed.

"No," I tell him. "It's time. Now."

"Now?" he squeaks.

"Yes, now," I growl. "Help me, please."

"Right." He steps into action, coming at me like he has no frigging idea what to do. Which he probably doesn't.

"Just take me to the… ugg."

I double over in pain with a contraction. "Take me to the hospital."

Conor gets me into the car and asks me what else we need to bring. But I don't know. Because I haven't packed anything. I barely have anything.

"Just take me," I groan.

And he does. He drives like a lunatic which only makes it worse. But I'm sweating, gripping the door handle, and trying to breathe through the pain.

Something isn't right.

I know it in my gut.

It's happening too fast. The pain is too intense. This baby is coming now.

"I don't know if I'm going to make it there," I tell Conor.

"You have to," he shouts. "I can't deliver a baby."

"Pull over!" I scream at him. "And call an ambulance."

He does. And while he's on the phone, I'm delivering in the backseat of the car.

"I need your help!" I yell. "Fucking Christ."

Conor comes around to help me and nearly passes out when he sees the baby's head.

"Just breathe," he tells me.

"I am fucking breathing."

I arch back in pain as the contractions come hard and quick. And it's happening. Three more pushes, and my baby is born. In the backseat of the car, in the middle of Boston.

The ambulance arrives just in time. And the paramedics quickly usher me and the baby onto a stretcher. Everything is in chaos around us, but I can only look at him as they bundle him into my arms.

He looks so much like his father.

I'm crying. I'm in shock. And I'm in love.

They start to close the doors with Conor still outside, looking lost and traumatized.

"You're coming with me," I tell him.

"What?" he looks horrified by the idea. "No."

"Yes."

He comes.

I grab onto his arm as they start checking our vitals. "You have to call him."

"Lachlan?"

"Alexei. You have to call Alexei."

He blinks in confusion.

"Now."

"Okay, okay. I'm calling him. What do you want me to tell him?"

"Just tell him I need him here. Please."

And then they are wheeling me into the hospital.

Fifty-Three

Alexei

I am vaguely aware of someone trying to wake me, but I ignore the hand on my shoulder and keep my eyes closed.

When they are closed, I can dream of her. I can forget for a brief time that it isn't real.

But the hand on my shoulder becomes more insistent. When I blink up and see Nikolai, I shove him away. He has not left my house for the last three days, and he is grating on my last nerve.

This is what I'm thinking when the ice water hits my face, followed by a stinging slap. I'm already wheeling back my chair, preparing to murder my half-brother once and for all, when I am met by Magda's angry gaze.

"Pull yourself together," she demands. "And drink this, you will need it."

I look down at the coffee in her hands and try to reach for my cognac instead. But she grabs the bottle and throws it against the wall, smashing it to pieces.

"Magda."

"No." She forces the cup into my hands, and I have never seen her look so crazed. "I have news for you, Alyoshka. But you must pull yourself together first. You look like death."

I don't know what other news she could possibly have, but when Magda is insistent I know there is no arguing about it. So I drink the coffee while they both watch me. When I have finished, I set down the cup and Magda hands me my jacket.

"I will tell you in the car. We must go, now."

"I am not going until you tell me."

"The news is about your wife," she says.

And then she walks out of the room, leaving me to trail after her and Nikolai in my annoyance.

"What about my wife?"

I try to reach out and grab her arm, but for a woman of sixty, Magda is surprisingly fast. The car is already waiting outside when they open the door, and my body is growing tense. Anxious.

Nikolai slips into the driver's seat while I reach out and stop Magda.

"Tell me now."

"She is not gone, Alyoshka," she says. "There is still hope."

It occurs to me as I yell at Nikolai to drive faster the reason they waited to tell me the news.

I need to get to her now.

To see it firsthand before I can believe it.

I need to see my sun.

Finally, my phone buzzes and Lachlan's name flashes on the screen. When I accept the video call, the first words out of his mouth are the ones I need.

"She is resting up now," he tells me. "She did a grand job of it, Alexei. Baby Nikolaev did not want to wait any longer."

It relieves me and angers me at the same time. I want to see her now. See her alive and breathing. But there is still so much distance between us.

"I should have been there."

"I know," Lachlan agrees. "I'm sorry, Alexei. I thought I was doing what was best."

Magda looks at me from across the car, and I ignore her. She does not need to tell me, I am already aware of my shortcomings.

"You were," I tell Lachlan. "But if you ever hide my wife from me again…"

"I know," he cuts me off. "I know, Alexei."

"We are still twenty miles out," I say.

"Mack and I are here," he assures me. "We'll hold it down until you get here."

"Don't leave her side," I order. "Don't let her out of your sight."

"She's not going anywhere, mate," he assures me. "She was the one who asked us to call you."

"Tell her that we are on our way," Magda says, grabbing the phone from my hand. "And I'm going to take good care of her."

She is tearing up, and so is Nikolai when I meet his gaze in the mirror.

We all look away from each other, allowing silence to settle over the car when Magda hangs up the phone.

My wife is alive. My baby boy has just been born.

And I am never going to fail them again.

Fifty-Four

Talia

My son is curled against my chest, both of our eyes closed when I feel his presence.

I am so tired. So, so tired.

But Alexei is here. So I force my eyes open, just in time to see him leaning down to cradle my face in his hands.

"Solnyshko."

His voice is rough, his eyes glassy. And the very word is an apology, filled with more emotion than I've ever heard in his voice.

"God, my Solnyshko. I have died without you."

And then he is kissing me all over my face, his other hand resting on our baby boy. When he turns his attention to him, I gesture for him to take him in his arms.

He does.

"Franco," I tell him. "His name is Franco."

Alexei seems surprised, but nods his agreement soon after.

"Franco. My son."

"He saved our lives," I manage to choke out.

I'm so emotional. Seeing him. Seeing them both together like this. It's overwhelming in a way that I wasn't prepared for.

Alexei meets my gaze, and his eyes are red and bloodshot. Filled with grief. And I have so much regret. So much agony and want for this man. The damaged half to my soul. We are both so damaged, but together, we fit perfectly.

I'm crying, I realize. Looking up at him with our baby in his arms.

"I'm sorry I let you think…"

"Shh…" He comes to sit beside me, reaching for my hand. "You did the only thing you could. I was so foolish, my sweet. But it will never happen again. I will never doubt your loyalty again. I will spend the rest of my life proving myself worthy of your…"

His words die off, and he looks like he's in pain.

"Of my love," I assure him. "I still love you, Lyoshka."

"And I, you," he answers, cupping my face in his palm. "You are my sun."

He kisses me, and everything else melts away. I don't doubt his assurances. I know with certainty that he will never allow anything to come between us again. Even the present distance is too much, he tells me, as he comes to sit beside me in bed. Franco nestled in one arm, and me in the other.

He is our foundation.

And despite the intensity of emotion between us in this moment, nothing has ever felt more solid.

The moment is interrupted when Mack and Conor step back inside of the room. Conor looks terrified when he glances at Alexei while Mack looks like she wants to murder him.

Alexei hands me back the baby and kisses me on the cheek before standing up to greet them. When he moves in their direction, Conor takes a step back.

"I didn't look at anything," Conor proclaims. "I swear."

Alexei extends his hand as a sign of respect. "Thank you, Conor. For being there when I could not. I owe you a great deal."

Conor's shoulders slump in relief and he smiles. Alexei smiles too. But Mack lays into him a second later.

"I don't like you." She pokes him in the chest. "You took advantage of her. You knocked her up. And then you hurt her. That wasn't the deal we had."

"I did do all of those things," Alexei replies. "I was wrong."

For the first time ever, Mack seems speechless.

"Damn right you were," she huffs.

"But she is my wife," Alexei tells her. "She is never leaving me again."

Mack looks set to argue, but then her eyes find mine. And she sees that I have no protests. This is just Alexei's way. This is his way of telling her that he is sorry. And that he will take care of me. So in the end, she chooses not to say anything, even though she really wants to.

And I am so grateful for her in this moment. For all that we have been through together, and that even after everything, she is still here for me. And I realize how much we have both grown up over the last two years. How much we have changed. I know that if we can get past all of that, then we can get past anything.

I also know the same is true for Alexei and I. He comes back to me and holds Franco for the remainder of their visit. He does not let anyone else hold our baby, except for Magda when she bursts into the room at the first available opportunity and doesn't take no for an answer. She sings him lullabies. And Alexei and I watch, his hand always touching me. Anchoring himself to me.

The rest of the day is spent much the same. Viktor and some of the other Vory come to visit, bringing lavish gifts for Franco and myself.

By the time visiting hours are over, I am exhausted.

"Please don't go anywhere," I tell Alexei.

"I did not plan to," he says.

He climbs into the bed beside me again, which is ridiculous considering his height, but he does not complain that his feet are hanging over the edge. Franco is cradled between us, and he simply strokes his face, his eyes moving between the two of us.

That is when I notice the tattoo on his hand. In the same space that I drew it before. My name, inside the sun.

I reach out to touch it, and Alexei takes my hand in his.

"You got it."

His eyes are glassy again. Vulnerable with emotion. But he does not try to hide it.

"You are the only woman for me, my sweet," he tells me. "Even in death, I could never let you go. You are it for me. And I am so sorry that I did not show you before."

"I don't want your apologies," I answer. "I just want your trust."

He expels a long breath and traces the lines of my face with his finger. "You have it. You have my word, I will not ever doubt you again."

"We need you," I tell him. "We need all of you."

"You have it," he assures me. "There is nothing without you. Tomorrow, I take you home. And I will make you mine all over again. Every day, for the rest of my life, Solnyshko. That is my promise to you. I will make you fall in love with me every day for a lifetime."

"A lifetime," I agree. "Because we are in this together."

He kisses me on the forehead, and then Franco too.

"Together," he echoes.

Epilogue

Talia

Some would say that happiness is fleeting.

I say that happiness is terrifying.

But it is also real. And possible.

And that doesn't mean that everything is perfect all the time. That doesn't mean that there aren't still lows. Or struggles. Or moments when the memories try to claw their way back into the present and blacken everything around you.

But I know now that if you just wake up every single day ready to do battle—ready to fight for what you have—then you have a real chance to hold onto it.

Alexei and I fight for each other every day. Without fail.

We argue. And we both repeat old patterns. But in the end, we always find our way back to each other. Because we promised we would.

He is my solace and I am his sun, and Franco is the entire universe around us.

Since Katya and Sergei's betrayal, Alexei is much more careful about who he lets into his home. And we never go anywhere without him. Without his protection and his diligent security measures.

Some would say that it is not right. To live so far away from everyone else. To be at home all the time. But this is our kingdom. He's my king, and I'm his queen. And we would do anything to protect each other. And we are happiest here. Where we have each other.

Mack and Lachlan come to visit often. Keeva and Franco will grow up together. The way that Mack and I did. But with people who love them. And they will never know the horrors that Mack and I knew. Or even Alexei. Because as a parent, I have realized one thing. So profound in its simplicity that it sometimes knocks me off balance.

My love for Franco is unending. And my mother's simply was not. She was broken in a way that I could never truly be. I am not like her. I will never be like her.

Because I have them. And for me that is all I ever need to know to keep fighting. To keep living. To keep cherishing every moment I get to spend with them.

When I watch Alexei now, speaking Russian to his son and earning smiles, I'm smiling too.

So is Magda, who has embraced the role of Babushka with gusto. Even Nikolai has earned his way back into Alexei's orbit. He is everything I could ask for in a brother-in-law and uncle. Always spoiling Franco when he comes to visit.

Today, he arrived with a blinged-out kid size hummer for Franco to cruise around the yard in. The only problem is that Franco isn't even crawling yet.

"It would be nice for him to have a cousin," I tell Nikolai.

He looks at me and shakes his head. I still don't know what's happening between him and Tanaka. She never leaves his sight, but the cold front between them is obvious to anyone.

"Maybe someday," he says.

"Maybe someday what?" Alexei asks as he passes Franco to me and pulls my body into his.

"I was telling him that he should start having some babies too."

Alexei shakes his head. "He could not handle it."

Behind him, Tanaka is smiling.

"Lunch is ready," Magda interrupts us.

"Nikolai, take Franco downstairs?" Alexei asks.

Nikolai takes him from me and everyone moves downstairs apart from Alexei and I. I already know what he wants. It seems like we always have visitors now. And sometimes, these stolen moments are all we get.

He reaches down and wraps his arms around my body, kissing me and groping me while he has a chance.

"Wear black for me tonight," he says. "And let's go to bed early."

"What about Franco?" I ask.

"Uncle Nikolai can have some practice," he answers.

I smile up at him, curious how long he's been planning this.

"Okay, Lyoshka. For you, I wear black."

I move to go downstairs, but he stops me again.

"I haven't told you yet today," he murmurs as his lips find mine. "But I love you, Solnyshko. Always."

The truth is, he does tell me that every day. Sometimes, he wakes up in the middle of the night just to tell me. To remind me that he has given me the one thing I never thought he could.

His heart.

I do not take that for granted.

Even when we fight, we always remember to never take each other for granted again.

So I guess in the end, maybe there's a little hope left for all of us. Even me.

The End

Works by
A. ZAVARELLI

Boston Underworld Series
CROW: Boston Underworld #1
REAPER: Boston Underworld #2
GHOST: Boston Underworld #3
SAINT: Boston Underworld #4
THIEF: Boston Underworld #5
CONOR: Boston Underworld #6

Bleeding Hearts Series
Echo: A Bleeding Hearts Novel Volume One
Stutter: A Bleeding Hearts Novel Volume Two

Twisted Ever After Series
BEAST: Twisted Ever After #1

Standalones
Tap Left
HATE CRUSH

Sin City Series
Confess
Convict

For a complete list of books and audios, visit:
www.azavarelli.com/books

About the Author

A. Zavarelli is a *USA Today* and Amazon bestselling author of dark and contemporary romance.

When she's not putting her characters through hell, she can usually be found watching bizarre and twisted documentaries in the name of research.

She currently lives in the Northwest with her lumberjack and an entire brood of fur babies.

Sign Up for A. Zavarelli's Newsletter:
www.subscribepage.com/bAZavarelli

Like A. Zavarelli on Facebook:
www.facebook.com/azavarelliauthor

Join A. Zavarelli's Reader Group:
www.facebook.com/femmefatales

Follow A. Zavarelli on Instagram:
www.instagram.com/azavarelli

Printed in Great Britain
by Amazon